MARIE TAYLOR-FORD

New Beginnings at Lilac Bay

LILAC BAY
SERIES
BOOK 3

To my sister, Luli.
I'd never have made it this far without you.
You're the best friend I'll ever have.
I adore you.

No part of this book may be reproduced in any form or by any electronic or mechanical means, including information storage and retrieval systems, without written permission from the author, except for the use of brief quotations in a book review.

This is a work of fiction and all characters in this publication are fictitious. Any similarity to real persons, living or dead, or actual events, is purely coincidental.

Text Copyright © 2022
Marie Taylor-Ford
All rights reserved

Cover design by Ana Grigoriu-Voicu

–

Author note: This book is set in Australia, and therefore uses British English spelling.

CHAPTER ONE

Marley hesitated as the frosted glass doors of the fertility clinic slid open. She'd spent the time it took to walk the few blocks from work gathering the courage to go inside. But now the air-conditioned chill of the foyer hit her, she had absolutely no idea how to start the conversation she wanted—*needed*—to start. She paused near the entrance, fiddling with the huge collar on her Hawaiian print jumpsuit and catching the eye of the attractive, inky-haired man at reception.

"Welcome to ReproJoy." He smiled warmly and Marley could see the blue of his eyes from where she stood. They were unusually deep in colour, even behind his thick-framed glasses.

She turned and walked straight back out.

Two days later she tried again. This time she made it halfway to reception. The same guy stood at the desk and Marley got close enough to see that his eyes were even more striking than they'd appeared from the doorway, contrasting against the jet of his hair and thick lashes.

"Welcome to ..." He broke off, tilting his head as though afraid he'd alarm her. "ReproJoy," he finished quietly.

Marley panicked and walked out again. "Sorry," she called over her shoulder as the doors slid open.

The next day, on her third attempt, he didn't say a word, though she made it all the way to the desk. She took a deep breath as he watched her calmly.

"Uh, how—what ..." The question wouldn't come out properly. Marley looked down at the counter, then resolutely back up at him. "I'd like to get my hands on some sperm."

He gently cleared his throat, his expression still smoothly professional and in the split second before he opened his mouth, Marley realised what she'd said.

"Crap. I heard it." Marley cringed and he shook his head to let her know it was fine. She sucked in a deep breath. "I've decided I want to have a baby. By myself. Obviously I don't have everything I need ... biologically speaking."

"Well, ReproJoy is definitely the right place for you. How much do you know about the process?"

"Only what I've researched and read in blogs. But ... no real life testimonials or appointments as yet."

"Don't worry, I can talk you through it and answer all your questions."

Marley smiled. His calm demeanour put her at ease and she could feel her nerves starting to subside. "What do I have to do to get some?" He blinked and Marley shook her head, annoyed at herself. "*Sorry*. What's ... how do we start, I mean?"

The clinic was dazzlingly white, about as different from the small GP practice where Marley worked as possible. Where Dr Martelle's office had worn orange carpet, this place had gleaming white tiles. Where they had faded wallpaper, ReproJoy had crisp white walls hung with framed microscope images. The desk at which the man stood, in his professional-looking long white coat, was polished to a gleam, clear of clutter and—of course—white. At least Marley had a chair she could sit in during the day, even if it was broken. It looked like this guy had to stand for his entire shift.

He reached under the desk and grabbed a branded folder, sliding it across the desk to her. "Our literature is a good place to start."

Marley gave it the briefest of glances. "I'm sure I already know what's outlined in there. Can't we just do it right away? The process, I mean," she added quickly. Dear God, what was wrong with her?

His look was sympathetic. "There's currently a two month wait for an appointment."

"Two months!" The words came out louder than Marley had intended.

"I realise how disappointing that is. It's like this at most places though. I can add you to our waiting list, and then if something else comes up before that, I can give you a call?"

She hesitated. "I guess I'll have to do that."

He adjusted his glasses with his thumb and forefinger, and clicked the mouse a few times. "To add you to the database, I need your name, address, date of birth."

"Okay ... a consultation is free, right?"

"Yes. That's free. Have you ... seen detailed pricing on the process itself?"

"I know the ballpark. It's hard to get *very* exact numbers."

He reached under the desk and pulled out a single sheet of paper, spinning it around to face her.

Marley ran her eyes over the cost breakdown and exhaled slowly. Roughly what she'd been expecting. Most places didn't publish their figures transparently, or if they did, they didn't include additional costs such as medication and bloodwork. Here on this sheet, everything was laid out. She appreciated the clarity, and though she'd already known she didn't have the whole amount saved, she did have options for getting her hands on the rest. The fact that those options made her slightly nauseous hadn't deterred her from marching into the clinic.

"There are some payment plans," he said kindly, after studying her face—obviously misunderstanding her expression. "Should I get you a pamphlet about them?"

She shrugged. "I guess it can't hurt."

He added another piece of paper to the folder and she placed the whole thing into her satchel.

A pretty woman with a blunt blonde bob slipped out of one of the white doors just beyond the reception desk. She stood beside the man at reception and flashed Marley a smile, holding up one finger. "Finley," she whispered. "When do you get a break?"

Finley shot Marley an apologetic look, then checked his watch. "Half an hour. But I'm taking a quick one. Just coffee at the Greek."

"I'll join you if I can."

After she disappeared, Finley smiled at Marley. "Sorry about that."

"It's fine." She shrugged. "Was that one of the doctors?"

"Yes." They held eye contact for a moment and Marley felt a faint movement in her core—like something had clicked into place. Colour rose to her cheeks and she looked down at the counter, momentarily flustered. Whatever *that* was, she was going to ignore it.

She could feel Finley's eyes on her. "Listen, we're not supposed to do this," he said, "but I can offer to tell you a bit more about the whole process if you'd like? In detail. A kind of informal information session so you can decide about booking an appointment."

"Are you that hard-up for business?"

He blinked. "We actually have more patients than we can handle. It's just that I understand how upsetting it is to find out about the waiting times. If we have a short chat, maybe you can better figure out whether this is for you."

"It is."

He laughed. "Okay. It was just a suggestion."

Marley was touched. There was something about him that made her feel comfortable and safe. "Thank you." She nodded her agreement. "Actually, I'd like that. If you don't mind," she added.

He smiled. "Not at all. Let's keep it quiet though. My girlfriend co-owns this place. I work here to help out and I'm not sure she'd exactly see this as helping out, although her business partner knows and approves. Actually, he encourages it."

Marley zipped a finger across her lips. "Wait. If that's your girlfriend, didn't she just say she'll join you on your break?"

He shook his head. "She never makes it. Meet me at the Greek restaurant just down the road in twenty five minutes."

"See you there." Marley turned to leave. She looked back and he smiled at her. "Thank you," she added.

He nodded, and Marley walked back out through the automatic front doors and onto the street.

With so much time to kill, Marley needed to walk off some nervous energy before she sat down to review the literature Finley had given her. She'd taken the entire day off after her boss, Dr Martelle, had reminded her that she hadn't had a break in several months. It seemed as good a time as any to use one of her vacation days up and let Tilda, the elderly former receptionist, step in.

Marley had power-walked two blocks when she noticed a small boutique. On impulse, she stepped inside, triggering a mechanical bell.

The heavily-pierced woman at the counter looked up from her phone and smiled. "Hi, babe," she called, her accent high-pitched and nasal. "Let me know if I can help you with anything. Your boots are totes adorbs by the way."

"Thanks." The orange cowboy boots were favourites of Marley's. She'd found them in a second hand store—where she bought most of her clothes—and the leather had been worn to a buttery-soft sheen. There were even arch support insoles inside, so she could stay in the boots for hours and her feet didn't ache.

Marley walked slowly through the shop, looking closely at every item. As well as racks of boho, floaty dresses, the store carried incense sticks, macramé pot plant hangers, books on crystal healing and Kashmiri homewares. Marley stopped in front of a shelf filled with bracelets made with strings of tumbled crystals. They had both adult and children's sizes. She spent a long time sifting through the different colours and shapes, eventually selecting a matching pair made of amethyst. One her own size, one much smaller.

Marley brought them to the counter and the sales assistant smiled as she wrapped them together in a piece of red tissue paper.

"Great choice, babe. Are these for someone special?"

Marley looked at her. The woman wasn't paying attention, her phone open on a string of texts she could barely take her eyes off.

"Me and my kid," Marley said slowly, enjoying the sound of those words and wondering whether she'd backtrack if the woman caught her out. If she demanded proof. "For when they're a bit older anyway."

"What a fab mum," the woman said, and Marley realised

she'd be forgotten before she even reached the door. "Your kid's going to absolutely love it."

Marley nodded her thanks and tapped her card to pay. Then she carefully took up the small red package and slipped it into an interior pocket of her leather satchel.

There were still ten minutes left until her meeting, but she headed slowly to the meeting point. The sun shone warm but not too hot, the sky was a bright turquoise without a single cloud in it. There was a spring in Marley's step as she headed to the little Greek restaurant.

The restaurant was sweet and small, with a leafy back courtyard filled with wrought iron tables and chairs. On the back wall of the courtyard, a huge mural depicted a view out to sea from what Marley recognised as Santorini, having seen it on a TV commercial. Marley chose a seat under a sun umbrella, with a view of the mural. It was quite well done and gave her the distinct feeling of being in a faraway place. She picked up the grimy, plastic-coated menu and then immediately put it back down, hating the feel of it on her hands. She wiped them on her sequinned pants and kept them in her lap as she waited.

He arrived five minutes late, shielding his eyes with his hand and squinting among the tables to find her. He'd shucked his coat and wore jeans, black runners and a graphic print t-shirt. He looked taller out from behind the white desk, and his arms were more muscular than Marley would have imagined. She waved.

"Hi." He scraped the chair out, cringing at the sound of the iron on brick tile.

"Thanks so much for coming. My name's Marley, by the way. And I know you're Finley."

"Actually, I prefer Finn. But yes, that's me."

They shook formally over the table, his hand easily engulfing hers. Tingles rippled up her arm where their skin touched, and Marley quickly pulled her hand back. Away from the harsh clinic lighting, Finn's skin looked impossibly clear and tanned, set off by the dark sheen of his thick hair and charcoal lashes.

"Shall we order some coffees?" she asked, waving the waiter over when he nodded. "I'll have a decaf cappuccino, please."

"No decaf." The waiter sounded bored and stood with his pencil poised above the paper.

"Seriously, you don't have decaf?" Finn looked up at him.

"Sure, we have decaf, and this is my stand up routine." The waiter rolled his eyes. "No. We don't have decaf. Like I said."

"Well, I'm trying to watch what I put in my body. So I don't want caffeine."

"Lemonade," the waiter suggested.

"Too much sugar."

"Juice."

"Is it fresh-squeezed here?"

"What do you think?"

She sighed. "I'll have a bottle of sparkling water then."

He scribbled onto his pad and looked expectantly at Finn.

"Espresso, please."

The waiter arched a thick brow. "Not the lactose-free mochaccino?"

Finn reddened as Marley looked at him questioningly. "You should get that, if that's what you want," she said. "Who cares?"

He gave her a half-smile and nodded to the waiter, who drew a line under their orders on his pad.

"They have that, but not decaf?" Marley said, once the waiter left.

"Weird, huh?" Finn grabbed a sugar cube from the bowl between them and crumbled it between his fingers as he looked at her. It seemed like a nervous habit, but Marley couldn't help staring at his hands. They were huge against the tiny sugar cube, strong and capable. Her eyes travelled up the corded muscles of his forearms.

"Why didn't you just order what you wanted?" she asked, snapping herself back to the present.

Finn looked down at the sugar and shrugged, colour still tingeing his cheeks. Marley had the distinct impression he was embarrassed about his order and she felt a surge of tenderness towards him.

She put her elbows on the table. "So give me the spiel."

He dropped the rest of the sugar cube into a nearby plant and dusted off his fingers. Then, as if on autopilot, he began, "Thank you for choosing ReproJoy Fertility Clinic, we're excited to be your partners on this journey."

Marley waved her hand. "You don't have to do the entire routine for me. Just maybe the key points?"

He grinned. "I know. It's just that I lived that speech on repeat for the first year I was with them and I can do it in my sleep. Do you have the folder I gave you?" When Marley nodded and held it out, he pulled a pen from his pocket and flipped one of the sheets inside the folder over, using the back of it to write on. Before he started writing, he looked at her. "One thing you need to know before anything else is that there's actually kind of a shortage in Australia. Of sperm, I mean. Have you heard that?"

"No. How's that even possible? You can get it on any street corner." He looked at her for a beat and she put her hand to her forehead. *"What* is the matter with me?"

He grinned reassuringly. "Okay, it sounds weird about the

shortage, I know. But we're not allowed to pay people for it, it has to be done voluntarily. There's a cap on how many families can use the same donor. And once the child turns eighteen, they're legally able to find out who the donor is. So, I guess that puts some people off."

"Huh. So even if I do this on my own like I want, there's still a chance the donor can become part of her life later?"

"Her?"

"I always imagined a girl. But I should stop saying that, I know. I'd love a boy just as much, I promise."

Finn twirled the pen in his fingers thoughtfully. "Have you thought about just having a one night stand or something? Or asking a male friend? Sorry to be blunt. I mean, assuming you're into guys, that is," he added quickly.

"I am." She sighed. "And the thought has crossed my mind. But I'd never do that to someone. Trick them into having a kid. It's different if it's a genuine accident, but I've never worked up the nerve to have a one night stand anyway." She gave him a sad look. "Anything more than that is a relationship. Which I don't want to be in."

"You sound very sure about that."

Marley nodded firmly. "It's the one thing I'm absolutely positive about. I'm doing this alone."

Finn nodded, biting the inside of his cheek. "Fair enough. And you're right. I guess a one-night stand to have a kid is a pretty shady way to go about it."

The waiter arrived with their drinks and left the bill in a metal cup beside them. Marley pulled it toward her.

"It's on me," she said. "Least I can do."

Finn smiled and started writing. As he wrote, Marley's mind skipped ahead. Maybe she could ask her best friend Lyra to lend her the rest of the money. Lyra had helped the third in their friendship group, Amy, set up her new interior design business—but then Amy had been able to pay a big chunk back quickly. Lyra would definitely say yes, Marley knew that. She'd need to think carefully about that option. Among others ...

She rolled her neck to give it a break from hunching over Finn's paper, and caught sight of the doctor from the clinic—Finn's girlfriend—weaving her way through the inside of the restaurant.

"Oh, she's here," Marley said, interrupting his talk.

Finn instantly knew who she meant, and quickly flipped the folder cover over the information he'd been writing. "Could you put that back in your bag, please?"

Marley did it quickly. "How are you going to explain me?"

"Coincidence."

Marley nodded. At the last minute, she had a flash of intuition and switched their drinks. Finn gave her a surprised look of gratitude.

"Finley, there you are." The woman reached them and bent down to peck Finn on the cheek. He tilted his head up to her. Marley caught a waft of her perfume—it smelled expensive.

"Hey, Bess. This is Marley."

"I saw you in the clinic earlier, right?" She spoke in an overly friendly tone, clutching her designer handbag in both hands as she stood beside the table. "And then you're also here. How odd."

"Well, there's nowhere else for a decent lactose-free mochaccino." Marley gestured to the almost empty cup in front of her.

Bess snorted. "Oh my God, not you too. Finley used to try and order those." She gave a short laugh that ended very suddenly. "Were you staying long, Marley, or ..." She trailed off, a smile frozen on her lips.

Marley stood. "No, I was just leaving. Please, have the seat."

Bess sat down just as the waiter came out. "Your outfit is super interesting, by the way." She looked Marley up and down with an unreadable smile. Finn shot Marley an apologetic glance.

"Oh, excuse me," Bess called to the waiter before Marley could answer, waving him over. "I'd like a Greek salad. Of course," she smiled like it was a joke and the waiter remained expressionless, "umm, but with no oil please? And can the lettuce be fresh? Last time it was all wilted. And the kalamatas should be pitted? I don't know *who* eats kalamatas with the pits."

"Greeks," the waiter said bluntly, shooting Marley a look.

"I'll head inside and pay," Marley said quickly, realising it was strange to just stand there beside them. "Have a nice day, both of you."

Bess flashed her a thin-lipped smile and then looked back at the menu, running a long manicured fingernail down it. Finn shot Marley a questioning look and she smiled back.

It was only once she was home and looked in the folder that she realised Finn had signed off one of the sheets of paper with his number. *Call me w/ any Qs. F.*

Marley smiled and put the paper on top of her hall stand, a warm glow spreading through her. She'd just taken the first steps towards her child.

CHAPTER TWO

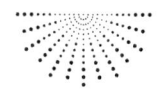

The next day, Dr Martelle arrived fifteen minutes after her first appointment should have started. The small GP clinic was usually booked several weeks in advance with appointments, and they kept a few slots free for urgent, walk-in cases. It didn't help that the doc cared so much for her patients that each slot usually ran over.

"Sorry, Marley." Dr Martelle swooped in breathlessly, the bottom three buttons on her blouse still open so it trailed behind her a little.

Marley thanked the heavens again that the waiting room had a door. She grabbed a patient file and followed Dr Martelle into her office, closing the door behind them. The doctor used the full-length mirror on the back to tuck her blouse into her knee-length skirt and slip her white coat over the top.

Marley glanced around the room to give the doctor privacy as she readied herself. The office made Marley feel calm—now. She had organised it to within an inch of its life, rescuing it from its former dishevelled state.

The doc herself was almost always running late, had the

handwriting of a six-year-old, and had been buried to her neck in random piles of paper before Marley started. As Marley looked back at the doctor, she closed the last coat button, completing her transition from disheveled to poised and polished. It was incredible how much a white coat and a good receptionist could hide.

Dr Martelle eyed Marley up and down and gave a small sigh at the sight of her checked golf pants, pineapple-print shirt and neon-yellow bolero jacket. "Marley, are you *sure* we can't invest in a uniform for you? You could even choose it. Something plain and simple?"

Marley shook her head firmly. "I am friendly, diligent and hard-working. Patients love me and I know all their names. I can even pronounce Mrs. Wiśniewska's name right," she tapped the patient file, "which she says you can't, by the way. I have reinvented your business and brought it into the twenty-first century. We have a *computer* system now, and almost all the patient files have been transferred across. It'll be finalised next week. We'll be moving to online appointment booking, and I'm planning a complete refurbishment of the foyer, reception and waiting room. And you care about my clothes?"

Dr Martelle arched an eyebrow. "A refurbishment?" she repeated.

"Yes. Do you know how many of your online reviews mention the horribly dated waiting room?"

"How many mention my oddly-dressed office manager?" she asked, a half-smile on her lips.

"None," Marley said proudly. Then it clicked. "Wait, did you just say *office manager*?" Dr Martelle nodded, grinning. "Is that a promotion?"

"It is." She winced. "It will be in name only for a couple of months, but after that, it will come with a pay rise. I just want you to know how appreciated you are. My turnover has increased by almost a third since you arrived. The least I can do is pay you a bit more like what you're worth."

"Thank you." Marley beamed at her. "I'll appreciate it even more when the money comes."

Dr Martelle laughed, then frowned. "Are you having some kind of financial trouble? You know you can always ask me for an advance if you are."

Marley shook her head. "No, I have a savings goal, that's all. This will help me get there quicker."

Dr Martelle nodded, adjusting her collar. "So, we'll discuss this *potential* refurbishment another time, okay?"

"Yes. But I was also thinking." Marley hesitated and the doctor eyed her expectantly. "We have way too much room for just you in these premises. If we got another doctor in here, you could split the rent and also get them to pay for half of the refurbishment."

Dr Martelle shook her head firmly. "We've discussed this. I don't play well with others. This is my space, I can afford the rent, and it's nice to have the two extra rooms for storage and lunch."

"But we could easily use the kitchenette for lunch instead."

"Marley, that's non-negotiable, sorry." The doctor gave herself one last glance in the mirror, hooked her stethoscope around her neck and moved to sit behind her desk. "For now, send in Mrs ... Whiz ..."

"Wiśniewska," Marley enunciated slowly.

"Wizneyuck ..."

"Try saying Vish-nyev-ska."

"Wish-nev? Oh, for God's sake, just send her in!"

The day dragged on, with Marley copying patient data from the old handwritten file systems into the specialist patient record database she'd installed several months ago. Tedious work, not helped by the fact Dr Martelle seemed to have written her notes during an earthquake. But it would be totally worth it once it she'd finished.

Marley found herself thinking about Finn as she clicked through the input fields on the system and entered patient data. His eyes were the most unusual shade of blue she'd ever seen, penetrating and warm at the same time—such a contrast with his black hair. Without warning, her brain conjured up an image of those same eyes and hair on a toddler, and she smiled.

A moment later, she was sickened at herself. Finn was in a relationship with Bess, and completely off-limits. Besides, Marley already knew she wanted to raise a child alone. With a past like hers, a history like her family's, there was no other way. She forced him out of her mind, but it didn't help that the very next file she picked up was for a patient named Flynn.

Marley hadn't given him her number, hadn't yet made an appointment with ReproJoy. She also hadn't had a chance to ask all she wanted to, about the specific way the clinic handled donor selection. The literature outlined the steps—most of which she'd already been familiar with—but she had a thousand detailed questions beyond that.

She decided to send Finn a text that evening. A short one, asking whether he could answer a few more of her questions.

She shifted on her seat uncomfortably. The first thing she would do if she got approval for the refurbishment would be to buy herself a new chair. The one she had was made of some kind of stained maroon fabric and had lost a wheel. It wasn't adjustable for her height and she often came home with a crick in her neck from sitting on it.

Marley would be meeting Lyra and Amy at their favourite bar, the Whistle Stop, after work, but she decided she'd pop home beforehand and grab Finn's number so she could send him a quick text. And perhaps also call the Thai massage place across the road, to see whether they could fit her in for a shoulder rub.

CHAPTER THREE

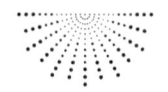

DARNEE, NEW SOUTH WALES, AUSTRALIA: 17 YEARS EARLIER

"Lena, come inside please." GamGam's voice cut over the top of Marley's conversation with Hayden. Marley rolled her eyes. She was fifteen now, far too old for her grandmother to still be calling her inside like that. Especially when Marley knew it was to stop her talking to boys. This boy in particular.

Hayden chewed a piece of straw, a habit Marley found interesting as it reminded her of the cowboys she saw in movies. The two of them were leaning on opposite sides of the chest-height wooden fence around GamGam's front yard, the long grass tickling Marley's bare feet and legs. She bent down to scratch a mosquito bite. They were bad this time of year, especially around twilight. It had been another stinking hot day and Marley looked forward to a cool shower after dinner. That usually calmed the itching, along with the calamine lotion GamGam dotted over her bites with a cotton ball.

"She's nice, your Gam. Even if she hates me," Hayden chuckled. "Must be great to have a hot cooked meal every day …" He flashed her a sad look with his huge brown puppy-dog eyes, and flicked his blond hair.

Marley hesitated. She knew there'd be hell to pay if she simply brought Hayden inside with her, and she also hated being at odds with GamGam. Besides, Gam definitely wouldn't have cooked enough for the three of them. She just wished her grandmother would let her invite Hayden to join them now and again. GamGam seemed to be the only one in Darnee resistant to Hayden's charms.

"I'll see you tomorrow," Marley said, deciding. "Sorry."

Hayden's eyes flashed with the briefest glimmer of annoyance, and Marley felt her heart lurch. Then they cleared and he smiled at her. "You're a good granddaughter. Hope she knows that and appreciates you. I sure will, when we're married."

Marley's stomach did flip-flops and she smiled shyly back. "Shouldn't you be getting home, too? Won't your parents worry?"

He frowned and shook his head. "Me and Brock are going down to the river." He leaned in to her conspiratorially. "He got a new kind of beer. Some fancy stuff like they drink in Sydney."

Marley nodded. She knew Hayden and Brock did that most evenings. Sat by the thick, slow brown river that ran through Darnee and drank beers Brock's father got for them. She didn't like it, but she'd told Hayden that once and he'd looked so pained that she hadn't mentioned it again.

"Lena!" GamGam called again, and Marley peeled herself off the fence, dipping her head forward to let Hayden peck her cheek as she always did.

"See you tomorrow, my girl." She nodded, turning from him and carefully picked her way over the bindi patches to the house. "Hey," he called as she neared the door. She turned. "You're heaps pretty, Lena."

She smiled the way she only did for him and went inside, the fly door slapping shut behind her.

GamGam frowned as Marley entered the kitchen. "I don't know what the devil you see in that boy," she said, not for the first time, as she violently whipped the already fluffy mashed potatoes. The kitchen smelled of grilled bream and Marley knew GamGam must have seen her old friend Lucas. They always ate fresh fish when she had.

Marley went to the wooden cupboard and pulled out the cutlery and crockery, setting the table for two places.

"He's my boyfriend," Marley said simply.

"You don't think you can do better for yourself?" Marley shrugged. "Boys like Hayden Gibbons are five a penny, Lena. I wish you'd just wait. Concentrate on school. You don't need a boyfriend yet, you're fifteen for God's sake."

"Exactly. *More* than old enough for my first boyfriend."

GamGam plated up their meals and brought the dishes to the table, setting Marley's down in front of her and taking a seat opposite. GamGam fell silent, watching Marley closely. Marley squirmed under her gaze.

"You're not sleeping with him, are you?"

Marley shook her head and made a face. "No. He says he wouldn't respect me if I did anyway. But I will once we're married."

GamGam's eyes bulged. "You're not going to *marry* him!"

"Yes, I am. I want to. Imagine how beautiful our babies will be."

GamGam's breathing had changed and she stared at Marley with a strange look in her eyes. "What do you think marriage is about?"

Marley cut a piece of her fish and chewed it thoughtfully.

"Well, I know you should do what the man says. And you have to sleep with him. And you have kids together, of course. That's the bit I'm excited about. I already thought of the names."

GamGam's face softened, but she still looked concerned. "The other stuff sounds appealing to you?"

"Not all of it, no. But ..." Marley trailed off. Of course she was going to get married. The alternative was to be an old maid, like Miss Grenville, and she didn't think she could handle the whispers everywhere she went in Darnee.

Hayden once said Miss Grenville had dried up *down there,* and that even if she wanted to do something, the area had grown over. There was even a rhyme that Darnee kids chanted as they jumped rope; *Old Miss Grenville / smells like a hen-ville / couldn't get a mister / now she's nothing but a spinster.* The rhyme always made Marley think of GamGam's friend Lucas, the fisherman. He'd never married, but no one chanted rude things about him. Most men spoke of him in admiring tones.

"Well, you're wrong, anyway," GamGam said.

Marley snapped her head up. "Which part?"

"Doing what men say, for a start. My marriage to your grandfather wasn't like that, and neither was your parents' marriage."

"What was it like then?" Marley lowered her cutlery, her eyes fixed on her grandmother. GamGam almost never spoke to her about her long-dead husband, Marley's grandfather. And she definitely never spoke about Marley's parents, who had both died in a car crash when Marley was three.

GamGam stayed silent for a long time. "It was a partnership, Lena. That's the most important part about it. The give and take, the support, the *love.* I don't think you'd get any of that with the Gibbons boy. In fact, I know you won't. I have a suspicion he wouldn't make much of a father, either."

Marley looked down at her plate, a fat tear plopping into her mashed potatoes. "I wish I'd been able to see how it was with them. With my parents. It sounds nice."

GamGam reached a hand across the table, laying it on top of Marley's with a squeeze. "Marriage doesn't tend to work out for us Phelps women," she said quietly. "My great-grandmother lost her husband when she was pregnant. My Nanna lost her husband in the war, when she already had kids. Her second husband died, too, falling off a cliff of all things. My father had a heart attack on the tractor, age of forty two. Your granddad, my beautiful Roger, well he only made it to thirty six. And then your parents ... except that time the curse took both of them at once."

"The curse?"

GamGam shook her head. "It's not a *real* curse. It's bad luck and coincidence. But it's how some people around here refer to it. If you looked into any other family close enough, you'd probably find a similar pattern. We just stick out a bit because Darnee is so small. You're going to hear people talk about it now and again. I'm surprised you haven't already, but I guess you aren't old enough. You're getting to be old enough now."

Marley nodded, taking it in. They ate in silence for a long time, GamGam watching her and Marley savouring the taste of fresh fish. Lucas went out in a motor boat, far up the river to where it met the huge lake several hours away. There, the waters ran clear and different kinds of fish swam. Most locals just fished from the dirty river, but Marley could taste the difference between river fish and Lucas fish.

"Was Grandpa Roger handsome?" Marley asked, as she stood up to clear their plates away once they'd finished eating.

GamGam shook her head. "Not especially. But he more than pulled his weight, he was mine alone and I loved him. I still love him."

Marley patted her grandmother's shoulder as she walked past, but deep down, she couldn't help feeling a little sorry for her. Marley knew exactly how lucky she was, being the girlfriend of the handsomest boy in Darnee.

CHAPTER FOUR

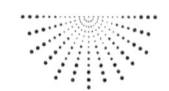

"The drinks are on me tonight," Marley told her two best friends, as they settled around their usual barrel at the Whistle Stop. It wasn't the trendiest place to grab a drink—Marley wasn't sure the sticky lino floor had ever been mopped and there was always a draught zipping through—but it was comfortable and familiar and they loved it.

"And why is that?" Lyra asked, smiling. She had her light brown hair pulled back in a ponytail and she sported her usual jeans and tee combo. The clothing hugged Lyra's shapely figure and Marley realised her red v-neck top had come courtesy of the record label she'd recently been signed to as a singer—the words "Teller's Music" were emblazoned in white just above her chest.

The server came over and they placed their drink orders.

"So?" Amy prompted, looking at Marley.

"I got promoted today," she said, and the girls jumped off their stools to hug her tightly.

"That's amazing!" Lyra squealed.

Amy sat back down and narrowed her eyes at Marley. "Does this mean you're still refusing my job?"

Amy had offered Marley a job at her newly-launched interior design business, Porter Lucas, but Marley enjoyed working for Dr Martelle too much to leave, even for one of her best friends. She knew Amy's business would do well—one look at her friend's ringleted blonde hair, her flawless mani and the vintage cream cardigan with the lace inset, and you knew you were dealing with a motivated perfectionist—but Marley found working with patients more fun than the snobby clientele she imagined Amy worked with.

Marley smiled. "I'm rather expensive now," she said, and Amy laughed. "Or at least, I will be when the pay rise kicks in."

"You're right, I probably can't afford you. Although, we're doing better than I had expected," she added with a note of pride, as their drinks arrived.

"That's awesome!" Lyra said. "Look at us all, doing so well in our lives. Well, I could do with more free time and less drama at the studio, but still. To us!"

They held their glasses up and clinked them.

"Oh, that reminds me," Marley said to Amy, after taking a sip of her sparkling water. "I'm trying to convince Dr Martelle to do a refurbishment of the doctor's offices. Know any good design firms, if she finally does come around?"

Amy grinned. "I do, as a matter of fact!"

"I even took 'before' pics today, when I was there alone." Marley got out her phone and swiped through some photos as Amy leaned in close.

"Oh my God, Marley." Amy put her hand to her heart in shock. "*That's* where you're working?"

Marley nodded. "Bad, right?"

Amy pinched and zoomed on a couple of photos. "Where did she even *find* those waiting room chairs?"

"You should see my desk chair!" Marley scrolled and zoomed in on it. "Please tell me you could do better than that?"

Amy looked at her in open-mouthed horror. "I think we could go to the dump right now and do better than that," she said. "I'm surprised you're not in hospital for the messed up back you must have!"

Marley laughed. "I'm getting close."

"It's not like you not to speak up," Lyra said. "Why don't you ask her for a new chair?"

Marley squirmed. "I think I can be assertive in certain circumstances. Not in others. And I don't usually mean to be blunt, it just kind of comes out. I've asked the doctor for a new chair before, and she's said she'll get to it."

"You should push for one though. You can't keep working like that," Amy said.

"I know."

A message pinged through and Amy squinted at the preview. "Who's Finn?"

Marley quickly withdrew the phone and swiped the notification away. "He was in our painting class, remember?" She felt a flicker of surprise at how easily the lie came to her. She and Amy had first met at a Wine & Paint course two years earlier and their connection had been instantaneous.

Amy frowned and shook her head. "Which one was he?"

"The quiet one always in the back corner. Used to carry a thermos with him everywhere and we'd always try and guess what was in it."

Amy gave her a blank look. "The one we caught eating his boogers that one time?"

"Uh, yeah?" Marley had absolutely no idea what she was talking about.

She felt a tug after she swiped away Finn's message. She was eager to read it, and that concerned her. Instead, she forced herself to concentrate on the moment with her girlfriends.

"Why on earth are you still in touch with someone like that?" Lyra asked, laughing.

Marley shrugged. "We just message now and again, haven't met up. You know those acquaintances you just can't seem to shake?"

Amy nodded knowingly. "Yes. God, that was me with Lauren."

"Rick's physio, or whatever she's called?" Lyra asked.

Amy nodded. "Physical therapist. I mean, she's doing amazing work with him. But I feel a hell of a lot more comfortable around her now she's dating."

Amy's boyfriend Rick had been injured in a car wreck several months earlier and was still to regain full mobility, though the prognosis was good. Amy had been slightly anxious about his extremely pretty physical therapist—until Lauren had started her own romance with one of Rick's friends.

"I also have some news," Lyra said shyly. They turned to her. "My first album is coming out soon and I'm going to do a short tour to support it."

They jumped up once again, squealing, and hugged her tightly, congratulating her.

"When will your next single come out?" Amy asked, once they'd sat back down.

"Three weeks." Lyra screwed her nose up. "They're making me do more social media first."

"Oh God," Amy laughed. "I can just imagine how much you're loving that."

"I can't believe you've avoided it until now," Marley said. "But surely they can just get someone else to actually do the posting and stuff though, right?"

Lyra shook her head, rolling her eyes. "You guys, it's

about *authenticity* and *access*," she droned, clearly repeating something she'd been told many times.

"Oh dear." Amy cringed sympathetically. "Well, shall we get a nice picture of you out with your BFFs?"

Lyra's face lit up. "That's exactly the kind of thing they asked me to put on there."

"Okay, well, let's crowd in." Amy beckoned Marley over.

Marley hesitated. "Why don't I just take one of the two of you?"

"No," Lyra insisted. "It's got to be the three of us. The three musketeers."

Marley couldn't think of an acceptable reason not to be in the picture. Aside from that if Lyra's social media account got big, someone would definitely see her. Someone from her past. And that was the last thing she wanted.

Amy seemed to sense Marley's hesitation. She was the only one who knew something of Marley's history—that she'd been married and that she'd previously gone by the name Lena. Amy winked at Marley now, looping an arm around her shoulders and raising her drink in a way that partly obscured Marley's face.

Lyra flicked through the images they snapped. "Oh, we can't see you properly, Marley."

"Sure you can," Amy said, leaning over, "and if not, all the more mystery." She changed the subject and Marley shot her a look of gratitude. Hopefully Lyra would have forgotten all about the photos by the time the record label pressured her to post something.

On the bus on the way home, Marley finally checked Finn's message.

Hey Marley, nice to hear from you. I'd be happy to answer your questions. Maybe you've got time tomorrow night? I could stop by after work since you're in the neighbourhood, but also happy to meet anywhere else.

Her heart pounded as she read the message and an involuntary grin spread across her face. She lowered the phone and stared out the bus window for a few moments, breathing deeply.

It had been so long since she'd felt flutters of attraction like this. So very long. Surely, there was no harm in just letting herself enjoy them—especially if she had no intention of ever getting involved. Finn was taken, happily so, and she was about to start the process of getting pregnant. Nothing could or would ever happen between the two of them. It was just that Finn was helping Marley bring her future child into existence—that was all.

Slowly, her heart rate returned to normal, and she typed a reply.

Sure. I'll have snacks. She added her address. *I'll be home from 5:30.*

The message was immediately marked as read and she could see he was typing. *5:30? Lucky you! I'll be there around 6:30. OK?*

Marley texted back the thumbs up emoji.

Her messaging app told her he was writing something else, but then his profile went offline. She waited a few more moments, then tucked her phone into her bag. Without even realising it, she smiled the entire bus ride home.

CHAPTER FIVE

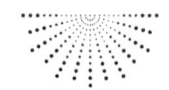

After a very long day at work, which had involved both an eleven-year-old patient *and* a seventy-three-year-old patient vomiting in the waiting room, Marley trudged up the stairs to her apartment, kicked her shoes off and flopped onto the sofa with a groan.

Dr Martelle had told Marley the amount she would raise her salary by. If Marley could wait that long, she could afford the donation process outright a few months after the raise kicked in. *If* she could wait ...

She desperately needed a shower to remove any chance of residual vomit clinging to her. She forced herself up off the sofa and into the bathroom, stripping off her clothes and immediately dropping them into the washing basket. She wished she could clean them with fire.

Maybe a uniform wouldn't be such a bad idea. If Dr Martelle ever did agree to the refurbishment, Marley would tell her that they could look for something together. But a uniform would be out of place in the current surroundings. They also needed to hire another permanent staff member. On the days when Marley was off they called Tilda back, and she struggled to cope with the computer system Marley had set up.

Marley ran the shower hotter than usual, trying to work out some of the knots in her shoulders. Her right side felt painfully tight, both from sitting in the oddly-leaning chair, and from hooking the phone into the crook of her shoulder as she took calls. She made a mental note to call the massage place for a slot at the weekend, having forgotten the previous day. Maybe she could even claim it back on taxes as a work-related expense.

She washed her hair and took a long time rubbing moisturiser over her entire body once she was out. Her skin had been feeling quite dry from the air-conditioning at work, and she needed to take better care of it. She'd once convinced Dr Martelle to turn the air-con off and open the windows instead. A giant cockroach had flown in and landed on a patient, so the windows remained firmly sealed and Marley imagined the ancient air-conditioning unit to be churning out Legionnaires disease her entire shift.

"You only get one skin, Lena," she could hear GamGam's voice in her head as she moisturised. "So you have to take care of it."

Marley smiled thinking about her grandmother. She missed her painfully. There wasn't a day that went by where Marley didn't ache in her bones to be able to see her again, though she'd been gone thirteen years.

Marley opened her medicine cabinet to get out her hair brush and her eyes fell on the necklace GamGam had given her, the gold one with the L charm hanging from it. She remembered with crystal clarity the day GamGam had given it to her—the jewellery shop smelling of new carpet and astringent polish, the watery look in her grandmother's eyes, the reverence with which the jeweller had handed them the chain.

For years, Marley hadn't taken that necklace off, and then when she'd moved to Sydney for her fresh start more than two years earlier, the L didn't make sense. Not when she was introducing herself as Marley. Lyra had found the necklace on her bedroom floor once. It must have fallen out of her jewellery box, but she'd told Lyra it wasn't hers. Even two years after leaving her past behind, Marley still wasn't ready to tell the girls the full story. Amy knew part of it, but not the whole thing.

Marley wanted to tell them. They were her best friends and she hated that they didn't know this about her. She would tell them soon.

She slipped the necklace on now, pressing it to her heart as she wandered into her bedroom to dress.

Afterward, she ran the vacuum through the apartment, tidied up everything out of place and then laid out a jar of olives, some bread sticks, an eggplant dip and some cubes of cheese on the colourfully-painted wooden crate coffee table. She filled her thrifted fish-mouth water pitcher and sat two mismatched glasses beside it.

She caught sight of herself in the living room mirror—it was shaped like a huge blob of dripping paint and Marley loved it—and wondered whether to tie up her hair. It was honey-coloured and thick, with a slight wave. She'd left it loose around her shoulders, the fringe slightly longer than she usually let it grow. Normally, she just scraped it into a ponytail without thinking, but maybe this was a nicer way to wear it. Maybe it suited her.

The doorbell rang and Marley's nerves jangled in response. She took several deep breaths before buzzing Finn in, telling him through the intercom to head up to the fourth floor.

"Hey, Marley." He smiled as he got to the landing. He handed her an expensive bottle of sparkling water and a pack of vitamin gums as he stepped inside and reached to take off his shoes. "I remembered you're not drinking, so I brought the nicest water I could find. And those gums have folic acid in them."

She was touched by the thoughtfulness of the gifts. "Thank you."

"That looks good," he said, eyeing the spread on the coffee table. "I'm famished."

"Sorry, I should have prepared more, then." She opened the sparkling water and poured them both a glass.

"No, no. This is perfect." He sank into the sofa. "Are you going to sit?"

She did so, awkwardly. Suddenly, her sofa felt incredibly small. It was also difficult to talk to Finn when she was sitting beside him, but her neck pinched if she turned to face him. She tried to angle herself in such a way that she could see him and keep some distance between them.

"Is there something wrong with your neck?" Finn asked, looking concerned. He dragged a breadstick through the eggplant dip and took a bite.

She rubbed her neck. "It gets sore from work. I have a horrid chair and I'm also holding the phone like this a lot." She demonstrated.

"What do you do for work?"

"I'm the office manager for Dr Martelle, on Avona Avenue."

Finn nodded. "Would you like me to try and fix your shoulder?"

Marley laughed. "Sure. That would be great."

"No, I'm being serious." His eyes were eager. "I'm actually a licensed physiotherapist."

She puffed out a breath, frowning. "Then why on earth are you working as a receptionist?"

"Yeah, it's a bit of a long story." He reached under his

glasses with one finger and rubbed his eye, looking suddenly very tired.

"You don't have to talk about it."

"No, it's fine. I've had a lot of questions about it from my friends over the years, so I'm pretty used to talking about it now. I met Bess at uni, I was studying physio and she was studying medicine. She always intended to specialise in reproduction. We dreamed we'd open clinics near one another. But then Bess started ReproJoy with one of her uni mates, and we both threw ourselves into it. We're going to get that off the ground and then focus on my clinic."

"Ah," Marley said, "That makes sense. How long ago did the clinic open? You must be impatient."

Finn seemed hesitant to answer, tracing his finger along the pattern on the sofa's fabric. "A couple of years ago now, I guess."

Marley frowned. "So, her dream won over yours and now you're a receptionist?" The instant the words were out of her mouth she regretted it. She could see she had offended him.

He shook his head. "It's not like that," he said quietly. "It's just we haven't found the finances for my clinic yet. And I've become indispensable at ReproJoy. For a while I went to work in another physio's practice. But things at ReproJoy got out of hand and I volunteered to come back for a while."

To Marley, it seemed horribly selfish of Bess, but she reminded herself Finn was a grown man, in control of his own life. If he was okay with the situation, what reason did she have not to be? He was basically a stranger to her.

"Alright," she said uncertainly. "It's none of my business anyway."

"And everything we're doing at ReproJoy is for mine and Bess's future."

"Oh, so the business is registered in your name, too."

Marley released tension she hadn't realised she'd been holding.

Finn laughed. "Wow. You're quite blunt, has anyone ever told you that?"

"Yes. Often," she said wryly, putting an olive in her mouth to stop herself from talking. She shot him an apologetic look.

He smiled to let her know it was okay. "No, it's not in my name. But I trust her." He picked up his water glass and sipped.

"Are you guys engaged or anything?" Marley asked. Instantly, she felt her face burn. Where had *that* come from?

Finn gave her a lopsided smile. "No. I did propose actually, long ago when we were just out of uni."

Marley blinked. "She said *no?*"

"Hmm. It wasn't the right time." He avoided eye contact, stroking his finger along the rim of the glass as they sat in silence.

Marley spent a few moments mesmerised by the stroke then cleared her throat, feeling warm. "Don't you miss physio? Aren't you worried you're going to forget everything you learned?"

"I won't forget," he said confidently, looking back up at her. "I practise on friends all the time, I keep my licence up to date and every now and again I attend seminars and things like that." Finn tilted his head at her. "You don't believe me, do you?"

When she didn't answer, he stood up and grabbed the green floor cushion from the other side of the living room. He set it at his feet and patted it, indicating she should sit there. She shook her head.

"Come on, Marley," he said in a singsong voice. "I have something to prove now. Just ten minutes. If you hate it, I'll stop." Alarm flickered across his features. "You don't need to worry, I'm not going to hurt you," he said quickly. "I just realised I'm a guy you barely know, asking to lay his hands on your body. That could come across as weird, I get it. No pressure." He held up his palms.

She laughed. "I don't get the feeling you're the Boston Strangler. That's not why I'm worried …" She didn't quite know how to explain that the words *lay his hands on your body* had registered differently in her mind than he'd intended.

"Come on, then." He slapped the cushion again. "Just ten minutes."

Her neck and shoulders *were* aching, and she supposed it wasn't inappropriate for a trained physiotherapist to work on a client for a minute, even if the client had no intention of paying. If there had been anything odd about it, surely he wouldn't have suggested it. After all, he was in a relationship.

"Okay," she said finally. "Just ten minutes. Then I want to talk about insemination." Their eyes caught and they looked quickly away. "God, there really is no good way to talk about that, is there?"

Finn chuckled. "Don't worry, I've heard it all."

She sat at his feet, glad she had her back to him so he couldn't see that her face was still pink. As soon as he touched his hands to her shoulders, he let out a low whistle.

"It feels like you have rocks under your skin. You must be in absolute agony," he said.

"It's pretty bad some days," she agreed, while he ran his hands over her back as though getting the lay of the land.

It was an effort not to make any noise as his strong fingers quickly found the source of her pain and started manipulating the muscles around it. At times, Finn worked so firmly that Marley almost told him to stop—the pain was worse than the pinch. But then he would switch to a more tender movement and she could feel a giant knot coming loose in her shoulder and neck. At the end of ten minutes, Marley felt like a new person.

"Shall I keep going?" he asked.

Surprised at how close his voice was to her ear, she sprang up. "No, but that was better than I thought." She grabbed two cubes of cheese and crammed them into her mouth for something to do as she sat back down on the sofa beside him. Even after that short session, she could turn her head without experiencing much pain.

"High praise." He grinned at her, waiting for her to swallow the giant mouthful of food.

"I don't want you to get a big head, that's all. But that helped a lot. Which makes it even sadder that you're not running your own practice," she added, shaking her head. "Bess is depriving the people of Sydney."

He smiled. "It's not her fault. We're in this together. I'll get my practice soon, once things are more steady."

"If they haven't steadied in a few years, do you think they're going to?" Again, the words were out of her mouth before she could stop herself.

Finn gave her a funny look. "Can we talk about something else, please?" he asked quietly.

"Yes. And I'm sorry. I've been like this since … for a while. I can't seem to shake the habit of speaking that way. GamGam would be so proud." Marley knew she was talking quickly, but couldn't seem to make herself slow down. "I can just imagine her saying, 'Lena, you finally found your voice.'"

Finn blinked. "Lena?"

Marley looked down at the sofa, grabbing a cushion and hugging it to her chest. She fell silent until she had steadied her breath. "My full name is Marlena," she said quietly, not meeting his eye. "Most of my life, I went by Lena. But I changed it to Marley a few years ago."

Finn seemed to sense the significance of what she had told him. "Well, that's a beautiful name. Any way you use it." He paused. "Is that what the L is for on your chain? Lena?"

Marley nodded, bringing her hand to the chain. She was mortified to find that she was blinking back tears.

"I'm sorry." Concern etched his features. "I didn't mean to upset you."

She shook her head and swallowed, trying to get rid of the lump in her throat. He reached out and unthinkingly put a hand on her arm. Her heart thudded out of rhythm and in the silence that fell, she could hear them both breathing. She didn't dare look at him.

He quickly released her arm and stood, glancing at his watch. "I totally forgot," he said. "I have somewhere I need to be."

"Yes," she said, standing. "Sure."

"We can talk about the other stuff another time, is that okay?" He was already headed for the front door.

"Of course." She kept her voice light. "No worries at all. Have a good night."

"Bye, Marley." He shoved his feet into his shoes and walked out, shooting her the briefest of farewell glances.

She locked the door behind him, pressed her back against it and slid down to the floor. She could hear Finn's footsteps going down the stairs. He was all but running.

CHAPTER SIX

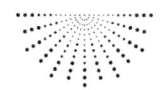

Several days later, Marley hadn't heard anything from Finn. She'd sent one text the day after their encounter, asking whether he had time to meet up somewhere public, to discuss the fertility topic. He'd read it, but had not replied.

She resigned herself to the fact she'd never see him again and felt a complicated mix of relief and disappointment. She spent the minutes between patients searching for other fertility clinics that weren't too far from her flat or work, or were at least on a decent public transport route. Without a car, it would otherwise be a bit of an issue to get to appointments without taking entire days off.

She returned to work after running an errand and found Dr Martelle sitting behind the reception desk, flipping through a huge office supply catalogue. She looked up when Marley walked in, a smile on her face.

"You didn't tell me you had a boyfriend."

"What are you talking about?" Marley joined the doctor behind the desk and tucked her satchel into the cupboard. She smoothed her paisley pencil skirt over her hips. It fit more snugly than she was used to and though she'd had several compliments on it, she made a note to give it to charity. She felt self-conscious in it. "I don't have a boyfriend."

"Well, he could have fooled me." Dr Martelle spun in the chair to face her.

"I honestly have no idea what you mean," Marley said blankly. "Are you open on the chair page?" She peered excitedly over Dr Martelle's shoulder at the catalogue. "Am I finally getting a new chair?"

She nodded. "And that's not all. See these stickies?" She ran her fingers along the edges of the thick book, which bristled with coloured place markers. "These are all the pages with options for things that a physiotherapist named Finn Mayberry came and told me are good for desk workers. Health and safety standard, actually."

Marley's heart punched against her ribcage. "Finn was here?"

"Yep," Dr Martelle nodded, standing. The chair spun a wonky half-circle. "And he gave me a proper talking to, as well."

"Oh, I'm sorry."

Dr Martelle grinned. "Don't worry. He wasn't rude. And he wasn't wrong. I've been sitting in this chair for the half hour you've been gone and I already feel like I need a hip replacement. I'm truly sorry I've been forcing you to sit like this."

"It's fine. You sort of get used to it."

Dr Martelle raised an eyebrow. "You do?"

"Absolutely not." Marley grinned. "I actually think it gets worse each day. And I did ask ..."

Dr Martelle winced and tapped the catalogue. "Well, you go through this thing and write down your choice of the items he's noted down here," she indicated a handwritten checklist beside the catalogue, "and give it to me when you're done. I'll take care of the rest."

"Thank you." Marley sat down and ran her eyes over Finn's note. He had listed a fully-adjustable chair with lumbar support and wheels, an ergonomic keyboard and mouse, a gel wrist-pad, an angled footrest, an LED light, a stand to lift the monitor up and down, a headset for the phone and a roll pad for the new chair so it would glide in and out from under the desk on its casters.

"You look way too happy," Dr Martelle said after a moment. "I'm the worst boss in the world for making you sit there!"

Marley shook her head, looking up at the doctor. "I'm just happy in general, that's all."

She nodded and headed back to her office, leaving Marley flipping through the catalogue, a warmth tingling through her body.

She picked up her phone to write a quick thank you message to Finn, but when she scrolled to his number, she saw her last message sitting there, read but unanswered. She put her phone away, determined not to bother him.

After all, he hadn't left a message for her with Dr Martelle, simply done a nice deed for someone who could potentially be a future client at his clinic—whenever that opened. Marley thought it was a lovely farewell gesture from someone who had almost been a friend.

CHAPTER SEVEN

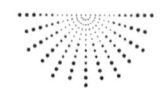

"I didn't like anything in that one either," Amy groaned, as she dropped a bridal magazine onto the growing pile on her living room floor. "God, I'm sick of spending my weekends trying to select things. I don't know why Rick and I can't just elope."

"Why don't you?" Lyra asked. She sat cross-legged on the carpet, a magazine open on her lap as she sipped a soft drink through a glass straw. Marley wanted to tell her it was a little early in the day for so much sugar, but she bit her tongue. "With me and Marley there, of course," Lyra continued. "And Rick should probably come, too."

Amy grinned, then sighed dramatically from her place on the sofa, flopping over. Her head landed near Marley's feet, which were tucked up alongside her. "Because Rick wants a wedding. Or, well I guess his mum does."

"Then let her plan it," Marley said. "That solves everything."

Amy looked up at her. "That isn't a bridal magazine."

"I went off-piste," Marley said, shrugging.

"You're reading *Knitting Weekly?*" Lyra squinted at her magazine.

"You're a terrible bridesmaid," Amy said, in a mock-serious tone.

"Then you should have asked me to be Maid of Honour," Marley joked. She saw Amy and Lyra exchange a worried glance.

Amy sat up. "Are you truly okay that I asked Lyra?"

"Yes, of *course*," Marley said truthfully, smiling. "I was only joking. You guys have known one another forever. I'm delighted to be a bridesmaid. I've never been one before."

Amy seemed satisfied and a look of relief crossed Lyra's face.

"But why are you reading a knitting magazine?" Amy asked.

"I figured I might learn. It's a useful hobby." Marley didn't mention that she planned on knitting for a small person. "And I found those wedding magazines boring. Sorry," she added when Amy pointedly cleared her throat.

"What about this?" Lyra said, turning her magazine to show them a beautiful, simple outdoor wedding at a long rustic picnic table.

"Oh, that's nice," Amy said. Then she frowned. "But I don't think Pam will go for it. She keeps using the word 'elegant'."

"Is she paying for the wedding?" Lyra asked. "Why's she getting so much say?"

Amy sighed. "Apparently when Rick's brother got married, the wife didn't let her get involved in the planning at all. Pam was upset about it and Rick always told her she could help with his."

Marley snorted. "He didn't think to consult the future Mrs Richard Ford?"

"Well, the future Mrs Amy Beth Porter isn't too pleased about it either."

"You're not going to change your name?" Marley asked, surprised.

Amy shook her head. "I don't exactly love my dad's name. But ... it's my name. I'd feel weird changing it. I've been using it for ages professionally as well."

"If you have kids, whose name would they have then?" Marley asked.

Amy made a face. "I have no idea. Maybe we'd hyphenate."

"The Ford-Porter children. Or the Porter-Ford children," Lyra said, sounding them both out.

"Or just Amy Porter and Richard Ford," Amy said. "I only have one ovary, so I don't know how easy it's going to be."

"Do you want kids?" Marley asked Lyra.

She nodded. "Yeah. Alex does too." Then she rolled her eyes. "But that would involve actually being at home together at the same time. That more or less never happens at the moment."

Amy studied her. "You don't look well, I have to say. I worry about you."

Marley nodded and Lyra flicked her eyebrows up in agreement. "You sound like Alex," she said wearily. "I know I'm working a lot, but this is what I've always wanted. There are some parts that maybe aren't ideal, but I'll take the bad with the good."

"Which bits are bad?" Marley asked.

Lyra sipped her drink and considered. "The owner and the producer and I still haven't agreed on a permanent keyboard player for my band, since Mick says he wants to retire. The one woman that I liked apparently had 'too much star power on her own' and was unsuitable. And the guy the producer liked turned out to be a massive homophobe who flipped out and quit when my brother and his boyfriend came to visit the studio. If he hadn't quit, I'd have killed him, so that was lucky. But ... we aren't exactly doing well on that front."

"Who's going to join the tour with you then?" Marley asked.

Lyra shrugged. "This is the question. And this is why I'm often at the studio at all hours. We need to do tryouts whenever the people the studio shortlist are available. And it's always at random times and there are *always* delays."

"Surely if they're being offered a permanent gig supporting a rising star, the studio should just name the time and they come running?" Amy said.

"You'd think so, wouldn't you? I don't know. Selena has an odd way of doing business I guess. But she owns the label, and she's taken a chance on me. There are people who'd kill to have this dilemma. I'm trying to just focus on the bright parts. And there are lots!"

"How does Alex feel about all this?" Marley asked.

Lyra's face fell. "We miss each other. Terribly. But at least we're living together now. And it shouldn't be so intense for too much longer. They want a three-piece band and we have two of the three. I have a drummer who seems pretty cool. He and I are starting to build some rapport. And the guitar player is a whiz but she hardly says a word. I feel like she could have an entire secret life as an assassin. But at least we don't disagree. It's just the keyboard player we're struggling with."

"Do you think that's just because you don't want to replace Mick?" Marley asked.

Mick—a grizzled rocker of an older man—had been like a father to Lyra for most of her life, and they'd played together for over a decade. He'd since decided he was too old to accompany Lyra on her rise to fame, and had turned down a contract so he could spend more time with his girlfriend.

Lyra looked at her sadly. "I mean, maybe that has a bit to do with it on some level? But I think if it was a match, I'd be open to it."

"Can Mick just do this one tour and *then* you find someone else?" Amy suggested. "He did the music for your first single, right?"

"Yeah, but he hated being away from Kathryn." Lyra grinned. "Amy, are you trying to change the subject away from wedding planning by any chance?"

Amy didn't respond, just flopped face down onto the sofa again. "Yes," she said, her voice muffled.

"Look!" Marley said. "I found the perfect dress!" She held up a page in her magazine where a woman sported a knitted tunic in shades of brown and green, several daisies woven into her hair.

Amy rolled onto her back to look at it. "It's perfect. We're done here, folks."

"Good, can we go for a walk along the beach then?" Lyra got quickly to her feet. "I'm starting to feel like Gollum, the amount of time I spend indoors."

CHAPTER EIGHT

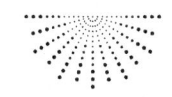

"I knew you'd get bubblegum," Lyra laughed, nudging Marley as the three women licked ice-creams from Amy's favourite vendor.

"I don't know why people waste their time with any other flavours." Marley shrugged at Lyra's chocolate cone and licked around the base of her own scoop. She had ice-cream so rarely that she couldn't pass up a chance for it.

Bondi Beach richly deserved its place as a jewel in Sydney's crown. The broad, long sweep of golden, sun-drenched sand cupped shockingly clear aquamarine water. At the edges of the semi-circular shoreline where the sand bank narrowed, big mossy stones added lush green to the colour palette. The waves were usually gentle, the sea scattered with surfers, the sand crammed with bathers.

Today, miraculously, it wasn't as crowded as usual so the girls went straight for the shoreline, letting the cool waves lick up to their ankles as they walked.

Lyra stopped and took long, deep breaths of the ocean air as she stood facing out to sea, watching gulls wheel over the surfers.

"God," she said, closing her eyes behind her sunglasses. "It's been *way* too long since I did this."

Amy nodded. "I start to feel sick when I'm away from the sea for too long."

"Like *Heidi* with the Swiss Alps," Marley said.

Amy laughed. "Exactly like that."

They walked on in silence, devouring their ice-creams and drifting in the direction of Icebergs—the open-air, Olympic-sized saltwater pool and the sun-bleached clubhouse that overlooked it.

As they walked, Marley found herself picturing what it would be like if she had a baby. Would she be able to do things like this?

As though in answer to her question, a young mother strolled past them with her baby strapped to her chest in a harness. She looked happy and relaxed. But perhaps she had a husband to go home to. Or a mother who took her baby several times a week so that she could have a break. Or an au pair. Or *she* was the au pair and could give the baby back at the end of the walk.

For a second, it felt overwhelming to even be considering having a child alone. Her life would be changed in the biggest possible way, and forever.

Still, if she closed her eyes, she felt the sun on her face, heard the roar of the ocean, smelled the sea breeze. She knew she wanted to give a child a chance to feel the same things. Marley already loved her baby so deeply that it was difficult to believe it wasn't yet real. She'd wanted a child so long, she could almost feel its weight in her arms. She wondered if these thoughts and feelings made her crazy, but she had no one to ask about it.

"Have you thought about the guest list yet, Amy?" Lyra asked suddenly.

Amy shook her head. "No. This is another reason I'm not

sure I want a wedding. Will I have to invite my father? I definitely have to invite my mum's husband, even though we barely tolerate each other. And if Dad *and* Bill are there..."

Lyra cringed. "Sorry. I hadn't thought of that."

Marley was considering the point when she spotted a couple up ahead, stopped in the sand and seemingly in the middle of an argument. They were both in swimsuits, the man's muscular, tanned torso on display. The woman had a trim figure and wore a skimpy bikini. She raised her voice from time to time and the man shook his head. Marley lowered her ice-cream and squinted at them, her heart beating faster. It was Finn and Bess.

"Can we go back the other way?" she asked, slowing down.

The girls slowed too and Amy frowned. "I was kind of heading for Icebergs, I thought we could get a bite there, sit on the deck."

"Okay. Or we could go back up? Find a place on Campbell?"

Lyra turned to face Marley, her expression unreadable behind her sunglasses. "Is everything okay?"

Marley nodded.

"Are you sick?" Amy asked.

"No." Marley took a moment to consider things. It was silly to want to avoid Finn and Bess, she decided. There was no reason for it. They likely wouldn't even notice her, but if they were content to disagree in public like that, they couldn't be surprised if they were spotted by someone who knew them.

"Never mind," Marley said, realising they'd all come to a stop and the girls were staring at her. "Let's just keep going. Icebergs sounds fine."

They started moving and Marley felt her eyes being drawn to Finn again and again as they got closer. She'd been vaguely surprised that his arms were so toned and now that he was shirtless, it was clear his arms weren't the only part of his body that rippled with taut muscles ...

The sight of him was having a physical effect on Marley.

Neither Finn nor Bess had noticed her, but as the girls drew closer, Bess lowered her voice. Still, snatches of the conversation reached Marley clearly enough for her to make them out.

"Discussed this over and over ... open *your* clinic when the time is right ... jeopardise *my* business, because you're too impatient ..."

Lyra and Amy didn't seem to have noticed them, or at least weren't paying attention to them. They resumed the discussion about the wedding guest list and Marley only half-followed along. Just as they were passing Finn and Bess, he looked up and spotted Marley. His face fell. She gave him a small smile of acknowledgement and he nodded ever so slightly, then put his head back down as Bess continued.

Marley felt a swirl of emotions. Were they arguing about his practice because of what she had said to him, the evening he'd come over? Or was it a discussion they regularly had, and she'd just been tactless enough to poke her finger in the hole? Either way, she hoped they resolved it. Finn deserved the chance to follow his dreams.

She knew from first hand experience how difficult it was to be with someone who didn't support you.

At Icebergs, Marley tried to push Finn and Bess from her mind. The girls chose a table on a bright, second-storey balcony overlooking the glittering pool and the ocean. Amy and Lyra both ordered an Aperol Spritz, Lyra determined to make the most of her time out of the studio. Marley ordered sparkling water and they all scanned the menus. She decided on fresh fish, which made her think of GamGam.

She looked out over the water and smiled contentedly, realising she would never get sick of seeing the ocean. She had dreamed about it during her childhood in Darnee, but she and GamGam had never actually managed a trip to the coast. She loved how fresh and clean the air smelled beside the sea and could fully understand why Amy had chosen to live in Bondi.

"How are you and Rick going with the house-hunting?" she asked.

Amy sighed. "It's actually hard. He's still living with Pam right now, and I'm spending a lot of nights over there. We don't want to be apart, and my building isn't accessible for his wheelchair. I'm locked in a disagreement with the other owners about getting a chairlift installed, but it might need to go to a vote and I have a horrible feeling it won't pass if it does. It blows my mind that they can say no. I don't want to give up my place, not when I'm relatively close to having it paid off and Bondi prices just keep going up. It's all a big mess." She put her elbows on the table and her head in her hands.

"You've just about paid me back the money I lent you when you were starting up Porter Lucas," Lyra said. "Why don't you borrow it again and use it as a deposit on a place for you and Rick? That way you don't have to give up your flat."

Amy shook her head. "Thank you for offering, but *you* should be using it. You and Alex could buy a place instead of renting."

"We're not renting. He owns his place. We'd sell it and get a bigger one that he'd flip, but ... I usually don't even have the time to look at the places he picks out."

"Why don't you just let him choose then?" Marley asked.

Lyra shook her head. "It doesn't feel right, delegating something big like that. It should be a huge first step for us, and I feel like I'm absent. I'll get there though. Anyway, what's going on with you lately, Marley?"

Marley bit her bottom lip, wondering whether now was the moment to fill them in on her plans. It would be a huge deal, going through the donor process and hopefully getting pregnant. She'd need them by her side, would want them there, cheering her on and helping her. They were the closest thing to family she had, just about the only proper girlfriends she'd ever had. But she almost felt as though she'd be jinxing things if she mentioned her plans now, at such an early stage. Still, she wanted them to know.

"I'm enjoying my job," she began finally. "And—"

"Well, that's a pretty big deal actually," Lyra cut in. "So many people don't get to love their jobs."

"So true," Amy added, raising her head off her hands. "I hated mine before I set up my own company. And I shouldn't have—on paper it was perfect."

"Paper isn't real life," Marley said simply.

"I swear to God, Marley," Amy said. "Sometimes you just say the wisest things. You're going to make an amazing mum one day."

Marley glowed. Here was her opening. She could say something now, it would be totally natural to slip it into the conversation here. She opened her mouth, but Lyra beat her to it.

"We just have to find you the right man now, that's all."

Marley smiled tightly. She wanted to point out that there were other ways, other options. But the moment had passed.

"So, no biggie then," she joked, and the girls chuckled. Their own paths to love had been so rocky. Watching them go through it all hadn't exactly changed Marley's mind about doing things by herself, let alone what she'd been through back in Darnee.

She wanted a child now. She had already waited far too long for one. Some days she felt like she'd been waiting forever and, in a way, she had. She'd dreamed of a child since she was fifteen, and those years had cost her a lot. There wasn't time to find the right guy now, and outside of the whispering gazes of the tiny town of Darnee, in a big anonymous city like Sydney, there wasn't any need.

Lyra suddenly sat bolt upright. "Ames, why don't you have the wedding here?"

"That's an awesome idea," Marley said, eyes widening.

Amy raised an eyebrow and tipped her head, a slow grin spreading across her face. She looked around, taking in the view, the sundeck, the pool below them. Then she slapped Lyra gently on the shoulder.

"I am *mortified* I haven't thought of this!"

"It would be a beautiful place to get the pictures done as well," Marley added. "And you wouldn't need to leave the party long to do it."

Amy's brow furrowed. She looked around again and her eyes fell on the stairs. Her shoulders slumped. "Crap. It's not accessible though." They heaved a collective sigh. "Back to the drawing board."

Two sparkling waters later, Marley stood washing her hands after finishing up in the bathroom when she heard a voice. She froze, looking to her reflection in alarm. The voice was coming from the bathroom foyer, which she'd need to walk through to get back to the girls.

"Yeah, he went home, so we won't make it to your place

for lunch, sorry," the voice said and Marley could just make out the tinny responses of someone on the other end of a mobile phone line. Her heart pounded as she chanced a peek into the foyer and whipped her head back quickly. Her hunch was confirmed. Bess.

Marley stood deathly still at the sink, wishing she'd brought her phone in so she could text an SOS to the girls to come and find a way to get her out. Then she realised she couldn't have explained the situation anyway. She put her fingers to her ears, but Bess's voice carried through.

"Of course it was about that," Bess continued, sighing. "It's always about that, he's like a broken record. Drives me absolutely crazy." She paused as the caller said something. "See, Mum I knew you'd say that." She sounded irritated. "I *knew* you'd take his side." She paused again, listening, then heaved another dramatic sigh. "Yeah, but it's not as easy as that. Now that we've got momentum at Repro. It just doesn't make sense to stop and do something else." Another pause.

Marley's chest felt squeezed. It was wrong to be overhearing this. She should make herself known. Except now she'd waited too long and it would almost be worse for Bess to realise she'd overheard this much. Still, she should stop it before she heard anything else. Resolved, she pushed back from the sinks and turned to the foyer, but Bess's next words made her freeze.

"Except he *isn't* my fiancé, that's the thing. He never has been. Never will be." A long pause. "No, he hasn't stopped talking about that. He still wants them. And I still don't. He's not going to change his mind and neither am I …" She snorted. "No, I'm not quite ready to break up with him, at least I don't think." A short exhale, almost like a growl of frustration. "Yes, I know it's been on-again off-again—sorry if that complicates *your* life." Her tone was sarcastic. "We want different things. I don't know. It's confusing." Another pause, then her voice took on an angry tone. "I can't talk to you about this, Mum. You always take his side. I've got to go. Sorry about lunch."

Marley held her breath, daring another glance into the foyer. Bess's profile was strained, as though she was fighting tears. Then she swore and tossed her phone into her bag, stalking out of the bathroom.

CHAPTER NINE

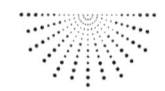

DARNEE, NEW SOUTH WALES, AUSTRALIA: 13 YEARS EARLIER

"You don't like it?" Marley asked, turning to her grandmother as she adjusted the neckline of the cream silk dress. They were standing in Darnee's only bridal shop, The Blushing Bride, and Marley was convinced she'd just found her wedding gown. GamGam didn't seem so sure, but then she'd hated every single one Marley tried on. The wedding was now just weeks away and Marley was getting anxious.

Marley knew it wasn't about the dress and she wished her grandmother wasn't so worried. Nineteen was a perfectly good age to get married—late even, for Darnee. They'd had *many* arguments on the topic and Marley had ended in tears after every single one of them, her heart heavy and her eyes swollen. She hated that her grandmother didn't approve of Hayden.

But Marley knew what she wanted and that was Hayden. He'd told her so many times about the way their lives would finally start once they were married. The things they could do, the places they could go. And to prove it, he'd even saved up the money to buy her a proper engagement ring. Years later, she would discover he'd actually stolen the ring. And technically, he hadn't asked for her hand in marriage, instead slipped the gold band with its tiny diamond chip, onto her finger during a picnic she'd organised for them along the river. But still, she'd have said yes if he *had* asked. They'd been together four years now, it was time. He'd been patient —as he always told her—and now he couldn't wait any longer.

It didn't matter that Marley was fairly sure he'd been getting "it" from Susie Baker for a year or two. Susie giggled uncontrollably whenever Marley was around. Marley had seen her ducking her head in the passenger seat of Hayden's ute going down Main Street. But Susie wasn't the one with a ring on her finger, and Susie wouldn't be the one walking down the aisle.

"It's perfectly fine." GamGam looked sadly at Marley in the dress. "But you shouldn't rush into anything. We can go for a drive out to Silton Town. Have a look around there."

"You keep saying that," Marley said, dropping her arms. "But we've never been."

"I think you'll find the range at The Blushing Bride to be just as extensive as the range in Silton Town, Petunia," huffed Margery Maple, the store owner. Margery always wore clothes several sizes too small and bleached her hair to a bright yellowish-blonde. "Although you might be able to find something if you want her going down the aisle with her bosoms on display, or her legs bare. Maybe you can even find something in red," she added, her eyebrows raised to points.

GamGam rolled her eyes and turned back to Marley. "Is that the one you want?"

Marley studied herself in the full length mirror, turning

this way and that. She looked nice. The dress was nice. Certainly prettier than any dress she'd owned before. So she didn't understand why she felt hollow inside. Wasn't this it? Wasn't this what it was all about? Getting married, having a baby, setting down roots?

She nodded at GamGam, who sighed.

"We'll take it then," GamGam said to Margery, who clapped her hands together.

"You're going to make a beautiful bride, Lena," Margery said. "And don't you pay any mind to those rumours. Once Hayden sees you walking down the aisle, there won't be room in his head for thoughts of anyone else."

It was the closest anyone had got to mentioning Susie Baker outright to Marley and it took her by surprise. So her suspicions *were* right. She wondered whether everyone knew. She felt heat rising to her cheeks and turned her back to Margery, hoping she wouldn't notice.

GamGam wasn't so easily deterred. "What are you talking about?" Her tone was sharp.

Margery rolled her eyes as she unbuttoned the back of Marley's dress. "Boys will be boys, Petunia. Pointless to pretend otherwise. And Hayden Gibbons could charm the pants off Mother Mary herself." She made a hasty sign of the cross. "But boys never buy the cow if they're getting the milk for free. And that Wilson girl should be about milked dry by now."

"Wilson?" Marley repeated blankly. Margery flushed and looked away. "As in Rosemary Wilson?"

"It's idle rumours."

Marley smiled tightly. She considered Rosemary a friend. Not a close one, but not one she thought would be doing … whatever she was doing with Hayden behind Marley's back. So Susie wasn't the only one. Marley felt sick to the stomach and was overcome with a sudden urge to get outside, breathe some fresh air.

"Wrap the dress up," she said to Margery, zipping the curtain back across to shuck the dress and pull her shorts and t-shirt on. She shoved her feet back into her shoes. "We'll come back and get it later."

She walked quickly out of the shop, GamGam on her heels. The cicadas seemed unusually loud and the ringing reverberated through Marley's head. The further her long strides took her from The Blushing Bride, the lighter the weight on her chest became. There were tears in her eyes and she dashed them away with the back of her hand, annoyed at herself.

GamGam struggled to keep up. "Lena, stop," she called gently. "I'm not as fast as you."

"Sorry." Marley halted. They were near the cemetery and she and GamGam linked arms and wordlessly headed through the gates, slowing to a dawdle. They paused by Father Joven's grave, where GamGam made a quick sign of the cross. Then it was past the Dwyer family plots. Marley had gone to school with Cress, who'd been killed by a kick to the head from a horse in third grade. He was resting beside his grandparents, and as everybody knew thanks to the gossip from the tiny local hospital, Cress's father would join him soon. Then the Lynches, then the Zanes, then the Dittmans. Marley realised there wasn't a name she didn't know in the graveyard, not a single family she wasn't at least on a first name basis with someone from. She'd always found it reassuring. Today, she found it suffocating.

GamGam heaved a sigh. "It's my fault," she said, and her voice shook. Marley looked at her.

"What's your fault?"

GamGam fell silent for a moment. "I should've taken you out of Darnee. When your parents died. Should've moved somewhere different. Somewhere bigger. Somewhere less ... Darnee."

"But Darnee is home. You love Darnee."

"I don't," GamGam said, as they stopped in front of the Phelps family plot. Their plot. Marley's parents' names were chiselled into the headstone, alongside her grandfather and great-grandparents'. This was the only way Marley had known her parents, or could remember them—names carved on a tombstone.

"I just couldn't bring myself to leave them," GamGam added in a whisper, staring at the grave with tears pooling in her eyes. Marley hugged her tightly and GamGam let out a small sob. "Now I've ruined it. I don't want you to disappear into this town. I don't want it to suck your soul like it sucks everyone else's. You deserve more."

"It's not like that." Marley laughed and released her grandmother to look her in the eye. "I'm getting *married*, GamGam. I get to have a baby soon, finally. I knew about Susie. I didn't know about Rosemary, but it doesn't matter. It's true what Margery said. There are two types of girls, ones that give out milk and ones that get married. You should be happy that I'm in the second group."

For some reason, this made her grandmother sadder. She reached out and cupped Marley's chin in her hand.

"You think that's all life is." She shook her head, heaving a sigh. "And that's what I'll never forgive myself for."

They walked slowly back the way they'd come, but GamGam stopped before the bridal store. She pulled Marley into the little jeweller two doors down from it on Main Street. The only jeweller in town. GamGam called it a wedding present, but when she looked back on the moment years later, Marley realised it was also a farewell gift. She'd seen her grandmother clutching her chest more and more often, getting into arguments on the phone with the doctor about the pills she was supposed to take, constantly being short of breath. But Marley hadn't yet connected the dots. Or hadn't wanted to.

The dainty gold L dangled from the delicate chain. It cost more than Marley had ever seen GamGam pay for something. Her grandmother stood right there in the store and fastened it around Marley's neck, turning Marley back around to face her.

"L for Lena. So you always remember, you're your own person. Your life isn't for anyone else. So you remember you are *so* very loved, and you can do anything you want." Marley hugged her grandmother tightly. "And we have one more stop before we go back and get the dress. But we'll need the car."

They drove together into Silton Town where GamGam pulled into the parking lot of Dr Trish Brenner's offices. She turned to Marley as she cut the engine. "We're going to get a script here, and I need you to promise me something."

"Okay?"

"You'll start taking these tablets before you get married, and you'll keep taking them for a year. One single year, Lena —that's all."

"Are you putting me on the pill?" Marley asked, her voice heated. "Why would you do that when you know how much I want a baby?"

GamGam sighed. "I can't stop the wedding, I know that. And if after a year of marriage, you still want to have children with Hayden Gibbons, then know that you have my blessing, wherever I am."

"You'll be right here!"

"I hope so." GamGam tenderly reached out to tuck a piece of Marley's hair behind her ear, then cupped her face in her gnarled hands. "But please, make me this promise now. It's the only thing I will ever ask of you." Marley held her grandmother's worried gaze and knew she couldn't say no. She nodded and GamGam pulled her in for a tight hug, kissing the top of her head. "My Lena. You are the joy of my life."

Just four weeks after the wedding, GamGam was buried in the family plot, beside every single other member of Marley's family.

CHAPTER TEN

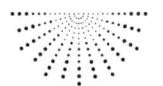

The ping of Marley's phone startled her slightly as she straightened the pile of papers on Dr Martelle's desk before heading home. She pulled the phone from her back pocket and swiped open the message. Finn. It had been three days since she'd witnessed his argument with Bess on the beach. And since she'd overheard Bess talking about him.

Hi Marley. Sorry I didn't reply to your last message. Can I pop round tonight? I thought of an idea that might help you. I can also cook if you have any interest, and I promise I'm good. Unless you have plans, of course.

She smiled at his words—the way he always gave her an out, tried not to apply pressure. But when she caught sight of her face in the mirror behind Dr Martelle's door, she saw the splotches of bright pink on her cheeks.

An image of Finn on the beach, his toned torso golden in the sun, flashed into her mind. She couldn't have him at her flat again, precisely because she *wanted* him at her flat again. She would be sliding into dangerous territory. It was difficult to admit, but even after only having met him a handful of times, she was anything but indifferent to Finn Mayberry.

Sorry, she texted back, her heart sinking as she wrote the words. *I have plans. But I've been meaning to thank you for talking to my boss about my chair.*

You're welcome. No worries at all about tonight. Next time, he wrote back a moment later.

Once Marley was home and showered and sitting on her sofa reading a book, doubts were creeping in about having pushed Finn away. After all, he'd said he had an idea that might help her. It had to be about the donor process. She tried to turn her attention back to her book, but it was pointless. She realised she'd been stuck on the same page, the same paragraph even, for over half an hour, so she got her phone out.

Tomorrow?

The message was quickly marked as read. *6:30 work? If so, see you at your place. Any allergies?*

Time works for me. Can eat everything except truffles. Never understood them, she wrote back, grinning as she typed the words.

What kind of animal sniffs out truffles on Sesame Street?

She frowned. *Miss Piggy?*

That's the Muppets! It's a truffleupagus;) Night, Marley.

His slightly dorky sense of humour was endearing. A little too endearing. She put her phone down, her smile replaced by a wave of anger at herself. She had no right to be grinning like this at the thought of seeing a man who was taken. A man who belonged to someone else, was in love with someone else. It didn't matter that she truly felt Bess may not be the greatest match for Finn—that Bess had all but admitted the same thing herself in the bathroom conversation she'd overheard. Bess was still Finn's choice. And Marley was not Susie Baker.

Besides, even if Finn had been single, Marley had nothing to offer him. She was never getting into a relationship, not again, not after Hayden. And she knew she needed to raise her child alone, *wanted* to. She had waited far too many years to start her family, and she would neither rush into something with a new guy and risk making another mistake, nor wait until she was in a steady relationship.

Those thoughts calmed her. She wasn't doing anything wrong seeing Finn. She was just meeting a new friend to hear what he had to say.

The delivery guy's hunched shoulders were Marley's first clue that he was irritated. The second was the rough way he long-pressed the buzzer to the office building. The office supply company hadn't warned her to expect her new desk equipment so early in the day. She knew there was no one inside to buzz the guy up, so she hurried across the street towards him.

"Have you been here a while?" she asked, slipping her key into the lock.

He huffed in response and she bit back the urge to offer to help him with the items. They rode the lift up three floors in perfect silence.

"Where do you want me to unload it?" he asked, when they reached the office. She gestured to the reception area, flicking on the lights. As he unloaded the cartons, Marley grabbed one, unboxing her new keyboard with such utter joy that the delivery man smiled.

"You look like you've won the lottery. It's not the usual reaction I get when I deliver office stuff."

"I basically have won it," she said, pleased with the turnaround in his mood. "Can you take this old chair away with you by any chance?"

He looked at it. "I'm doing a run to the tip later, I can drop it off."

"Set fire to it if you get the chance."

He chuckled. By the time Dr Martelle rushed in, moments before her first appointment, Marley had everything connected, plugged in, sanitised and operating. Her chair had been perfectly adjusted to her settings, and typing was a joy when she didn't have to hammer the "g" key to get it to work.

"Living the dream?" Dr Martelle asked her, stopping by her desk to grab the patient file. Marley knew her boss was joking, but actually, in a way she was living her dream. A humble dream, sure, and it wasn't her stopping point. But for so long in Darnee, with Hayden, even something as simple as this had been out of reach.

CHAPTER ELEVEN

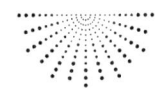

Marley was feeling extremely grateful to Finn as she tidied up the apartment ahead of his visit. Without him approaching Dr Martelle, it might have taken Marley another year to work up to asking for all those items. Probably longer, since she hadn't even known some of them existed. It was the first time since she'd started working for the doctor that her shoulders weren't hunched up around her ears when she came home. How had she ever managed to work at that desk before?

At 6:30 on the dot, her doorbell rang and she buzzed Finn in. As soon as she saw him, she realised it had been a mistake to have him over. Her heart rate picked up and she felt colour rising to her face.

"Hey," he said, smiling widely at her as he took his shoes off in the entryway. He carried a shopping bag bulging with ingredients.

"Hey." She avoided looking him directly in the eye. "Listen, thanks so much for taking time out of your day to think of this idea for me ... let alone cook." Their eyes locked.

Marley cleared her throat and looked away. "What are we having?"

It seemed to take Finn a second to answer. Marley scrutinised the carpet during that silence. "I'm going to cook a mild vegetable curry. If that's okay?" he said finally.

"And if it's not?"

"I'm going to cook a mild vegetable curry."

"Good thing I love curries." They smiled at each other. "But I warn you, I sometimes eat at Spice of Mumbai, soo …"

"Pssht," Finn scoffed, straightening up and hoisting the bag onto his shoulder as they headed for the kitchen. "No competition."

She grinned, realising that despite the way her heart behaved when he was around, she found his company relaxing. Reassuring. Finn was fun to hang out with.

"Tap water?" she asked, moving to grab a glass from the shelf.

"That the best you can offer when you're entertaining distinguished guests?"

He was laying out vegetables, spices and tinned goods from the bag along the counter. The cheeky wink he gave her made her quickly turn her head back to the cupboard.

"I might actually have some sour milk or …" She opened the fridge. "Oh, you're in luck. I have some soft drinks. Amy must have brought them round once."

"Well, give Amy my thanks. I'll take a can of something. Lady's choice." She pulled one from the fridge and popped it open, pouring it into a glass. "So you don't usually drink alcohol?" he asked. "It's not just something you're doing to prepare your body for …" He trailed off, pulling her knife block towards him and examining the blades. She shook her head. "Do you mind if I ask why you don't drink? I mean, I think it's a good idea not to. It's just I don't actually know that many people who manage it."

"I do drink very occasionally, but ..." Marley decided to be truthful. And blunt. "My ex-husband was an alcoholic."

Finn froze, then turned to her with a carving knife in his hand. "You were married?"

She nodded. "Can you put the knife down when you make sudden movements towards me?"

Finn swallowed and lowered the knife. He turned to the groceries for a moment, and then back to her. "Does your ex still live around here?"

Marley shook her head. "No, he never did. He's ... in my hometown."

"Oh? Where is that?"

"Darnee. No one's ever heard of it. It's a tiny town, quite far inland. About a nine hour drive north west from here. Getting close to the Queensland border."

"It sounds ..." He struggled for the right word.

"It's not much," she cut him off. "But it was home for a very long time."

He nodded. "At least you won't run into him then. That's probably the worst part."

He sounded thoughtful, and Marley had the feeling they were no longer talking about her.

"So, what can I do to help?" she asked brightly, hoping to change the topic. She didn't want to end up in a long conversation about Darnee and Hayden.

"Uh, you can dice that onion." He slid it over to her.

"Saving the best jobs for me, I see."

He grinned. "And you can show me where your honing rod is before I give you a blade. These are so blunt it's dangerous!"

Marley had never known the proper name for the metal stick that she pulled now from a drawer, let alone used it. She watched in fascination as Finn swept the blades along it in quick movements, and when he handed her back the smaller knife to cut the onion, it sank straight through the flesh with ease.

"So *that's* what it's supposed to be like."

He shook his head in mock exasperation. "I need to hook you up with some kitchen shows." He chopped through a carrot in a movement so fast the motion became almost a blur.

"No, you just need to come over more often!" Marley said, and an odd silence fell between them. She'd meant it as a joke, but it had come out wrong—changed the atmosphere.

After a moment, Finn put the knife down and turned to her. "By the way, I'm sorry you saw Bess and I arguing at the beach at the weekend."

Marley busied herself searching for the right sized pot. "I'm sorry I saw you, too. I hope everything's okay. Actually," she straightened up and met his eye. "I was going to apologise in case that argument was brought on by what I said when you were over last time."

"So you heard."

"Bits and pieces. Not the whole thing."

He shook his head. "No. You didn't cause it. It's an argument we've had before." He sighed. "I can see things from her point of view. She wants to keep ploughing money back into ReproJoy, making it the best it can be. And she truly believes we'll get to my clinic sooner or later. But ... I can see it fading into the horizon. I sometimes feel as though it's never going to be the right time. We just need to do it, but she doesn't see it that way. Our fight at the beach ended up being a bit of a doozy and carried on the whole weekend."

Marley had stopped moving as he spoke, trying to give him her full attention. But something strange had happened. In her mind, she was suddenly back in Darnee and the overwhelming feeling of being trapped, of having life pass her by, swept over her. She felt the familiar hallmarks of that very specific panic, the one that had kept her company almost from the moment she lost GamGam: hot, prickling skin, a wildly beating heart, blood rushing noisily in her ears, a sensation like being smothered alive.

She realised Finn was staring at her in concern. "Marley?"

"Huh?"

"Are you okay?"

"Yes."

He put the knife down and took her gently by the elbow, guiding her to a chair at the dining table and bringing her a glass of water. She took it gratefully, and then paused between sips.

She hadn't thought through the words before they came spilling out of her. "It's a mistake to marry someone who doesn't support you. A big, *big* mistake. I hope it's not a mistake you make with Bess."

Finn froze, looking at her oddly. She watched his chest rise and fall. Then he turned back to the kitchen counter. "I'll keep making the curry. You relax for a moment."

―――

"Oh this is *good*," Marley said, savouring a mouthful of the curry. She and Finn were sitting opposite one another at her small dining table.

"The secret's in the way the onion's cut," Finn said with a grin, and she smiled back.

He had accepted her apology for having blurted out her thoughts about Bess, and seemed to have genuinely moved past it. But Marley was mortified and couldn't quite relax.

"So, what was it you wanted to tell me?" she asked. "The idea you had?"

"Oh, God! Sorry, I should have told you that right away."

He lowered his fork. "I have a cousin who went through the sperm donor process, with ReproJoy actually. Rebecca. She has a kid, a boy who's two now. I didn't know if you already had someone like that in your life, but I thought it might help for you to talk to her if not."

Marley beamed at him. "I love that idea! And no, I don't have anyone like that to talk to. I've hovered around some chat forums, but it's not the same."

He nodded, looking pleased. "She's open about it. You could ask her basically anything, and if she isn't happy to answer, she'll just let you know."

"Thank you."

Finn smiled and their eyes held a beat too long. He cleared his throat and looked down. Marley quickly stood up and went to the sink to refill her water glass, running her hand under the water and keeping her back to him as she pressed her cold fingers to her cheek. When she sat back down, they both acted as though nothing had happened.

"I've actually been having second thoughts about asking your boss to get you a new chair," he said, after a moment.

She stopped with the spoon halfway to her mouth. "Oh?"

"Yeah. I've realised I've done myself out of a repeat customer when I open my practice."

"Well, you might not have me, but don't forget where I work. I can speak to Dr Martelle and we can keep your business cards on my desk—refer people to you if they need a physio." She smiled brightly.

Finn stared at her, and she couldn't read the expression on his face. For a moment, it seemed as though he was fighting his emotions. Then he stood so abruptly that his chair almost toppled backwards.

"I have to go," he said. "I'm sorry. I feel like I always run out of here."

Marley got up and followed him out of the kitchen,

watching as he put his shoes on. "I hope I didn't say anything wrong … again." He shook his head but didn't reply. "Shall I pack you a Tupperware with some leftovers before you go?"

"No, you eat it. I'm glad I could cook for you. And you're right. I do need to come over more often."

He stood and their eyes caught for another long moment, then he turned and left. Marley stared at the door after he was gone, her emotions in turmoil. Something had happened between her and Finn—she just didn't know exactly what.

A moment later, she went back to the kitchen to clean up, her appetite gone.

CHAPTER TWELVE

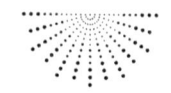

For a split second, Marley genuinely thought she was looking at the actor Jon Hamm. She'd watched enough *Mad Men* to find the likeness to the man standing before her uncanny. He had nervously cleared his throat, dragging Marley's deep concentration away from the database at work and onto his jaw-droppingly handsome face. Thick, dark hair, bright grey-green eyes and three-day growth on his chiselled features—he was a work of art.

"How can I help you?" Marley asked.

"I'm Don Hamlet."

Marley had to struggle to suppress a laugh, his name was so similar to the actor's. He said nothing else, but stood smiling at her.

"Okay, and are you here to see Dr Martelle?" she prompted.

"Oh, sorry. Yeah, I should have mentioned that." He looked slightly embarrassed. "I've just moved to the area and I wanted to get on the books."

"Our books are unfortunately closed to new patients at the moment."

"Only, I think I was here maybe a few years ago? Dr Martelle's the one with the big grey beard, right?"

Marley snorted. "Uh, no. Dr *Elizabeth* Martelle is a very attractive woman in her mid-thirties."

"Crap." He was actually blushing.

"I'll check our files for you anyway. Maybe you were here once."

Now that the majority of patient records had been entered into the database, Marley could simply type his name into the system. Previously, she'd have had to root through the filing drawers and hope that the card had been put back in the right place.

"I do have a file under the exact same name, however …"

Don's face fell. "Is the address Chelsea Street?" Marley nodded. "Yeah. That's my Dad. He's gone. Two years ago."

"I'm sorry to hear that." Marley bit her lip. "If you like, I can give you his place at the clinic? I'll deactivate his file so you won't get any awkward mail or phone calls."

"Thanks so much, that's kind of you."

She grabbed a clipboard and new patient form from the pile she had pre-stacked, and handed them to Don with a pen. "Take a seat in the waiting room while you fill that out," she said, pointing. "Bring it back to me when you're done and I'll get you added in."

Don nodded and disappeared. When he brought back his form ten minutes later, he seemed anxious. The pen slipped from his hand as he held it out to Marley and she saw him wipe his palms onto his jeans as he bent to pick it up.

"Hope I filled it all out right," he said.

Marley smiled and nodded, putting the clipboard aside. "I'll type it all in later, but as long as we have your birth date and contact details, that's the main thing. You can call up whenever you need an appointment."

He hesitated. "Could you just check it now, real quick?"

Marley frowned. "Do you think you spelled your name wrong or something? I'm positive it's fine."

He seemed edgy and remained at the desk. Finally his arm shot out and he grabbed the clipboard back. He handed it to her, pointing to a business card under the clip. Above his name, he'd scrawled: *Your eyes are beautiful, like a fresh cut lawn at dawn, I don't want to be gone without asking ... go out with me?* Apparently he worked as a gardener.

Marley blinked. Really? A guy who looked like *that* was interested in her? She felt deeply flattered, if a little confused. Still, though he was incredibly handsome, he wasn't her type. And there was no point even going out for a drink with someone when she was looking into having a baby alone.

"I'm kind of ... it's not the best time in the world for me," she said.

He nodded, exhaling a shaky breath. "I thought you'd be taken. But I wanted to try anyway."

"Oh, I'm single," she said. "I'm just not looking for someone right now."

"I understand." He smiled warmly. "No problem at all. I'll see you when I need an appointment then."

Marley smiled, pleasantly surprised with how well he'd handled her rejection.

Later that day, clearing up her desk to go home, she slipped Don's business card into her satchel. It would make a very funny story to tell the girls next time she saw them.

CHAPTER THIRTEEN

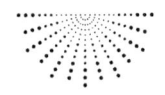

DARNEE, NEW SOUTH WALES, AUSTRALIA: 7 YEARS EARLIER

"Lena, it's your duty as his wife to accept Hayden as he is, and to encourage and support him to be the best version of himself that he can be."

Marley bit her lip, staring at the priest across the table from her. She tried not to be repulsed by the white hairs sprouting from his nose and ears, tried not to think about the fact that if the priest had lived strictly to his vows he would never have laid hands on a woman, let alone navigated a marriage. Something she found increasingly difficult.

"I know that, Father Curtis," Marley said, forcing herself to hold the priest's sceptical gaze. "At least in theory, but … Hayden and I have been married six years now and the drinking is just getting worse. This is the third time I've come to see you. I don't know who else is supposed to help. I'm genuinely worried for him."

Father Curtis folded his hands and looked at Marley. "Is

there any harm in a man letting off steam with a few drinks among friends?"

"No." Marley shook her head. "But Father, he doesn't have any steam to let off. He doesn't work. *I* do."

She'd obviously known before they had married that Hayden drank, but assumed it was a boyish trait he'd grow out of once he was a proper married man, taking up his place in the town. That was the other thing. He hadn't taken up anything, aside from squandering the money she brought home from her job in the Super Saver Mart.

She was trying to save to take a business administration course in Silton Town, so they could have a better future. Trying to put a little aside for when they had a baby. But the money seemed to slip through their fingers, and had done for years. There simply wasn't enough of it. No matter how hard Marley tried to put money aside, they needed every penny. Either they had nothing to eat near payday, or something in the house needed fixing, or Hayden discovered her hiding spot and used the money for beer.

Whenever she asked him what he planned to do for work, he turned it into a joke, or told her she should be grateful he'd married her since he knew about "the curse" or worst of all, tried to kiss her and distract her that way. She was irritated with herself, but she still couldn't resist his smile. He'd been a cute teenager and he'd matured into an incredibly handsome man—rough around the edges, effortlessly strong, tall and broad-shouldered. She felt her body pull towards his whenever she saw him, and she was still filled with desire whenever he reached for her.

But she'd been true to GamGam's promise and had taken the pill for a full year after they were married. And then she hadn't stopped. She told herself she still wanted a baby with Hayden, that she was just waiting until he became more stable. It was a hard decision and one that caused her pain—

she'd wanted a baby for as long as she could remember. But she knew why GamGam had made her wait.

Things hadn't stopped between Hayden and Susie Baker either. Marley had come home from work more days than she could count, just in time to see Susie disappearing through the side gate into the wasteland behind their house. Rosemary was no longer an issue, having married a guy from Silton Town, where she'd ended up moving. But Susie hadn't found a beau, so she still contented herself with Marley's husband.

Marley had made a kind of uneasy peace with it, and now found the most upsetting part of it to be the fact that it was taking place under her own roof. When GamGam had died—Hayden had turned up drunk and late to the funeral—she'd left Marley everything she had. It hadn't amounted to much, mostly just the house she'd grown up in, and Marley had thought she and Hayden might sell it and perhaps move somewhere else, start over. Ideally in Silton Town, but if not, at least to the outskirts of Darnee.

But Hayden had said they weren't going anywhere. They'd been born in Darnee, and they'd be buried in Darnee. Did she think she was too fancy for the town now?

Marley couldn't shake the feeling that her grandmother was looking down on everything going on under her roof—and feeling sorry for Marley. Feeling furious with Hayden. And feeling contemptuous of Susie Baker.

Marley realised her fingernails were pressing so deeply into her palms that she had drawn blood. It jolted her back to the present.

Father Curtis sighed. "It's a heavy burden to be a man in this world," he said solemnly. "Perhaps if you had children …"

Tension rippled across Marley's jaw. "If we had children, what? He'd miraculously get a job? Stop drinking? Stop with

Susie? Wouldn't that just put *more* pressure on him, if he's already finding life so difficult?"

"Children bring love into a home, Lena. They can heal many wounds."

For a moment, Marley felt real pain. How many nights had she sat alone in her house, a hand to her stomach, feeling its emptiness. How much fuller her life would be with a baby in it. She was prepared for every part of motherhood, knew beyond a doubt that crying wouldn't bother her, nights awake wouldn't bother her, none of the challenges she saw other women go through would bother her. What she couldn't have coped with was leaving a child with Hayden all day while she worked for their money. She knew he couldn't handle it, that he'd end up drinking, and their child would be neglected. Life with Hayden was a mess she'd walked into, eyes wide open. It wouldn't be fair to make that problem a child's as well.

"It's a big *if* to assume he'll change for a baby," Marley said.

She wasn't sure when she'd started talking like this—so bluntly. She supposed she'd developed the habit over the years with Hayden. If she wasn't blunt, he would still try to get around her by charming her, snaking his arms around her waist, planting kisses over her that left her tingling. The bluntness confused him, stopping him in his tracks. She used the tactic more and more often. It was definitely not the way she'd grown up speaking and she saw many people flinch when her words hit their ears. But she was also learning to take enjoyment in the flinches, and the surprised looks on people's faces.

Father Curtis tilted his head at her. "I can see the hesitation in your heart, Lena. And I wonder whether that's why God hasn't blessed your marriage with children yet."

Marley wasn't sure what she'd been expecting when she

asked to speak to Father Curtis. There was no-one else though. He was the person Darnee folk went to when something troubled them, the closest thing to a counsellor they had. Now, Marley wondered why she'd bothered. Father Curtis always seemed more intent on making excuses for Hayden than helping her get his drinking or womanising under control.

Marley took a deep breath. "Thank you, Father. You've given me a lot to think about."

He raised an eyebrow, detecting the dismissive note in her voice. "Marriage is a lifelong commitment, Lena. You made a vow before God. It's not supposed to be without its trials and tribulations."

"Oh, I'm keeping my vows," Marley said confidently, letting the unspoken words fall between them. *Hayden isn't.*

Father Curtis nodded and stood, bowing his head. "I'll pray that you hear the pitter-patter of little feet before long. I think it would do Hayden a lot of good to have a proper family."

As Marley walked out of the rectory and back to the supermarket, she thought about Father Curtis's prayers. She had no idea how powerful they were, although several people in town claimed his prayers had helped them.

Still, no matter how strong, Marley knew they were no match for the pills in the secret pocket of her handbag. Choking each pill down felt like a daily act of sacrifice for a child that would never even know what she'd spared it from. Sometimes she fought tears while taking them, she wanted so badly to be pregnant. But the longer her marriage went on, the more convinced she was about her decision.

CHAPTER FOURTEEN

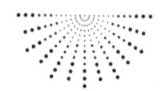

The other bus passengers were shivering, and even the driver was wearing a State Transit-issued jumper as Marley bumped along on her way to Lilac Bay on Saturday morning. The sun was blinding and the sleepy warmth of the day had fooled her into wearing a balloon skirt and neon tank top, but the bus's air-conditioning was turned so low that she was worried she'd get frostbite.

Finn had passed on his cousin Rebecca's number and she'd suggested they meet in the little horseshoe beach of Lilac Bay for their chat.

Marley arrived at the harbour shivering and the sun spread a welcome warmth back into her bones. As she wandered towards the park from the bus stop, she caught herself thinking about Finn. She'd had a single text from him after their dinner at her place the previous week—telling her he'd managed to get an appointment for her at ReproJoy in six weeks' time. She'd thanked him, but aside from that they hadn't spoken. She'd also continued her search for different fertility clinics in her area, trying to find a quicker appointment. She thought it might be safer and smarter for her to just stay away from Finn altogether. Though she was keen to press ahead with her plans, she still hadn't made any firm decisions about the finances. But she told herself anything could happen in six weeks ... maybe she'd win lotto. Someone had to, didn't they?

Marley had written down scores of questions about the more emotional side of using a donor, but she was also curious to hear from Rebecca about life as a single mother. Arriving at the bay, she looked around for a woman with brown hair and a red top, as Rebecca had described herself in the text messages. Instead, her eyes landed on Finn, dressed in shorts and a t-shirt, leaning up against a tree with his arms folded. He stared out at the water and Marley turned away as soon as she spotted him, her heart instantly becoming unsteady.

"Hey!" he called out, and she turned back to see him waving and jogging towards her.

"I didn't realise you'd be here," she said once he reached her. "I can't see Rebecca."

"She's on her way. Few minutes late. I'm actually going to take Walter for her, so that you guys can have some peace while you talk."

"Oh, that's good of you." Marley suddenly felt awkward in Finn's presence.

"It's actually good of *her*," he replied, smiling. "I love Walter and I never usually get to spend time with him. Or, I haven't up till now—" There seemed to be more to the sentence, but he cut himself off with a short shake of the head. "Anyway, I get to do it today, and more often, hopefully."

Marley opened her mouth to ask why, and heard their names called.

They turned to see a young woman pushing a pram and walking quickly towards them, wearing red yoga clothes. In the stroller, a chubby, ruby-cheeked boy with a mop of coppery-brown curls strained against his straps.

"Pinn! Pinn!" he called, and Finn broke into a huge grin.

"Hey buddy!" he shouted back, moving towards them. Marley trailed him.

Finn and Rebecca embraced tightly as they met, Finn reaching a hand down to ruffle Walter's curls at the same time. Rebecca smiled warmly at Marley over Finn's shoulder, then she seemed to remember something and frowned.

"God, I'm so sorry to hear about you and Bess," she said in a low voice to Finn.

At the mention of Bess, Marley's chest tightened. She was still randomly startled awake at night by the memory of what she'd blurted to Finn—that he might be making a mistake in staying with her.

"Oh, it's okay," Finn said quickly, pulling back and obviously trying to cut Rebecca off, "let's talk about it later."

"I know it's been a bit rough for a long time," Rebecca continued with a sigh, oblivious to his hint, "but breakups always suck, no matter what."

Marley turned abruptly to face the other direction, making a show of rooting in her backpack for her sunglasses, trying to get her emotions under control. When she turned back to them, Finn had managed to get his message through to Rebecca, who'd clapped a hand over her mouth, her eyes wide behind her sunglasses. Finn was bending down to undo Walter's pram straps.

"Hi, I'm obviously Rebecca," she said, quickly, smiling at Marley.

"Marley." She smiled back. "Thanks so much for doing this."

"Oh, it's no trouble at all," Rebecca said breezily. "Look at that cherub. If I can help anyone else to have a Walter in their lives, I'm happy." Marley smiled. Rebecca pulled her purse out of her handbag and shoved some notes at Finn. "As long as you bring him back to me alive, you can take him wherever you like. But he's only allowed *one* treat per day."

"A fairy floss stick the size of his head?" Finn joked, and Rebecca raised an eyebrow. He grinned. "I'm just kidding. I'll make it the size of my head."

"Fainy foss!" Walter yelled, and Rebecca mock-glared at Finn.

"Now you've done it," she said, smiling. "Do you want to take the pram?"

"Nah, we'll just toddle around here a bit. I can carry him if he gets tired."

"He's a lug, just to warn you. Weighs about thirteen potato sacks now."

Finn bent down and scooped Walter up, tossing him effortlessly into the air. Walter squealed with delight.

"I can manage him." Finn grinned at the girls' horrified faces. He hoisted Walter onto his shoulders, biceps bulging as he did so, and Walter took chubby fistfuls of Finn's hair into his hands like reins. "Come on, Wally, let's go." He turned from them.

"I've told you not to call him that!" Rebecca said, rolling her eyes. "And wait, I haven't kissed him goodbye."

"He calls me Pinn. It's a fair deal," Finn said, and tipped forward so Rebecca could loop her arms around Walter, covering his face in little kisses.

Finn straightened up and set off at a jiggling trot, bouncing Walter on his shoulders. Walter shrieked happily and kicked his legs.

"Okay, well I'm not going to relax until they're back,"

Rebecca said, but her light tone told Marley she was joking. "Shall we go sit on the bench over there?"

Marley nodded and Rebecca wheeled the empty pram over to the wood and stone bench, then sat down with a sigh. Marley perched on the other side, uncertain how to begin the conversation.

"Sorry," Rebecca said, sliding down and tilting her head to the sun. "I get so few moments of peace like this, that I have to soak them up." She sighed happily and stretched her arms, enjoying the warmth for a moment.

Marley loved being at Lilac Bay. The semi-circle bite out of Sydney Harbour featured a tiny, white-sand beach. The bay bobbed with moored boats whose owners lived in the sandstone mansions ringing the inlet. Today, everything was calm—barely a ripple ran across the water which shone like glass. Marley stared out at the Harbour Bridge in the distance. She'd never get sick of this view. She'd grown up beside a body of water in Darnee, but this couldn't have been more different.

Rebecca turned to Marley. "Okay, so what would you like to talk about?"

Marley felt put on the spot, even though this was the whole reason for their meeting and she was armed with a load of questions. "I guess I'm a bit curious about why you decided to do it this way. But we don't have to talk about that if you don't want to."

"It's fine," Rebecca said, leaning forward to pull a metal water bottle from the bottom of the pram. She took a sip and considered for a moment before answering. "I honestly haven't been in a relationship with someone I'd want to co-parent with, it's as simple as that. I could keep waiting, and I *am* on the dating scene—as much as I can be with a kid. But I felt as though it would make things easier if I could decouple having a baby from meeting the person I wanted to have a baby with. If that makes sense."

Marley nodded slowly, thinking of all the years she'd spent with Hayden, deliberately not getting pregnant for the same reason. "We're lucky we live at a time where it's possible," she said.

Rebecca nodded. "Yeah, we really are." She sighed and looked in the direction Finn and Walter had walked. They hadn't gone far and Walter's occasional giggles floated back to them on the breeze. "Finn's such a great guy. I hope he finds happiness." Rebecca's voice was low and thoughtful—she didn't seem to have meant that comment for Marley, but it still brought her heart closer to her throat.

"So, how did you decide on the donor?" Marley's voice came out too loud and Rebecca jerked slightly.

"Uh, I had some criteria." Rebecca tilted her head as though trying to remember. "I wasn't specific about physical stuff. But, I wanted the guy to work in a caring profession—like a firefighter, teacher. That kind of thing."

"That's definitely something to consider."

Rebecca nodded. "It is weird how much information you get about them. I mean, I even have a letter from this guy and a baby pic of him and everything."

"Really? A letter?" Marley couldn't keep the note of surprise out of her voice. Somehow she'd imagined the process to be less intimate. Certainly, no one on the forums had mentioned such a thing.

"Yeah. I think I have the files on my phone, if you want to take a look? You can see the kind of information you'd get about your donor."

"Yes, please," Marley said eagerly, and Rebecca dug into the bottom of the pram again to fish out her phone.

Marley watched Finn and Walter while Rebecca scrolled

on her screen. Finn crouched down in front of Walter, holding something out for him to examine. A bug, she guessed. Walter poked the object tentatively with his finger, engrossed.

Rebecca handed the phone to Marley. "That's the form you get, the letter is in another folder. I'll show you when you finish reading."

The form listed everything about the donor. His height, weight, physical characteristics and those of his parents. Marley scrolled and found another section listing his blood group and ethnic background, as well as answers to a questionnaire on family medical history.

But what interested her the most were the personal details—hobbies, interests, goals and skills. Even his favourite films and books. It was an incredibly revealing document and Marley felt slightly overwhelmed by it.

"It's a lot, isn't it?" Rebecca said, studying Marley's face.

"Yes, I didn't know you'd get to find all that out. It's more than I ever knew about my husband and we were married almost ten years."

Rebecca seemed to freeze. "I hadn't realised you were married," she said gently.

"It wasn't a … good marriage," Marley said, not making eye contact.

"I can see why you might be hesitant to get into a relationship then." Rebecca looked out to the water for a long moment, then back to Marley. "Do you want to see the letter he wrote?"

Marley nodded eagerly, and Rebecca took her phone back and flicked through some files, passing it back to Marley once she found it. Marley saw a short, scanned note, handwritten in all caps. "I WANT TO HELP PEOPLE MAKE A FAMILY, MY HOPE IS THAT YOU RAISE ANY CHILDREN THAT COME FROM ME WITH LOVE AND RESPECT, HOW I WAS RAISED."

Marley smiled, touched.

"It's a bit yelly with the caps," Rebecca chuckled, taking the phone back. "But it's sweet, and it's something I can show Walter later."

Rebecca spun the lid on her water bottle, and Marley noticed that she scanned the shore for Walter and Finn. Her gaze relaxed once she spotted them slowly meandering back. Walter turned to Finn and held his arms up, and Finn hoisted the child onto his shoulders. His delighted squeals made the women exchange a smile.

"Did you have to give yourself injections?" Marley asked.

Rebecca shook her head. "I did it unmedicated, via insemination. You can also take meds and have your eggs harvested, then do IVF. They limit the donor selection unless you do it that way. But I wanted to see if simple insemination would work and it did. ReproJoy will probably still suggest you do use some meds, to have a greater chance of it working. Of course, then you can always end up with twins or triplets or something. I would have switched up the method if it didn't happen on the first try. But one shot and bang—Walter."

"Do you find it overwhelming alone?"

"Yes," Rebecca said without hesitation. Then she laughed. "I mean, I knew what I was getting into. And I wouldn't have it any other way. But there are some nights where, like, Walter's throwing spaghetti all over the walls and I have a cold and the phone is ringing for work and all I want to do is lie down. But then I think about some girlfriends who are married and still need to juggle all that. Then I don't feel so bad!" She chuckled. "Are you worried about that side of it?"

Marley tilted her head, thinking as she stared out over the water. "No. I was raised by a single woman. I learned a lot from her."

"And look how well you turned out," Rebecca said with a smile. "I'm sure it will all be a breeze for you."

"I hope so," Marley said, watching as Finn took Walter down to the small sandy beach of the bay. He pulled both their socks and shoes off and sat in the sand beside Walter. Something in Marley's chest tightened, watching how natural and tender Finn was with the little boy.

CHAPTER FIFTEEN

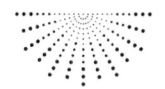

By the time Marley and Rebecca had finished chatting, Finn had waded into the water up to his calves, carrying Walter. Marley squinted out at them, Finn's perfect form cradling little Walter, who snuggled into him as Finn pointed to the Harbour Bridge beyond the bay. Then Finn dangled a delighted Walter's feet into the water, bouncing him up into the sky and pretending to let him fall—catching him again before he dropped into the crystalline bay. Marley had to force herself to look away from the mesmerising flex of Finn's biceps.

"Do you think you and Finn could watch Walter for about twenty more minutes?" Rebecca asked suddenly. "I'd love to nip off and do a few errands without him."

"Uh, sure," Marley said, feeling a warmth light up in the pit of her stomach. Whether at the thought of spending time with Walter or Finn, she decided not to examine too closely.

"You're a gem." Rebecca stood and jogged down towards the boys, calling out the plan to Finn.

Marley wandered down to the sand once Rebecca had gone.

"Come on in!" Finn said, tossing and catching a giggling Walter once more. He held Walter still and waited for her to join.

Marley peeled her socks off and waded in. It was colder than she'd anticipated, and she tried not to flinch. The edges of her balloon skirt brushed gently against the water.

"Say hi to Marley," Finn said to Walter, who ducked his head shyly into Finn's shoulder.

"Hi Marmey," he mumbled, and Marley flushed with pleasure. It sounded so close to Mummy.

"Do you want her to hold you?" Finn asked him.

He peeked out at Marley, studying her for a long moment. Then he shook his head. "No."

Marley laughed. "That's totally fine." Walter frowned at her and she smiled warmly. "Look!" She dipped her hand into the water and picked a small, pale-pink shell from the sandy surface below.

Walter bit his lip, watching her dripping hand. "See?" he asked finally.

Marley moved towards them, her breath hitching at the closeness to Finn, who smiled at her. She held her palm flat with the little shell resting on it.

"Pity," Walter said, poking a chubby finger at it.

"It's very pretty," Marley agreed. "Do you want to give it to your mummy?"

Walter nodded once, snatching the shell from Marley. "Potet?" he asked Finn.

"Yeah, we can put it in your pocket until she comes back." He helped Walter angle the shell into the tiny pocket of his shorts and Marley thought her heart might explode.

"Shall we go back and play in the sand?" Marley asked, and Walter nodded.

The three of them built a small sandcastle that wouldn't have kept out so much as an army of ants, but they had a lot of fun doing it. Marley was put in charge of carrying over small handfuls of water to keep the sand sticky enough for building. Walter enjoyed watching her do it so much that he soon abandoned castle building and started a game with her where they raced to the water, scooped a handful and dashed back to Finn to drop it on his castle. Walter's giggle was one of the sweetest sounds Marley had ever heard.

When the two of them sat down to catch their breath a while later, Walter flopped into Marley's lap as though it was the most natural thing in the world. She looked at Finn, who grinned and nodded slowly in appreciation of the perfect moment.

All too quickly, Rebecca was back.

"I missed you, bug," she said as Walter toddled towards her. Then she felt his nappy. "Oh God, come here." She moved to the grass to pull off Walter's shorts and swiped a fresh nappy from the bag on the back of the pram.

Marley stood in the sand, dusting off her skirt. She put her hand on Finn's arm. "I wanted to say, I am so sorry that you and Bess broke up," she said in a low voice. "I *really* hope—"

"Stop," he interrupted, and the smile he flashed her was heart-stopping. "I was worried you'd think it was about what you said. Actually ... I'd already broken up with her when I came over to cook the curry."

Marley swallowed. "Oh. You had?"

He nodded, looking down at the grass. "Yeah. It was ..." He puffed out a breath. "It was long overdue, but it was still hard. It's going to *be* hard. She fired me," he laughed tonelessly, "of course. And she's going to make my life difficult. With our apartment, with everything, basically. But that just makes me even more certain that I did the right thing."

Marley shook her head angrily. "That isn't right. I'm sorry

you're going through this. It's brave to break up with someone. I wish …" she cut herself off. "Well, anyway. I was worried that my big mouth had something to do with it. I'm glad it wasn't me."

He twisted his mouth and looked up at the sky, then back down at the grass. "In a way it was you though," he said quietly.

She laughed, thinking he was joking. But he didn't look up. "What?" she asked, alarmed. "Why?"

He raised his eyes to hers and drew a deep breath.

"Alright! He's got a fresh bottom. We can get on our way!" Rebecca called, wheeling Walter back towards them in the pram. "Are you still coming back with us for lunch, Finn?"

Finn tore his eyes from Marley's face and nodded to Rebecca, smiling tightly. Rebecca beamed at them both and reached out to hug Marley.

"Thank you so much for today," Marley said, returning the embrace.

"Honestly, anytime," Rebecca said. "Now that I have my favourite cousin slash future babysitter back, we can do it as often as you like. Seriously, give me a call if you have any questions." Finn had bent down to pay Walter some attention and give the women some space. "And despite Bess, it's a great clinic. It will all work out," Rebecca whispered.

Marley forced a smile. Knowing the way Bess had treated Finn, she wasn't sure she wanted to go anywhere near the clinic again …

Marley jittered with nervous energy once Finn, Rebecca and Walter had left. She didn't want to sit on a cold bus, nor did she want to be back at her empty apartment. She decided to take the longest route possible home. To cross the harbour back to the city, she considered walking over the Harbour Bridge, but instead headed for the wharf. She passed The Pie-ganic—the pie truck Lyra had previously run with her brother—which was closed. She boarded the next ferry to Circular Quay.

Despite the crowd on the top deck, she still found a place on one of the wooden benches as the green and gold vessel sliced its way across the harbour. She closed her eyes, enjoying the ferry's gentle rocking, the sun on her face and the breeze in her hair. Despite her emotions being in turmoil, she felt a deep sense of contentment in the moment.

She opened her eyes again as they neared the Harbour Bridge. Some kids beside her were waving up at the blue-clad bridge walkers high overhead, strapped to the railing that ran over the top of the bridge. Marley had been meaning to make time for the experience since she'd arrived in Sydney. Somehow she hadn't, but it was still on her list. Along with staying overnight at Taronga Zoo and seeing a show at the Opera House, which they were now passing. She decided she'd stop for lunch on the outdoor lower concourse of the Opera House. It looked busy but not packed and it would be great to grab a bite with that view of the bridge and harbour.

She chose a simple pasta dish with a side of grilled bread and some water, then picked her way to one of the last empty tables in the sunshine. She chose the side facing out over the water, slipping her sunglasses down against the brightly glittering water. The harbour bustled with yachts, jet boats and ferries and she enjoyed the buzz of happy conversation and activity around her. Laughter, glasses clinking, the sun bouncing off the clear blue water, the bright blue sky decorated with a few fluffy clouds—Sydney truly was a beautiful show-off.

Once she finished, she set off walking, heading for the

Inner West. Thoughts of Finn started crowding in, and she increased to a punishing pace to try and distract herself.

It was pointless. The whole way, the same train of thought looped on the tracks in her head. Finn was single, Finn had broken up with Bess ... Finn was single. And Finn had been about to tell her something. Something about why she'd been responsible for the breakup.

By the time Marley finally arrived home and dragged herself up the stairs, she'd decided to make a phone call. She needed to do something to put some distance between herself and Finn. She was frightened of the way she felt about him and about how those feelings might interfere with her plans. The phone call probably wasn't the best idea she'd ever had, but it made her feel slightly calmer.

She first took a long shower, washing her hair twice and using a lemon and sugar scrub all over her body. She slathered her most nourishing moisturiser from head to toe once she got out. She sat on the closed toilet seat to massage cream into her throbbing feet.

Then she fished through her satchel and found the card she was looking for. Her call was answered on the third ring.

"Don Hamlet? It's Marley from Dr Martelle's office."

CHAPTER SIXTEEN

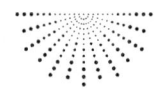

DARNEE, NEW SOUTH WALES, AUSTRALIA: 4 YEARS EARLIER

A hammering at the front door tore Marley from her sleep. She sat up in alarm and switched on her bedside lamp, finding Hayden's side of the bed still tidily tucked in, untouched since she'd made it three days ago.

She hadn't seen him for those three days, but that was nothing unusual. He often stayed away for days at a time, and she knew he spent that time with *her*. Nine years into their marriage and not a thing had changed, except that Marley had slowly disconnected herself from it all—unplugged from the marriage, from him. The arguments were few and far between now, because she simply couldn't bring herself to care.

This latest one had been triggered by him forgetting to pay their council rates. The single task she'd entrusted him with in nine years, and that because he'd begged her to give him something to do, so he could prove himself.

He must have decided to finally come home and lost his key again. It wouldn't be the first time.

The hammering continued and Marley slipped into her robe and scraped her hair back into a ponytail as she headed towards the front door. She switched on the porch light and saw Constable Drew Norman standing there, his chubby stomach cinched into a B shape by his thick leather belt. Marley had gone to school with both Drew and his wife Crystal. She didn't know them well, but they were friendly acquaintances—Crystal worked the occasional shift at the Super Saver Mart with Marley. Drew looked nervous.

Marley opened the door a crack, poking her head out and frowning at the constable. "What's he done now?" she asked, her voice croaky with sleep.

He looked at her ruefully and Marley's stomach lurched with a premonition. She suddenly felt wide awake. "Drew? What happened?"

He let out a slow breath. "Can I come in?"

———

"I don't want to identify him," she told Drew shakily as they sat at her dining table blowing on their cups of tea to cool them. "I just don't think I can see him that way. I'm sorry."

Drew nodded sympathetically. "I get it."

"Is there anyone else who can do it? His parents, if anyone can find them. Susie Baker, maybe?"

Drew cleared his throat and peered into his mug.

"She already knows, doesn't she?" Marley asked, a cold finger of shame poking her stomach.

"I didn't tell her," Drew said quickly. "Brock called her after calling me ... She was there when I spoke to him."

Marley fought the odd urge to laugh. Hayden's affair had

gone on so long and so publicly that his best friend actually considered Susie Hayden's partner instead of her.

"Brock was with him when ..." Drew nodded. Marley was silent a moment, before sheer curiosity got the better of her. "How did Susie take it?"

Drew pressed his lips together and shook his head. "Not well. I dropped her off with her Mum about half hour ago ... I used the word 'hysterical' in my official notes."

Marley sighed. "I'm sorry to hear it."

Drew frowned. "I gotta say, you're taking this better than I thought you would. But then, we're all different when someone ... when something like this happens."

Marley sipped her tea. "I suppose it hasn't quite hit me yet. What ... what happened?"

"Fell in the river," he said quietly. "He was pretty drunk, Brock told us. Acting like a bit of a galah. Not to speak ill of the dead. Seems he slipped and hit his head and went under. Brock couldn't find him until ... well, until he could. We're waiting on the coroner, coming from Silton in the morning. They're going to want to do toxicology."

The thought of the thick, slow-moving waters of the Darnee river made Marley feel nauseous. She closed her eyes, picturing Hayden's face the last time she'd seen it. Sorrowful and confused, as though he genuinely couldn't understand why his wife was pushing him away. Years earlier, that face would have brought her to her knees. Three days ago, she'd been able to stay strong against it. Had that been a mistake? Would he still be here if she'd broken down and shown him affection again?

Drew helped himself to a biscuit from the serving plate Marley had set out. She wasn't certain of the etiquette on hosting police officers who came in the middle of the night to tell you your husband had passed away, but she thought biscuits likely covered it.

Drew was staring at her strangely when she opened her eyes again.

"Say it," she prompted, holding his gaze.

He cleared his throat. "You know they're going to flap their gums? The folks here. About ... 'the curse.'" He used a mocking tone and air quotes as he said it, but Marley could tell from the slightly reverent look on his face that he wasn't *entirely* sure the curse was made up.

"Yes."

"Well, I just wanted to say it is all."

"Thank you." Marley sighed. "Maybe I'll get my own rhyme, like Miss Grenville. Lena rhymes with ..." She smiled wryly. "Not a lot. They're going to have to be more creative with mine."

They were silent for a long moment, sipping their teas.

"What'll you do now?" he asked her.

She shrugged vaguely and didn't answer. But her thoughts were buzzing. She was twenty eight years old. An orphan twice over and now a widow. She worked a crappy job in a dingy supermarket in a dying town that time had forgotten. And she'd been stuck there because of her husband. People in Darnee didn't get divorced, and they certainly didn't just up and leave. But now ... with Hayden gone, it suddenly felt as though there were options for her again. Something inside her was slowly whirring to life, but she suppressed the urge to examine it too closely—especially with the constable still there.

She would have a lot to process with the loss of Hayden. But she had to admit, her feelings weren't what most people might experience at the loss of their "other half". Because Hayden had never been that for her. Not even a partner.

What she wanted was to leave Darnee. She'd wanted that for years. But it would take a while. She couldn't just up and run from everything she knew. Not yet. Especially not right after Hayden had died—it would look as though she had reason to run.

After the constable left and Marley stood at the kitchen sink washing off the cups, she hatched a plan. And set herself a deadline. Before she turned thirty, she'd move to the big city. Not Silton Town, further.

She'd move to *Sydney*. And she'd use a donor to finally have the baby she'd waited so long for. Before she went to bed, she fished through her handbag and pulled out her packet of pills. Then she marched to the bin and tossed them straight in.

Only hours later, when she was lying in bed struggling to get some sleep before dawn, did the reality of Hayden's death hit her. She grabbed his pillow and hugged it to her, inhaling deeply to try to catch any lingering traces of his scent.

And she finally let herself cry.

CHAPTER SEVENTEEN

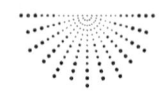

"You're going to bring the wedding *forward?*" Lyra repeated to Amy, a corn chip screeching to a halt before her mouth.

Marley shifted on her sofa and stared at Amy, who sat in the armchair on the opposite side of the room. Amy's feet were tucked up beneath her, her blood-red vintage shirt dress smoothed over her knees and matching polish on the fingers wrapped around a wine glass stem.

"Just by five weeks. But the venue is perfect and honestly, I can't believe it's available at this short notice!"

"So when will it be?" Marley asked, struggling valiantly to keep her mind on the conversation. She kept waiting for an opening but she was finding it hard.

"Early Spring."

"But that's," Lyra counted on her fingers, "that's only like nine months away. That's not very long to plan everything."

Marley gulped. Nine months...

"It's not going to be big, at all," Amy continued, shaking her head. "That's the other thing. We *really* scaled it back. Rick's only having a handful of his army buddies. I'm obviously having Pop and Hazel, you guys, Silas and Ernie, Kristina and Martha from work. And then of course, both our immediate families. Unfortunately there isn't any way to avoid that."

"I hadn't realised it was so soon," Marley said unsteadily. "Sorry. I guess I wasn't paying attention. Good thing I'm not the maid of honour."

The girls exchanged a quick glance then looked at her in concern.

"You don't seem yourself tonight," Lyra said gently. "Are you sure everything's okay?"

"Uh, actually …" Marley took a deep breath. Then she waved her hand. "Wait, tell us more about the wedding, Amy."

"Okay," Amy said uncertainly, looking quickly at Lyra who discreetly shrugged one shoulder. "Uh, it's going to be in the Hunter Valley. It's actually going to be pretty similar to that pic you found in the bridal magazine, Lyra. The long outdoor banquet table."

"Ooh, wine country," Lyra sighed, bringing her hands up to her heart. "I can't wait."

"Me either. It'll be simple and classical. String quartet, short vows, no dance floor. I just want us to be married already."

"How's everything going with the owner's group for your building?" Lyra asked. "Have they agreed to make the building accessible for Rick's wheelchair?"

Amy shook her head, pinching the bridge of her nose wearily. "No. And I haven't had the heart to tell Rick yet. I think we're just going to look for a place to buy together. I'll rent out my Bondi unit, much as that will kill me. And I think I'm going to have to accept the idea that we probably can't afford to buy in that same area."

"Can anyone afford to buy in Sydney at all?" Lyra joked.

She shot another glance at Marley, who smiled mechanically at her. "Uh, did you decide what to do about your dad, Ames?" Lyra tried valiantly to keep the conversation circulating. Marley felt a rush of gratitude towards her.

Amy nodded. "We're inviting him ... I feel good about it."

Amy had recently reunited with her long-estranged father, but the connection was still shaky and new.

"Oh wow." Marley said. "That's pretty big."

"Wait. Is he going to walk you down the aisle?" Lyra asked.

Amy twisted her mouth. "No. Pop will. He'll talk to Dad about it. I'm seriously worried about Mum's stupid husband being there at the same time as my dad but," she shrugged, "nothing I can do."

"Maybe you can hire minders or something," Lyra said. "Ooh, the record label probably has some bodyguards on retainer. I'll see if I can bring one."

They both laughed, and Marley joined in a second later.

"Okay," Amy said gently, leaning forward to set her wine glass on the coffee table. "We can't ignore this anymore. Marley, you *have* to tell us what's going on."

Marley looked up at their faces, both etched with identical tenderness and distress. Her stomach lurched. She was going to tell them everything tonight. Everything about her past and her plans for her future. That was why she'd invited them to her place instead of suggesting the Whistle Stop ... it was a deeply private conversation and one she was apprehensive about. She also wasn't sure how they'd react. It didn't come naturally to her to share things, to open up. She was learning though—Amy and Lyra shared so much with her that she felt odd keeping secrets from them. She hoped they understood why she hadn't mentioned some things until now.

"It's kind of a long story," Marley said finally. "And there's bits I haven't told you before." She blew out a breath, grabbing a cushion and hugging it to her chest. "I'm sorry that I'm about to dump a lot on you. I don't want you to be offended that this is all news to you, but I know you might be. I'm prepared for it …"

Lyra clicked her tongue. "Marley, of *course* we won't."

"What she said," Amy added quietly.

Amy watched her closely. Marley had often wondered whether Amy had broken her trust to fill Lyra in. She had her answer in both their expressions. Amy had kept the secret.

Marley looked at the girls for another moment, then she took a deep breath and started the story. She began with Hayden. With dating him in her teens, with their too-early, ill-fated marriage, with his drinking problem and with her previous name. As she spoke, she watched the curious anticipation on Lyra's face cloud over. She was struggling to school her expression, but Marley could see she was upset.

"Wait. That woman who called you Lena," Lyra said finally, holding a hand up to interrupt. "At the Whistle Stop?" Marley nodded and Lyra raised her eyebrows, remembering something else. "And the L necklace I found right here, in this flat when you moved in. That was *yours*?"

"Yes."

"The box I tried to look inside of that day—"

"Documents. Marriage certificate … other things …"

Lyra looked torn between frustration and sadness. "I'm sorry. I know this isn't about me, but … *why* would you not tell us this? Marley, this is such a huge part of your life! Don't you trust us?" She frowned towards Amy for support and Amy averted her gaze, toying with a button on her dress. Lyra inhaled sharply. "You *knew*?"

"She found out by accident," Marley said quickly as Amy shot her a look of panic. "And just some of it. Not all. It was my plan never to tell either of you."

Lyra's mouth hung open. "I'm sorry, I just don't get *why.*"

The question hung in the air.

"It was never anything personal," Marley said finally, her voice wobbling. She looked fiercely at them. "You're both the best friends I've ever had, it's just that … I actually don't have that much experience with friends at all. With letting people in. After GamGam—" She bit her lip, unable to finish. She swallowed. "When I left Darnee, I wanted to start all over again. I didn't want to be reminded of what I'd left behind."

Lyra's shoulders slumped and her expression softened. "What's the matter with me?" she asked, her voice full of emotion. "I'm sorry, Marley."

"No, it's okay." Marley reached a hand out to Lyra. "I shouldn't have kept this to myself. I just didn't know how to get started talking about it after not having brought it up for so long. But …" She swallowed. "I don't want secrets from you guys anymore."

Lyra squeezed Marley's hand and Amy shot Marley a sympathetic look. "Go on, when you're ready," she said in the gentlest voice.

Marley took a long sip of her drink, feeling their eyes on her. Then she continued. She told them about her long-held dream of having a child and about spending years on birth control. When she got to the part about Hayden's death, Lyra clapped a hand over her mouth, tears welling in her eyes.

"I'm so sorry," she whispered.

Marley rubbed her arm. "It's okay. It's really okay now. But thank you." She took a moment to compose herself then blew out a shaky breath. "Anyway, I've decided to do it. Now. Alone."

Lyra frowned. "Do what?"

"Have a baby."

Amy gasped. "Have a *baby?*"

"What, with a sperm donor?" Lyra asked, perplexed.

Marley nodded. "I've only just started the process. Nothing's happened yet. But that's where I know that Finn guy from, the one who texted me that night at the Whistle Stop. He's not actually a random guy who picked his nose in painting class."

The girls were silent, Lyra's mouth hanging open. "Marley, I might come at you later again for not having told us all this earlier. I can't promise that I won't. But right now, I'm just *so* glad you did."

"Same," Amy added, slowly breaking into a grin.

She and Lyra exchanged an excited glance. "We're going to be aunties!" they yelled in unison and the three of them laughed.

As the girls bombarded her with questions and she happily answered, Marley felt lighter than she had in a long time. She wasn't overly affectionate by nature, but she wanted to wrap both the girls into tight hugs and never let them go.

Maybe the universe had denied her close friendships for most of her life, knowing it would gift her Lyra and Amy. Knowing they would make up for everything. And she was so relieved they finally knew her story. It had been the right thing to do, to let them in. She wished she had done it sooner.

CHAPTER EIGHTEEN

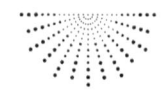

When her doorbell rang, Marley frowned and checked her watch. She was getting ready for her date with Don Hamlet, but there was still an hour to go and he didn't have her address anyway. Figuring her elderly downstairs neighbour must have locked herself out again, Marley pressed the buzzer without asking any questions, then went back to her wardrobe.

She had made a very deliberate choice about her clothes when she'd left Darnee. First, she would never again buy anything brand new. Partly because she didn't have the money and partly because if she looked less like the neatly-combed, Sunday-best version of herself that GamGam had raised, less like *Lena*, there would be a smaller chance of anyone recognising her. She'd stopped doing anything fancy with her hair for the same reason, and had also quit wearing makeup.

She'd hoped it would keep men at bay—keep herself at bay from them. The last thing she needed after finally being free of Hayden and Darnee was to get into another relationship or fall for someone. She had a lot to work

NEW BEGINNINGS AT LILAC BAY

through and needed space to do that. Not to mention she needed to set up a new life from scratch.

And there was part of her that also knew dressing this way was an act of rebellion. She'd leaned into it and had a *lot* of fun—much more than she'd expected to. She'd found a style she liked—playful and colourful and mismatched. Occasionally, she went over the top, her outfits becoming almost a parody. But overall, she enjoyed the way she dressed now. In Darnee, she'd done *everything* right, followed all the rules and played the game exactly as the town had raised her to. All it had gotten her was a wasted decade and a drunken, cheating husband.

Tonight, she wanted to wear something a little calmer and more subtle than her usual outfits. She wanted Don to at least ask her out on a second date. There was absolutely no chance of her falling for him, and she didn't want him to fall for her either—she just wanted something casual and slow and arm's length with Don. Something that would act as a barrier between her and Finn.

She'd just decided on fitted jeans and a v-neck emerald-coloured top when she heard a tentative knock on her door. She made her way to it, looping a belt around her waist as she walked.

"Berta, are you locked out again?" she asked loudly, fiddling with her buckle.

"Uh, no," Finn said. Marley froze, and then pulled the door open.

"What are you doing here?" The words came out more aggressively than she had intended. They hadn't spoken since the Saturday at Lilac Bay with Rebecca, and now the sight of him sent Marley's heart off-kilter. His tan had deepened since the weekend, somehow making his thick lashes look even darker and his blue eyes more striking. His strong jaw was shaded with stubble, and Marley could barely take her eyes off him.

"Sorry to just show up unannounced," he said, frowning. "I should maybe have texted but ... I have something to tell you." He ran a hand through his thick hair. "Can I come in for a quick minute?" Marley opened the door wider and beckoned him in, closing it behind him. "Are you going out? I don't want to keep you."

"I have a date."

"Oh."

Marley could hear the surprise and disappointment in his voice, and it made her feel sick.

Finn recovered quickly, but the heat remained in his face. "Well, I hope you have a nice time," he said finally, his voice stiff.

"Thank you. It's, I'm not ..." Marley bit her lip and stopped talking. She'd instinctively wanted to tell him it wasn't a real date. But that would defeat the purpose of keeping herself distant from him—a decision she was questioning now that he was standing before her. She shakily closed her belt buckle in the awkward silence that fell.

"I won't keep you long then," he said. "I wanted to tell you that I managed to get you a quicker appointment. It's not at ReproJoy ... I thought that might be odd, with Bess and all. But it's an excellent clinic—MacArthur Fertility. An acquaintance of mine runs it."

"What?" Marley looked at him sharply, frowning. "How did you organise that after Bess fired you?"

Finn's mouth quirked. "The details don't matter." His voice dropped. "It just matters that you'll be able to follow through on your dream quicker."

Marley's heart stopped, then started pounding hard. She felt an almost overwhelming urge to pull him close. It took a moment for her to master herself. Then she took a deep, shaky breath. "Thank you, Finn. Thank you."

He nodded, cheeks flushing with colour. "That's not all. You, uh, you won't actually have to pay ..."

"Huh?" Marley squinted at him, thinking she'd misheard.

"I've seen how upset you look when the issue of cost comes up—" he began.

"No, Finn! It's not because of—"

He held his hand up. "It doesn't matter . Part of this, part of what I've organised ... you won't have to pay."

"No. I cannot accept that." Marley was horror-stricken.

He held up a hand to cut her off, proffering a business card. "Ring the clinic tomorrow. They're expecting your call. And I really do hope you enjoy yourself tonight."

"Finn, wait! I'm not accepting—"

Before she could finish, he reached behind himself to open the door, gave her a quick, searching look and was gone.

"Are you also a doctor?" Don asked, smiling nervously at Marley. They were at a large window table, in a modern Australian restaurant on King Street in Newtown. Don lived on the Northern Beaches, but had insisted they choose a place convenient for Marley. She'd been meaning to try this place out and was glad of the chance.

In a desperate attempt at novelty, the restaurant tables and chairs were all adult-sized replicas of school desks, complete with lifting lids where the menus could be found, scrawled in faux-childish writing. The specials were written on an old chalkboard and bunting hung from the ceiling, while green croupier lamps served as lighting. To Marley's amusement, the staff were all in some variation of a school uniform: the women in pinafores and knee-socks, the men in ties and blazers. She couldn't figure out if they were going for nostalgia or fetish.

Don and Marley's entrees had just been cleared away and they were waiting on their mains.

Marley had been relieved to note that upon meeting him for the second time, she still found Don's freakish good looks almost amusing, but not necessarily appealing. But while she seemed resistant to his charms, the rest of the world did not. A waitress had almost tripped over another table with a tray of drinks while busy gazing at him. The host had upgraded their table and they'd already been given one round of complimentary drinks. Their waiter was cloyingly attentive and Marley was drawing looks of ire from women at other tables.

"No, I'm the office manager," she said, smiling at him.

"That's cool. How did you get the job?"

"Actually, I just walked in for an appointment one day and there was a very ... a much older lady there at reception. It was a bit chaotic in the practice and she seemed overwhelmed. We got to talking and she told me she wanted to cut back her hours but the doctor didn't trust anyone else and she didn't want to leave her in the lurch. I asked for a trial and it went well. She still works there on the days I have off."

Don looked at her for a moment, a half-smile on his lips. Then he closed his eyes and began to orate in an earnest voice. "She walked into a mess and decided to bless / the doctor's place with her pretty face. They couldn't know she'd make it glow / and they didn't want to take things slow. With her," he added after a slight pause.

Marley was stunned into silence, colour rising to her

cheeks. "Oh, that's—that was … Wow. Did you just make that up?"

He nodded proudly. "It's kind of what I do."

"I thought you were a gardener?" Marley took another long sip of her water.

"Yard maintenance. But that's just what I'm doing until I get big. That's not my real passion."

"Get big as a … poet?"

"Spoken word, yeah."

"I hadn't realised you could get big in that." For once Marley chose her words carefully. She felt embarrassed on Don's behalf, but he seemed genuinely proud of himself. Besides, what did she know about poetry? Perhaps he was actually very talented.

"I have a YouTube channel and everything."

"Oh? That must be a lot of work."

"No, I just get in front of the camera and the spirit takes me." He closed his eyes again. "I can think of a rhyme even short on time / to help my fans put a smile on their dial. I can't help it, I was made for this / made to be the rhyming specialist."

Their waiter approached with their mains as Don spoke. He set them down on their table and applauded loudly. Don opened his eyes and smiled, shifting his gaze to Marley to take in her response. She was thankfully spared having to react by the waiter's effusive praise.

"Bravo!" The waiter leaned between Don and Marley and put his hands to his heart. "That was *wonderful*. What a treat! We have to get you something on the house for that."

"Thanks." Don looked pleased.

The waiter hovered for a few more moments, asking Don about his "special talent" and Marley learned that Don's YouTube audience was mainly female, in the thirty-five to sixty age bracket, and that he'd had to employ his mother to monitor the comment section since a lot of the feedback was borderline indecent.

"I mean, it's a *poetry* channel," Don said, practically wringing his hands. "I don't know why they don't comment on my art, rather than ... well."

Marley stared at him. It was as though he had absolutely no idea how good-looking he was, or the effect he had on people around him. In a way, it was lovely that he'd made it this far into his life without becoming arrogant about his looks.

The waiter tutted, shaking his head sympathetically. "Despicable. Absolutely shameless some people are ..." He cleared his throat. "What did you say the name of the channel was again?"

When the waiter finally left, Marley tried to steer the conversation away from Don's poetry, in the hope she wouldn't need to sit through another performance.

"Tell me more about your gardening business." She had ordered the fish and she flaked off a piece with her fork. It was perfectly cooked and for a moment, she was whisked back to Darnee in her mind—the smell of Lucas's fish frying in GamGam's pan, her grandmother smiling as she steamed greens and mashed potatoes.

"Well, I love mowing grass. I find it relaxing. It's nice to see the before and afters as well. Take something messy and make it nice and tidy."

Marley thought of her work and nodded. "I can definitely understand that. And it must be nice to be outside most of the day, that's something I don't get in an office." She took another bite of her fish.

"I do like it. I'm not sure I could work inside all day."

"It's pretty strange that's what humans have evolved to, isn't it?" When Don didn't answer, Marley looked up. He was poking at his kangaroo steak. "Is something wrong?"

Don set his fork down and screwed his nose up. "I just realised I don't want this. I feel like something else."

"Would you like to try some of my fish?"

"No, it's okay. I'll just tell them I changed my mind and get them to bring me something else. They can take this back."

"Don," Marley half-laughed. "You can't change your mind about food! They're a business, they're not just going to give you a new dish."

Don frowned at her and gestured to the waiter who rushed to their table. "Sorry, I don't want this anymore. Can I have the shrimp pasta instead?"

Without so much as blinking, the waiter whipped the plate from under Don's nose. "Immediately, sir. With our apologies."

Marley's mouth dropped open as the waiter zoomed toward the kitchen. "Is that how people usually respond when you change your mind?"

Don looked genuinely puzzled. "In restaurants? Yes, of course. You're allowed to change your mind, they just bring you something new."

"Do they charge you for the first dish?"

He laughed. "Of course not. I didn't eat it!"

Marley drew her head back in surprise, then looked slowly around the restaurant. What she'd noticed when they'd first sat down—people glancing at Don—had only become more pronounced during the course of their meal. Almost *everyone* was staring at him. Women were twirling their hair as they gazed in his direction, pupils dilated and teeth sinking into bottom lips. Men were shooting him glances somewhere between envy and admiration. The wait staff were tripping over one another as they went about their tasks with their heads craned towards Don.

And Marley felt a small shiver as she realised something

else. He had no effect on her whatsoever. If she compared how she felt when she looked at him with how she felt when she looked at Finn, how her body responded in Finn's company ... she had no right to be here. It wasn't fair to Don, and it had been a bad idea from the beginning. She'd been hoping for a casual distraction from Finn and instead she'd ended up with, well, *Don*.

She pictured Finn's face as he told her he'd found a way to help her out and her blood started racing as a horrible thought occurred to her: Bess must have made Finn give up something *big* in exchange for that favour. Not that she was going to accept it. Still, she couldn't bear that thought. She'd call Finn first thing in the morning to clear everything up.

For now, she just had to get through this date.

"Can I see you again?" Don asked eagerly as they finally walked out of the restaurant and into the fresh night air. They'd been given free desserts, followed by coffees and then two rounds of after dinner mints. Marley had begun to think the waiter might actually take them hostage to keep Don around.

"Oh. Don, I don't think that's the best idea." Marley kept her voice light but firm.

Sadness flickered across his face and he nodded slowly. Then he closed his eyes and placed a hand on his chest. "He had a great night, full of delight / but for her the feeling wasn't right. He hopes that despite, she'll remember him right / and maybe one day they'll reunite."

Marley paused until he opened his eyes. "Good night, Don. You're going to make someone very happy."

Don looked down for a long beat, then back up. "Well,

thank you for a wonderful evening anyway. I had a lovely time."

"I'm glad," Marley said, and rested her hand gently on his upper arm in a gesture of farewell. He smiled sadly, then he saw her into a taxi. She could easily have caught the train, but didn't want to risk him offering to see her home.

She kicked off her shoes at the door, smiling and shaking her head at the evening's events. If nothing else, Don had indeed provided a distraction. Although not for the reasons she'd hoped. She couldn't wait to see the girls again—she knew they'd get a kick out of the story.

Marley showered and got changed into her pyjamas, then flopped onto the bed, phone in hand.

Got time to talk tomorrow? she wrote, before she could think better of it. Finn immediately read the message.

Yes.

The Greek? Lunch time?

He sent the thumbs up emoji and started writing something else. Without even realising it, Marley held her breath. *Not a late night, then?* His message appeared and then vanished, withdrawn seconds after she had read it, but she felt a grin spread over her face.

She was about to respond with something flirty when she caught herself. The smile fell from her face and she put the phone away.

It took her a long time to fall asleep.

CHAPTER NINETEEN

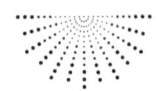

A summer rain shower took Marley by surprise on her way to the Greek. By the time she got there, she was drenched. Her hair was plastered to her head and her leopard-print skirt and basketball top clung to her body, but Finn didn't seem to mind. He had already claimed a table for them inside the restaurant and his whole face lit up when he saw her. He stood, and then sat quickly back down again as though remembering something.

"Hey." She took her seat and hoped he would think her cheeks were red due to the walk in the rain and nothing else.

"You didn't need to shower for me," he joked.

She grinned and turned to order a sparkling water from the waiter.

"And the usual for me," Finn added.

"The usual?"

Finn tilted his head sceptically. "*Now* you don't remember?"

The waiter shrugged. "I got a ton of customers. You think I remember everyone?"

Finn sighed. "Lactose-free mochaccino, please."

The waiter tapped his pen on the pad. "Already had it written down."

Marley giggled as he walked off and Finn shook his head, smiling. Then an awkward silence descended between them. Finn pulled the sugar jar over and started crumbling a cube while Marley dried off her face with serviettes and pulled her hair up into a topknot. Then she cleared her throat.

"Finn, so far you've given me a secret meeting to pass on more details, cooked me an incredible dinner, introduced me to Rebecca and now …" She blew out a breath. "I can't ever thank you. I don't even know how to try."

"You don't need to," he said, eyes trained sharply on the sugar cube. "I want to help you."

"For nothing at all in return?"

He looked up, frowning. "I … your happiness. That's what I get in return."

Marley was silent, struggling with her emotions. Unable to stop herself, she reached a hand across the table and grabbed Finn's. He froze with the sugar-cube mid crumble and Marley saw his chest rise and fall in perfect unison with hers.

The waiter plonked their drinks on the table with a wink. "We don't rent by the hour here."

Marley quickly pulled her hand back and laughed a little, trying to lighten the mood. When the waiter left, she leaned her elbows on the table. "I haven't contacted them yet," she said. "MacArthur Fertility, I mean. I need to know something first."

"What is it?" Finn stirred his coffee, his cheeks slightly flushed.

"How did you make this happen? And what did you have to give up to get it?"

He shrugged. "It doesn't matter."

"It does," she said firmly. "It matters to me."

He bit his lip and cast his eyes down. Marley stared at his thick lashes, the waves of his biceps. She swallowed hard and turned her gaze to her water glass.

"All your costs will be invoiced to ReproJoy. And I'm just walking away," he said finally. "I'm not taking anything, any part of the business, any severance or anything. It's what I want. But I made Bess think I'd fight if she didn't do what I asked. And she was scared of that."

"But that's silly," Marley said quickly. "You're going to need money to set up your practice. She owes you a lot—you can't walk away empty-handed. I'm not saying you try to take her down, just get a bit of what should rightfully be yours."

"I don't want it," Finn said. "I feel bad for breaking up with her. I mean, we were together for a long time."

"But you'd already asked her to marry you. She'd said no." Marley didn't mention the conversation she'd overheard in the bathrooms at Icebergs that day. That was a secret she planned to take to her grave.

"Yeah, I know." He sounded irritated. "Maybe I'm an idiot about Bess. My friends have told me that enough times that I should probably believe it. But I want to do it my way and that's my way. So go to your appointment—if you want. There's no need to feel guilty."

Marley struggled with her emotions, sitting silently as she took deep breaths. "It's time."

"Time for what?" He looked up and frowned at her. "Marley, you've gone pale."

"I just made a decision." She puffed out a breath. "I will go to my appointment. Maybe even let the costs be invoiced to ReproJoy, if you're not going to take anything else from Bess. But … then I can help you set up your business. As repayment."

"Marley, are you okay? You're not making sense."

Her eyes were round as she looked at him, and everything she was feeling was written in their depths—a nervous kind of excitement, tinged with sadness. And something else. Fear. "Finn, I have a way to get my hands on a bit of money. I just haven't wanted to do it until now."

"Does it have anything to do with street corners? Because—"

"No!" She couldn't help but smile. "It's a little hard for me, but I know it's right. And once I've done it, I can help you set up your physio practice. In return for what you've given up for me."

He recoiled slightly, shaking his head. "I'm not taking any money from you. Sorry. You can use it for tons of other things. Put it aside for your baby. This isn't even something I'm willing to discuss."

Marley met his intense blue eyes and nodded slowly. "We don't have to discuss it, but I'm going to make it happen."

Marley's second experience with a fertility clinic was slightly less reassuring than her first. The young woman on reception at MacArthur Fertility seemed flustered and confused, accidentally swiping clutter off the desk as she frantically clicked the mouse and glared at the computer screen.

"I can't find you in the system." She sounded irritated.

"I called you yesterday afternoon," Marley said calmly. "We spoke then and you said you had added me in for today. You said it was noisy in the background and I said that's because I was sitting at a cafe."

"Okay, then I don't think it was us because I know we don't have appointments available for a couple of months."

Marley patiently drew a breath. "We spoke about how

they had made an exception for me. I'm a referral from ReproJoy. I'm going to be meeting with someone called," Marley quickly checked the notes she'd taken in her phone, "Dr Adam Coleman."

The young woman frowned into the screen and clicked a few more times. "Are you Marlowe Phop?"

"Marley Phelps."

Her face lit up. "I did put you in there. Okay, you can take a seat in the waiting room and fill out this form."

She handed Marley a clipboard, but the form under the clip was smudged with coffee, so she bent under the desk to get a new one. It sounded like something dropped behind there, and she swore softly, but she came up with a fresh sheet and smoothed it into the clipboard for Marley.

"Could I grab a pen?" Marley prompted gently.

The girl scanned the mess of her desk and came up triumphantly with a ballpoint—the top end of it scarred with teeth marks. Marley pretended not to notice, but took it gingerly between her fingers and doused it with hand sanitiser once she was sitting in the waiting room.

She quickly texted Finn. *Are you sure this place is legit? I'm not getting the best impression ...*

It's good, I swear. They have a temp on reception at the moment. I know she's not ideal. But trust me.

She clicked her phone off and carefully filled in the form with her most elegant writing. That wasn't saying a lot—as much as she mocked Dr Martelle for her shocking writing, Marley's wasn't much better. When she finished, she laid the pen down on the clipboard and closed her eyes, taking some deep breaths. Excitement flooded her body and she felt almost giddy with anticipation. Maybe this time next month she'd even be pregnant. It was an exhilarating thought that brought her close to tears. She quickly grabbed a magazine from the coffee table to take her mind off things.

About fifteen minutes later, she heard her name called. A friendly-looking man in a long white coat and with a prematurely receding hairline stood waiting for her.

"Dr Coleman," he said, extending his hand. She shook it and they walked to his room, taking seats opposite one another at the white desk. "So," he began, scanning his eyes over her form, "I understand we have a special case with you and you'd like to get started right away." He folded his hands together on the desk and looked at her in a friendly way.

Marley knew she should probably be embarrassed that she was there because of what Finn had given up with Bess, but she wasn't. Especially not when she thought he deserved more, and when she had already found a way to make it up to him.

"Yes. As soon as humanly possible."

Dr Coleman chuckled. "Okay, let's begin, shall we?"

After a physical exam and ultrasounds—during which Marley answered as many questions as she could about her family medical history, her own health and her cycle—Dr Coleman drew blood. "We'll get these lab results back in a couple of hours, but based on your cycle history, you're actually at the perfect point to start with clomiphene, if you want to."

"Yes."

"Five tablets over five days. You could opt not to take it and try naturally. At your age I'd expect a high success rate—"

"I want the tablets."

Dr Coleman chuckled. "Well, alright then." As he walked her through the rest of the plan in very human terms, Marley's mind ran ahead. This was it. Her lifelong dream of becoming a mother would become a reality. She knew there were no guarantees, but she was closer now than she ever had been.

"Are you okay, Marley?" Dr Coleman broke off in concern, peering at her. "You look as though you might cry. Am I going too fast with the explanation?"

She shook her head, swallowing the tears of happiness back down. "There's no such thing as too fast, with this," she whispered.

Marley left the clinic with a script, login credentials for the app where she could select her donor choices, and a long list of detailed instructions and dates. She was glad Dr Coleman had written everything down, she'd tried hard to concentrate but her mind hadn't exactly been cooperating. He would phone her once her lab results were in, and she could start with the tablets that day if everything checked out.

She needed to submit her donor selection within the next few days, to ensure it was reserved for her. She decided going back to work would be pointless, so she messaged Dr Martelle to say she wouldn't be in for the rest of the afternoon—Tilda was thankfully happy to stay—and got the script filled at the pharmacy near her flat.

At home, she made herself a cup of tea, set some soft music playing through her bluetooth speaker and flopped onto the sofa with the app.

It was surreal selecting the criteria for the father of her future child from a series of dropdown menus and baby pictures. Humans had evolved to this. They'd moved through eras where women were bought and sold as chattel, through generations where women had no choice in their partners, to a place where she could toggle through parallel universes and alternate versions of her child with some simple swipes and taps. Marley found it clinical and empowering at the same time.

She also felt odd, choosing a potential partner from his baby photo. There were many other criteria, but visually that was all she had to go off. It made her feel strange, sizing up random toddlers to determine whether they had the genetic goods she was looking for. And the pool to select from was painfully small, the consequences of her choice life-changingly huge…

Dr Coleman had said she needed to submit three choices through the app—her first choice and two backups in case the first wasn't available. By the time the sun set, she had narrowed it down to seven. She phoned her local Thai place for delivery, replied to a text message from Dr Martelle warning her Tilda had done something strange to the computer system that afternoon, and ignored one from Don asking how her week had been.

She wished GamGam was around. This was the kind of thing she could imagine them doing together, sitting at the kitchen table in the house in Darnee. GamGam would give sensible advice like "check their profession" or "make sure they have kind eyes in their baby photo" and Marley, or rather the old Marley, would simply try to find the best-looking one.

Amy texted in their group chat, asking how the appointment had gone and the conversation quickly turned to requests from Lyra and Amy to send screenshots of the donors as Marley shortlisted them. But she felt funny doing that, instead promising to show them her phone on their meet-up the following day.

The only other person she considered discussing the donor selection with was Finn. But that was obviously a terrible idea. If she closed her eyes and pictured them sitting side by side, swiping through profiles and discussing the pros and cons of each potential father for her child, she felt ill. And there were other reasons too, not least of which was the fact the donor she was most interested in could have been Finn's younger brother in the baby picture...

At midnight, Marley woke with a start, the phone having fallen on her face as she lay on the sofa.

She dragged herself to bed, half-hoping GamGam would visit her in a dream and tell her which donor she should choose.

CHAPTER TWENTY

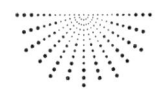

"Ohhh, that one is super cute." Lyra held the phone up beside Marley's face, the screen showing a picture of a donor as a child. "Ames, don't you reckon these two would make beautiful babies?"

Amy leaned forward on her barrel and squinted, crinkling the perfect wings of her eyeliner as she considered. "He's already a baby in that pic. I find it hard to tell. But he's definitely cute. That black hair!"

Marley grabbed her phone back from Lyra and put it face down on the barrel, blushing. "What if it's someone here?" she hissed, glancing furtively around the Whistle Stop.

"If it is, you'd be better off knowing now, right?" Amy reasoned. "You can size them up and see if you want to reconsider."

Marley couldn't argue with that. She flipped the phone back over and the girls cooed over her other choices and read the letters from them several times. They both agreed—they liked the donor with the black hair best.

"Have you submitted them yet?" Amy asked.

Marley shook her head. "I've *pretty* much decided, but I'm

yet to click the actual button to send them through. I need to do it though."

"Is it expensive?" Lyra wondered aloud, as Marley tucked her phone back into her satchel. "Can I help?"

"I can, too," Amy added eagerly. "I'm so excited to be an aunty!"

Marley shook her head. "Thank you both so much. Really, you have no idea how much that means to me. But … that's actually a big part of what I want to tell you about tonight. I've decided to sell my house in Darnee. I'm driving back this weekend to go get it ready for sale."

Lyra blinked. "You forgot you had a house?"

"No," Marley laughed, then turned sombre again. "I just … I *really* didn't want to sell it before now, even though there have been times I badly needed the money. It's too full of memories of GamGam. It's been standing empty for two years. But now I realise this is exactly what she would have wanted. For me to sell it. She always wanted me to get out of Darnee." A wave of emotion hit Marley unexpectedly and she struggled against tears. The girls enclosed her in tight hugs until she felt better.

"Are you … worried about seeing the people you knew again?" Lyra asked gently.

Marley's eyes were mournful as she nodded. "I did kind of disappear. But it wasn't as though I fitted in there anyway. I never did. Still …" She drew a deep breath. "It's time to face them all again. I feel ready. Or, as ready as I ever will."

"When are you leaving?" Amy asked.

"Sunday morning," Marley said. "I'll stay there until Friday and drive back Saturday. If anyone's up for a spontaneous road trip, let me know."

She'd arranged everything for her trip back—Dr Martelle had given her a week off which Tilda would cover, she'd rented a car and mostly packed her bags. It had actually taken her a full hour and quite a bit of panic to find the old house keys, but she had them tucked in her satchel now.

She'd wanted to meet with the girls before heading off—even hoped one of them might be randomly available for a road trip, although she knew it was unlikely. Amy was still getting her business off the ground, plus she was planning a wedding. Lyra was generally locked in a studio.

"I wish I could come," Amy said sadly, "I'm sure if I asked Kristina and Martha they wouldn't have a problem at all. It's just that we have a big pitch coming up and I don't want to dump it on them."

"It's fine," Marley reassured her. "I didn't think either of you would be able to make it. I just wanted to make sure I asked, and let you know where I was going."

"Is Darnee pretty?" Lyra asked.

Marley twisted her mouth. "It can be. The problem is actually the river, which I guess at one time was a feature. GamGam had a beautiful painting of it from the 1920s. But now there's a lot of pollutants in it and it probably needs to be dredged or something. It can stink in summer. Other than that, Darnee's just like a normal Australian small town, I guess. One Main Street, barren on the outskirts, everyone knows everyone. Stuff like that."

"I'm a bit worried about you driving nine hours alone." Amy's brows knitted together in concern. "Make sure you take lots of rest stops along the way and message us every couple of hours."

"I might not be going alone." Marley looked into her drink.

"Who's going with you then?" Lyra frowned.

"I do have other friends aside from you two, you know," Marley said lightly. They stared at her. "Okay, I pretty much don't," she admitted. "Finn offered to come when I told him about it. But it's probably a very bad idea."

"Finn? From the clinic?" Amy arched an eyebrow. "Bad idea in what way exactly?" Marley flushed and Amy made a small "ah" of understanding. "Still, is it enough of a bad idea that you'd want to drive all that way alone? Lyra and I would both feel way better if you had someone with you."

"Is there any chance he's dangerous?" Lyra added worriedly.

It would definitely be dangerous to go all that way with Finn, let alone spend a week with him in her old house, although not for the reasons Lyra was thinking.

"I haven't decided if I'll really make him come all that way," she said finally. "The thing is, Finn got me the appointment at MacArthur Fertility. When he broke up with his girlfriend, he sacrificed a lot so that my treatment would be paid for. I'm not accepting it," she added quickly, "or, well I am but only temporarily. Then I'll pay him back with the startup funds he needs. That's why I'm selling the house. I've always known I'd probably have to, but I was hoping I might have saved up enough to avoid it."

"Wow, that's amazing of him," Lyra breathed, touched.

"Do you need to sell the house?" Amy asked. "Can't you just borrow from us and then pay it back over time?"

Marley smiled. "Thank you. But it's time to sell it. It feels right."

"It will be good for you to have closure, too," Lyra added gently.

"If Finn wants to go with you, let him. It will definitely make us feel better." Amy winked. "Maybe you, too."

"I agree," Lyra said. "We don't want anything happening to you. Not when we're so close to becoming aunties!"

"I don't know," Marley said, stirring her water and taking a chip from the basket of fries they'd ordered to split. "Darnee's not exactly a riveting place to be. And I'll have lots of running around to do, I guess. He might just be bored."

"He wouldn't offer if he was worried about that," Lyra said.

"And you might need to do some repairs or whatever," Amy added. "It would be useful to have a second pair of hands. Not to mention moral support if things get heavy or weird with your old ... connections."

"Yeah, I suppose you're right. It's just that I'm attracted to him, and now he's single. I don't want any complications. I want to have my child with a donor so it's clean and there's no involvement. I want to do things my way. I don't want any risk of things getting messy and that's basically the only outcome if you rush into something. Plus, I just don't want to wait anymore."

Lyra nodded in understanding. "Yeah, I get that."

Amy looked thoughtful. "It's not like you *have* to get together just because he's going with you. Besides, a nine hour road trip both ways and five days in the same place ... maybe you'll find out you hate one another and then you'll actually be relieved once it's over."

Marley couldn't imagine that happening, but she nodded anyway and changed the subject to Lyra's album. They chatted for another few hours and Marley was grateful to hear their latest news, and even more grateful for the distraction. But in the back of her mind, she couldn't stop weighing up whether or not to have Finn come with her to Darnee.

CHAPTER TWENTY-ONE

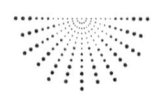

"Well, GamGam," Marley said into thin air as she stirred a cup of tea in her kitchen on the morning of her road trip, "I've chosen the baby's father."

She sat at the dining table, feeling the warmth from the light streaming in through the window and yawned. She'd stayed up into the small hours working up the nerve to submit her donor selection in the app. When she finally clicked the button, she half expected a proper adult to knock on the front door and ask her who she thought she was, making a decision like that alone.

After a lot of consideration, she'd marked her first preference as Finn's-could-be-brother. Part of her had known she would do that all along. She'd resisted it for a while, purely because of his visual similarity to Finn, but then decided that wasn't enough of a reason *not* to choose him. She would never know the man's real name, but she'd decided to call him Tim. It may have been because a Tim Minchin song came on at the moment when she pressed the button, or more likely, because she'd polished off a packet of TimTams while working up the nerve to finalise everything.

Now she sipped her tea as she mentally ran through her packing list. Enough clothes for a week, because she wouldn't have access to a washing machine, several bright torches and a bumper pack of batteries, since the power would be disconnected, a small bag of toiletries that included her remaining clomiphene tablets, a bag of food, the deeds to the house and the keys. She'd loaded most of it into the boot of the rental car the previous night, and hoped she wasn't forgetting anything. Nine hours was a long way to come back if she did.

Her worst fear was driving all that way to find out the house had been destroyed somehow. That, or it was infested with mice. Or that squatters had taken up residence. God, why had she left it so long without once going back to check on the place?

A message from Finn lit up her screen and Marley felt a now-familiar warmth as she read his words and pictured his face, those deep blue eyes and the sweep of his thick lashes. *Not too late for me to come with you ...*

She clutched the phone to her chest, heart racing, and let herself enjoy the feeling for a moment. *I'm about to leave, otherwise I might have reconsidered your offer :)*

She showered quickly and threw on a comfortable driving outfit, tamer than her usual choices. Going back to the place where she'd been known as Lena, a well put-together and respectable young lady, made her want to tone down her outfits.

She heaved her backpack onto her shoulders and opened her front door to find a basket on her doormat. It bulged with healthy snacks, bottles of sparkling water and a little note that she bent to examine. *Wanted to make sure you didn't starve on the way. F.*

She felt heat tingle through her and exhaled a short

breath, a huge smile spreading over her face as she grabbed the basket and headed for the street.

She looked up and stopped short just outside her apartment block doors. Finn stood in the street, arms crossed, leaning against a car. His hair looked blue-black in the morning sun and a duffel bag was slumped at his feet. He grinned at her and her heart flickered wildly in response as she stood stock-still, eyeing him with what she hoped was a calm expression.

"Does this mean you're accepting my offer to help you set up your business?" she asked finally.

"One hundred and fifty percent not. I just hate the idea of you spending all that time alone in the car."

She adjusted her backpack and twisted her mouth to stop herself from smiling. "I'm perfectly capable of driving nine hours alone."

"Oh, I'm certain of that. It's just going to be *puh-retty* boring, isn't it?"

"Don't you have anything better to do? It's five full days away, seven with the drive each way."

He shook his head and held his palms up. "I'm unemployed, remember? And I've always wanted to see Dungaree."

"Darnee," she corrected, grinning. "Oh yeah? Which specific part of it?"

"The …" he tilted his head at her, "hot springs?" She shook her head. "The big … rock?"

She laughed. "Finn, you really don't need to do this." She knew even as the words were out of her mouth that she would let him come. And that it was a huge mistake.

He sensed the acceptance in her words. "I'm not pushing, just so you know. I only wanted to let you know I was serious about coming."

Marley grinned, nodding and relief flooded his face. "Do

you want to take my car?"

"No, but thanks. I rented one and it's already packed. Besides, if that's yours ..." She jerked her head to indicate the one he'd been leaning against. It was hot pink with flower decals above the wheels. "We'll be skinned in Darnee."

He chuckled. "Nah, mine's a few blocks away in an unrestricted zone. It's a green one."

"A *green* one?" She clicked the button on her keyring and the rental beeped and flashed its lights as they headed towards it. "You don't know anything about cars, do you?"

"Not a single thing." He grinned.

"Oh my God. They're going to eat you alive."

———

Marley glanced down at Finn's legs and fought a smile. They'd been on the road for two hours, headed inland. The scenery had changed from inner city traffic snarls, through quiet suburban streets, to low scrub, high rock and wide dual carriageways.

"What?" He paused with a gummy worm halfway to his mouth. While he'd loaded her basket with nuts, dried fruit and vegetable chips, the front pocket of his duffel had been rammed with sweets for himself. "What are you smiling at?"

"Nothing!" She kept her eyes on the road.

"You're clearly laughing at me. What is it?"

"It's just, are you wearing *zip-off pants?*"

"Oh, *you're* going to talk to me about fashion." He waved the worm at her. "You. The woman who usually looks like she got dressed running through a flea market at high speed."

Marley burst out laughing. "I like my outfits!"

"And you want to confuse your predators. I get it. I've seen it in nature documentaries."

"So you are wearing zip-offs?"

"I wasn't sure what to dress for," he said finally.

"You think we're going to a farm, don't you?"

"No."

"The outback."

He paused. "Hey, I can't even find Darnee on the maps app."

"Were you looking for Dungaree?"

"Irrelevant! I packed for everything. Hot, cold—"

"The nineties."

He flicked the gummy worm at her. It landed in her lap and she chuckled, returning her concentration to the road as Finn changed the playlist on his phone, which they'd hooked up to the car's sound system.

Her thoughts swung between alarm that she'd actually let him come on the trip, to trepidation as to what awaited her in Darnee, to pleasure at Finn's company. She felt relaxed around him, but she vowed to be on guard against getting any closer. Well, any closer than five days in the same house would necessitate.

That would be heading into dangerous territory. Territory Marley wanted to stay well away from.

Finn's phone rang and he let out a small sigh. "It's Bess."

"I can pull into the next petrol station so you can call her back? We need to take a break anyway."

"I'll just answer it now, I'm sure it's going to be a quick call." Finn swiped to answer, and Bess's voice boomed through the car's sound system.

"Finley? Where are you?"

"Uh," Finn tapped furiously at his phone, trying to disconnect it from the speakers, "I'm going to be out of town for a few days."

"Why didn't you tell me?" Her aggressive tone made Marley cringe.

"I don't need to tell you anymore, remember?"

A pause. "You're not with that weird girl are you?" Finn cast a mortified look at Marley, still unable to get the phone to play through the handset.

"Bess, what do you want?" His voice was tight.

She gave a sigh that could peel paint. "I need you to retrain Ebony, the new receptionist. She's crap."

Finn frantically pressed several more buttons, finally uncoupling his handset from the system. He lifted it to his ear and Marley kept her eyes firmly on the road, attempting to tune out of Finn's side of the conversation.

She studied the car in front, a bright orange ute with the mudguards flapping, and the car in the other lane, an older Mercedes whose driver wore a large hat. She focused on the metal guardrail separating the traffic flowing in the other direction, on the remains of a wombat they passed. But she couldn't tune out Finn's voice.

"Bess, I can't. Also, I don't want to. You're responsible for hiring and firing. If she's not working out, get rid of her. She wasn't my choice ... but that's the thing Bess, it *doesn't* affect me. You're the one who fired me ... I'm not being difficult, I'm stating facts ... look, I need to go. I'll be back next week. Maybe we can talk then." He clicked to disconnect and they drove in silence for a few more minutes. "I'm sorry you heard that," he said finally, his voice low.

Marley shrugged. "It's totally fine. Don't worry about it."

"She shouldn't have said what she said."

"That I'm weird?" Marley glanced at him. He was biting his lip. "I am weird." She turned back to the road. "And it's something I'm very happy about. You should be too."

"What do you mean?"

"It's not everyone who gets to travel to Dungaree with an escapee from the flea market."

He fell silent, but from the corner of her eye she could see him grinning. She picked the gummy worm off her lap, tossing it back at him.

"Oh God." His voice was suddenly terror-stricken. "There's going to be snakes, isn't there?"

CHAPTER TWENTY-TWO

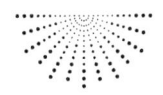

They reached Darnee at midnight. Marley was driving, the car silent as Finn dozed lightly in the passenger seat. They'd driven in shifts and made several long breaks at truck stops. Marley was reluctant to admit it, but she doubted now she could have made the trip alone. It was one thing moving to Sydney on a Greyhound, where she could shuffle up the aisle to the bathroom, read books and nap, and quite another to stay alert and in the driver's seat for a nine hour drive.

Having someone to talk to, someone to take over while she closed her eyes and reclined for an hour, having a second pair of eyes along winding country roads had made a huge difference. She was feeling very grateful to Finn for his persistence in wanting to accompany her. Her heart swelled as she looked at his sleeping form, his glasses slipping slightly down his nose. He'd tried to broach the topic of her appointment at MacArthur Fertility and had seemed gently curious about whether she'd made her donor selection. Marley had quickly changed the subject and Finn had taken the hint, not raising the topic again on their long drive.

The roads of Darnee were dark and eerie, the few street lights shining weakly through the waving trees, dappling the tar with amber patterns. The river gleamed black in the pale moonlight—Marley swallowed and turned her gaze from it, thinking of Hayden.

She was overcome with emotion as she rolled slowly past the graveyard, towards the grocery store where she'd previously worked. A light wind swirled trash and loose newspaper sheets around the empty parking lot. She drove quickly past the church and the rectory, and turned onto Main Street. The Blushing Bride was still there. The bakery. The butcher. The hardware store. She spotted a new cafe and tried to remember what had been in its place when she'd left. The locksmith? No, that was still there. For the life of her, she couldn't remember.

Two years. Almost two-and-a-half. She'd only been gone that long, but it might as well have been a lifetime. She wasn't the same person coming back as the woman who'd left.

She drove past the three other houses on the quiet cul-de-sac street where she'd spent the first thirty years of her life, almost certain she saw a curtain twitch as she passed the Hayworths—if it still was the Hayworths—and pulled up outside the single-storey red brick house, fighting tears. The wooden fence was still standing, and she took that as a positive sign. She let Finn sleep for another moment as she squeezed back tears. She could almost hear GamGam's voice, smell her lavender soap, feel the pressure of her hugs. If only she could walk through the door and see her again.

"**F**inn." She shook him gently awake and he yawned and stretched.

"That was quick." He opened one eye and grinned at her.

Marley's heart pounced in her chest. "Let's get the torches. There won't be any power. Or a lot of water."

"Now you tell me," he grumbled, undoing his seatbelt.

They got stiffly out of the car, taking a few moments to stretch their legs. The night air was chill and their breath billowed in front of them, making ghosts in the air. Marley opened the boot and they grabbed their bags and the torches. She reached a hand over the fence to unlatch the gate.

"Huh."

"What?" Finn asked, rubbing his palms against his upper arms.

"There's a different clasp on the fence than there used to be."

"Okay? Did you have anyone looking after it?"

"Not really. I sort of told Mr Hayworth that I'd be gone awhile."

"Well, maybe he fixed it. Let's get inside. I'm freezing."

"Lucky you brought zip-offs."

He swatted her as she opened the gate. Her flashlight beamed over neatly trimmed grass that had recently been edged. Good. Those monthly yard maintenance service bills weren't for nothing then.

Standing on the small concrete front porch, Marley slipped her key into the lock. It wouldn't turn. She pulled it out and shone the torch on it to check whether she'd accidentally used her Sydney key. No, she had the right one. She tried again. Nothing. The key wouldn't budge. She swore lightly under her breath.

"Marley?" There was an edge of concern to Finn's voice. "Do we definitely have the right house?"

"Yes! Of course. I know my own place."

"Sorry. It's just then when keys don't fit, it's usually a sign you might not have the right door." Finn dropped his duffel and pulled out a thick woollen jumper, slipping it over his head. "It is *bitter* around here, aren't you feeling this?"

"Yes," Marley admitted, jiggling the key again. "Welcome to Darnee, where the nights are freezing and the days are so stinking hot they have you begging for the nights. What the hell is going on, why doesn't my key work?"

"Is there a hotel or something we can check into for now? One with heating? We can look at this fresh, tomorrow. When it's less like a horror movie."

"Finn Mayberry, are you scared?"

"Not even a little." He grinned. "So about that hotel."

"The closest one is in Silton Town, but I don't even think they have 24 hour service at check in. But Finn, this is *my* place. Something's going on. The key should work."

"Okay. Do you want me to try and break a window?"

"Let's try one around the back first. We never got locks for those."

Marley guided them around the narrow path to the small backyard, the Hill's Hoist looming eerily in the moonlight. She stepped up onto the small back deck and tried the sliding door that led to the kitchen and dining room, but found it locked. Her flashlight bounced back against curtains and Marley pulled her hand away from the door like she'd been burned.

"What?" Finn asked in alarm.

"I never had curtains on this door!"

"Alright, clearly something is going on and we need to get out of here. This is creepy as hell, Marley. If you wanted to take me somewhere and murder me, you could have just done it in Sydney."

Marley smiled tightly, her mind racing. Who could have changed the locks? Added curtains? The house had belonged half to Hayden when he was alive, but had passed fully back to her when he'd died.

Marley knocked firmly on the back door, the crisp rap echoing in the still night. Finn grabbed her hand as she pulled back for a second knock.

"What are you doing?" he hissed.

"Seeing if anyone's in here."

Finn sighed. "They're not just going to casually answer if they are, especially if they're not supposed to be here. If you're determined to get in, I'll try the other windows."

They split up, both tugging at the sash windows. Finn gently called her name and Marley breathed a sigh of relief when she saw that the window to her old bedroom lifted.

Finn had already levered the fly screen out and she hoisted herself up and through the window, leaning back to Finn. "Go to that sliding door, I'll let you in."

"Are you kidding?" He tossed their bags in, then heaved himself up effortlessly behind her, swinging his legs around and landing lightly on the floor. "We have no idea who's in here. I'm not letting you go alone."

Marley's heart swelled and she was excruciatingly aware of how close they were standing, their breathing rapid. Something about the strange situation made her want to reach out and touch him. He was watching her in the dark, his eyes black and huge. She swallowed and took a big step backwards, breaking the spell.

Marley swung the torch around the room. The double bed, the nightstands, the wardrobe—everything was the same. She was surprised it didn't smell musty, but that might have been the blast of cold night air they'd just let in. She spun on her heel and headed for the door. Before she reached it, Finn gently caught her arm, pulling her behind him. Her skin broke out in goosebumps around his touch, her heart thundering in the silence as he smiled at her.

She'd told him there would be no power, but he instinctively reached for the light switch. They both inhaled sharply as light flooded the room. Once their eyes had adjusted, Marley found Finn staring at her questioningly.

"Maybe they forgot to disconnect it?" she whispered, uncertain. "Let's check the rest of the place."

They conducted a thorough search of the small house. As they flicked on the light in the smaller second bedroom, Marley gasped.

"What?"

"This isn't my furniture! Like, at *all*." The room held a short, narrow single bed—a child's bed. There was a crib shoved into the corner and a changing table stuffed with supplies beneath the window. "What the *flipping hell* is happening?"

"Well, at least if whoever was using the place has a kid, they're less likely to be a serial killer? Let's check the rest of the place."

There was no one inside the house. Not even behind the shower curtain Marley whipped back with a racing heart. Everything had been recently cleaned and there was barely a speck of dust. The fridge and cupboards were empty—save for a box of teabags—the sink scrubbed and the garbage bin sparkling. Clearly, there was no one living there now. But there *had* been. The new curtains in the kitchen, the kid's beds, the changed locks ...

"Should we call the police?" Finn asked, as they headed back toward the dining room.

Marley considered. It was probably the safest and most sensible option. She just hadn't imagined her return to town beginning with a call to the cops. "I guess," she said reluctantly, taking a seat at the scoured dining table where she'd eaten almost every meal of her life until she'd moved to Sydney. She toyed with her phone. "I mean, it doesn't look like they're coming back any time soon, but ... you just never know."

"Aren't you glad I didn't let you come alone?" Finn said, taking a seat opposite her. His eyes were deep pools in the warm tungsten light. Marley's heart squeezed.

"Yes," she said simply. Then she dropped her head into her hands with a groan. "I just wish we had some coffee. God knows how long the cops will take to get here. All I want to do is sleep."

"There's a kettle. Shall I make us some tea while you call?"

"Thanks." Marley dialled triple-0 and forced her eyes away from the sight of Finn's toned form as he moved around the kitchen. "Emergency services? I'd like to report a ... very tidy break and enter."

CHAPTER TWENTY-THREE

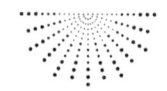

They'd moved to the living room to wait for the police. The combination of soft sofa, a long day of driving, and a warm cup of tea had proved too much for Marley and at some point, she must have dozed off. Finn had dimmed the lights and thrown a blanket over her, so the room was dark when Marley heard the noises. Disorientated, she shot awake, her heart already hammering and her skin prickling with a cold sweat as though her body had sensed danger before her mind had. Something was moving around outside the living room window. She could see the beam of a torch slicing through the side of the house. She sat up and moved to prod Finn, who was slumped in the armchair, asleep.

"Finn, there's someone outside," she whispered urgently.

He was instantly wide awake, sitting upright in a single movement. He fumbled to put his glasses on. "It's probably the police," he said.

"Then why are they sneaking around instead of knocking on the door?" Marley hissed.

"I don't know. Do you have a rolling pin or something?"

His voice cracked with tiredness and Marley wondered whether he was sleep-talking.

"A rolling pin?"

"To whack them over the head. Unless you have a cricket bat?" He scrubbed his hand over his face, then looked up at her widened eyes. "Where do you think this person is?"

They sucked in sharp breaths as a torch beam cut through the window, waving just above their heads. Finn spun Marley to push her into the armchair, sheltering her with his body. They were pressed firmly together, and Marley was acutely aware of their breaths rising and falling in rapid unison. He was warm and firm and she could feel the shape of his pecs and abs, leaving her tingling in a way that had nothing to do with the fear she was feeling.

"Stay quiet," he whispered in her ear, sending echoes shooting downwards. She nodded, her cheek grazing his as she did so. God, she couldn't stay like this. He was far too close and it was scrambling her mind. They might be about to get killed and all she could think of was melting their bodies together, pulling his mouth to hers...

Then she heard a noise that chilled her—a key turning in the front door lock. Finn scrambled to his feet, protectively shoving her behind him as he faced the door.

The door opened and the torch cut a swath through the room, landing on Finn, who shielded his eyes with one arm and tucked Marley further behind him with the other.

"Police! Stay where you are!"

Marley frowned, stepping out from behind Finn. *"Drew?"*

The torchlight rushed over her face, then hit the floor as the light came on. Marley flinched against the sudden brightness.

"Struth. *Lena?* Is that you?"

"Yes!" Her hands were over her eyes, which smarted

against the light. "And I'd love an explanation as to what the *hell* is going on!"

Drew re-entered the kitchen with the packet of biscuits he'd gone to fetch from his patrol car, just as Marley set down fresh cups of tea on the dining room table. Drew looked uncomfortable—seeing him in her kitchen again felt like an eerie reminder of the night he'd come to tell her about Hayden, and she wondered whether he was remembering the same thing. The night Susie Baker had found out before her.

"What took you so long?" Marley asked accusingly, trying to shake the memory off.

Drew eased his bulky frame into a seat opposite them and fixed Marley with an apologetic glance. "Whitey was exposing himself on the main road again. Took longer to wrangle him in than I anticipated. Dispatch said your call wasn't urgent, and I didn't recognise the address right away, otherwise…"

"Tell me everything," Marley said, meeting his eye. "And make it quick. I'm beyond tired."

"We both are," Finn added, glowering silently at Drew, who kept throwing edgy glances his way.

Marley felt a warmth in her belly at the use of the word "we". Her chair sat close to Finn's, their elbows almost touching as they wrapped their hands around their cups of tea.

"Father C had your locks changed."

"*What?*"

"I tried to tell him. I didn't want to press charges because of the … of why he did it. Anyway, I didn't have a way to get hold of ya. Left without a trace." There was a slight accusation in his look, and Finn turned to her as well.

She felt her face grow heated. "I didn't realise I needed the town's permission to move."

He waved his hand. "Course you didn't. But the only reason I knew not to file a missing person's was that someone had seen you getting on the Greyhound. I called the utilities companies, found out you'd had things switched off. I know," he cleared his throat, "the *situation* hadn't been top notch."

"Please," Marley shot Finn a quick glance and found him staring at her. "Let's just ..." She waved her hand to indicate they should drop it. "Why did he change the locks? What happened."

Drew sighed and pinched his nose. "Rosemary Wilson and her two kids were in a bit of trouble."

Marley's eyes widened. She hadn't heard Rosemary's name for years, since she'd moved to Silton Town after her marriage. Marley had been hugely relieved at the time—one less person to worry about Hayden fooling around with. Now she was surprised to feel a pang of fear for the other woman.

"What kind of trouble?"

Drew shook his head. "Look, I'm not one to gossip. But she went to Father Curtis and he needed a place to hide the three of them for a while. I'm not sure Father C was thinking straight, but he," Drew cleared his throat, "he got old Willie, the locksmith, to bust the locks and get Rosemary in here. Chose a night when the Hayworths were hosting a card evening. Got the cot and stuff in and no one noticed. We're the only three knew. She's been gone a week now, though."

"She was hiding here?"

"Yeah. A kind of temporary emergency shelter, I guess you could say. It was perfect—fenced-in yard, off everyone's radar, not too close to other neighbours, and the ones who are around aren't exactly Nosy Nellies anymore."

"That explains the curtains on this window." Marley jerked her head to indicate the floral yellow set that had been hung up. "I'm back here to sell this place. Do you think the church would buy it? They could use it again in another situation like that if they did."

Drew crunched down a biscuit, looking thoughtful. "Can't say's I know. I doubt it though. I think it was fine for Rosemary, but in a place like this ... wouldn't be a secret for long."

Marley nodded slowly, stifling a yawn. "I'll call a real estate agent tomorrow. And have a strong word with Father Curtis."

Drew nodded and drained his tea. "I can't apologise enough to you and your fella—"

"Oh, he's not ..." Marley began, waving her hands. She didn't want a rumour circulating before she'd even put the coffee pot on.

"I'm a friend," Finn cut in, his voice hoarse. "Someone who cares about her. Good thing, since you almost scared us both to death."

Drew looked sheepish. "I thought I should check the perimeter before coming inside." He stood and walked his mug to the sink. "You can keep the key I had, obviously," he jerked his head towards the table where it sat, "and I'll have Father C drop his copy round in the morning. At least you can take a hot shower and turn on the lights and whatnot." He hesitated a moment, scratching his head. "There's something else I should probably mention." He cast a look at Finn, as though he wasn't sure whether the topic should be discussed in front of him. Marley shrugged wearily. "If you're going to call an estate agent ... Susie Baker runs the one in town. In most of the other towns round here too, actually."

Marley frowned. "She came back?"

In the months after Hayden's death, Susie had left town. No one knew exactly where she'd gone, although it was known that her mother had contact. But by the time Marley had left two years later, Susie still hadn't returned to Darnee.

"Yeah. She and—" Drew broke off sharply, his eyes widening. Marley had the distinct impression there was more to the story, but she was too tired to fish for it. "She's back."

"Okay." Marley yawned. "Thanks, Drew. Tell Crystal I said hi."

Drew nodded, a warm smile playing on his lips. "I'll introduce you to our girl if I see you around. You staying long?"

"Congratulations," Marley said, genuinely happy for him. "We'll be here a week. I hope I get to meet her."

Marley closed the door behind Drew, clicking the deadbolt shut. She slumped against it and then turned to Finn, who was watching her.

"Well. Who knew a trip to Dungaree would be so hair-raising?" he said.

"Finn, I am so, so sorry."

He raised his hand and cut her off. "Don't be. I'm glad I was here."

They smiled at one another and Marley's heart rate increased, thinking about the moment their bodies had been pressed together on the armchair. She felt colour stain her cheeks and she ducked her head.

"Are you okay to take the sofa?" she asked.

"Yeah, of course."

"Sorry it's not much. I'm going to bed. I'll see you around midday tomorrow, I guess. I plan on sleeping late." She risked a glance at him and found him watching her with an almost bashful expression. "Night, Finn."

"Night, Marley," he called gently after her, as she hurried to her room and closed the door. Despite being bone-tired, it took her a long time to fall asleep.

All she could think about was how it had felt to be pressed up against Finn Mayberry.

CHAPTER TWENTY-FOUR

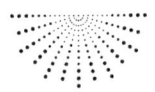

Kookaburras. How she'd missed their laugh. She rarely heard them in the city, but her mornings in Darnee had been sound-tracked by their riotous calls. She opened her eyes and lay there, smiling as their song filled her ears. This part of Darnee felt like home. The noises.

For a second, she could almost believe that GamGam would be in the kitchen, making breakfast for the two of them, her gnarled hands kneading fresh dough or frying bacon. Marley could almost smell the eggs cooking. Funny, the tricks the mind played.

Marley sniffed the air. There *were* eggs cooking, and toast and coffee and something else she didn't recognise. But how had Finn managed to get groceries? Had he been to the grocery store? Dear *God*, had he been to the grocery store?

She sprang out of bed to find him freshly showered, hair still wet, stirring a skillet of scrambled eggs on the hob while the coffee dripped into the pot. He turned to her with a smile that paused her heart.

"Good morning, sleeping beauty."

"Why are you so chipper?" she asked suspiciously. "And where did you get all that food?"

"I had a refreshing night's sleep. Well, a good couple of hours after our visitor left, I mean. That couch is comfortable. And the food?" He turned his back to her as a second set of toast ejected from the toaster. "That was from the Super Saver Mart."

Marley's heart thumped. He'd been at her old work. With her old colleagues. One of whom was married to the cop. By now, the news would be all over Darnee that Lena had returned with a stranger in tow and was back at her old place getting cosy with him.

She kept her voice light. "Oh? Did you, uh, find everything you needed?"

"I did, yes." He flipped some small white rectangles on a second frying pan. "Would never have guessed they had halloumi here." That was the smell she couldn't identify. Halloumi.

"Probably got sent over from one of the city stores just before going off." Marley grabbed a glass of water from the tap, her elbows brushing Finn's as she did so. Then she took a seat at the table.

"Probably," Finn agreed. "The sales assistant who rang it up hadn't seen it before. But it's perfectly in date, don't worry."

Marley cleared her throat. "Were you there long?"

"Hmm? Oh, not that long." He held up a piece of toast to her. "Is that brown enough?" She nodded. "Breakfast will be ready soon. Do you want some orange juice? Fresh squeezed," he added with a wink.

She smiled. She could get used to this—an insanely good-looking man in her kitchen, making a proper breakfast for her. She usually just had a bowl of cornflakes or grabbed a croissant on her way into work. She caught herself in the thought and her spine went rigid. This wasn't something she could get used to. Nothing she *should* get used to. She and Finn were friends, that was all, and he was simply keeping her company on this trip. She'd need to cut back the amount of time they spent together once they got back to Sydney. And *especially* once she was pregnant.

The countdown app she'd installed on her phone told her there were only eight days to go until her appointment. Not that she needed reminding. The date was branded in her brain. She'd swallowed her last tablet and she'd chosen her donor. Now she was a single step away from a baby. A step that definitely didn't involve Finn.

"All done," Finn said grandly, setting a plate in front of her. It smelled heavenly and the juice he put down next was brightest orange. Darnee grew world-class oranges.

Finn took his place opposite her and smiled warmly. "Bon appetit."

"Thank you so much for this, Finn." She lifted her cutlery and took a big bite, washing it down with a sip of the fresh, cold juice.

Finn smiled and cut himself a chunk of halloumi. It was almost to his mouth when he said, ever so casually, "So what's all this about a curse?"

"I swear to God, I am going to strangle Crystal Norman." Marley's face felt hot, and she knew it was probably bright red. She'd almost spat her orange juice out at Finn's words. This was what she *hadn't* missed about Darnee. Every busybody knowing every other busybody's stupid busybody business. Now it seemed even more unlikely that Rosemary hadn't been discovered while hiding out at Marley's house. A sheer and utter miracle, in fact.

Finn seemed to be taking great pleasure in her discomfort. He shook his head and grinned as inky locks tumbled over his eye. "This lady's name tag said Phoebe."

"Phoebe? I don't even know a Phoebe. Who the heck is Phoebe?"

"Red hair, greyish eyes, quite skinny?"

"Ah. Gemma's younger sister. A Pullman. That's right."

Finn paused. "Do you all know one another? Is it like the small towns in movies?"

"Apparently."

Marley took a long sip of her orange juice, Finn's thick-lashed blue eyes twinkling at her. "So are you going to tell me about it?"

"About a dumb rumour? No." Marley wished he'd drop it. Surely he could tell she didn't want to talk about it.

"Phoebe made some compelling points," he said with a grin. "Sounds like any future partner of yours needs to beware."

"Well, that won't be you, so don't worry," Marley snapped. She instantly regretted the words.

Finn recoiled slightly, the grin disappearing from his face. "Oh, my God, Marley. I'm sorry." He looked devastated, mortified—and Marley hated herself. Her chest heaved as she stared down at her plate, unable to bear the hurt in his eyes.

Why had she said that? Why did she care if he knew about the "curse"? It wasn't real anyway. It was just stupid town gossip, like GamGam had said. A series of unconnected events that had just been more prominent in her family than others.

She did hate the feeling of being branded though. She hadn't had to hear about the stupid curse for over two years, since she'd been in Sydney. And she realised now what a relief that had been. How freeing and how wonderful to just be "Marley", not "Lena of the Curse." She should have known someone would tell Finn. Should have realised that if he came with her, he'd find out about it. She just couldn't explain to herself why she was so upset that he knew ...

"I'm sorry," she mumbled into her plate. "That came out wrong."

She met Finn's eye and he gave her a sad smile. "It's okay. I shouldn't have joked about it."

Marley nodded dumbly. She looked back down at her plate, her appetite gone. A beautiful breakfast and she'd ruined it. She felt close to tears. "I'm going to go take a shower. I'll eat this later. I'll clean up."

He nodded. She turned back when she reached the door. "Finn, I'm really sorry."

"Don't worry about it, Marley. Truly."

CHAPTER TWENTY-FIVE

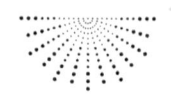

The river looked even murkier than Marley remembered. She also couldn't see anyone fishing in it. Maybe it had gotten so bad that it couldn't be used—a shame, as it had once been the lifeblood of the town.

She and Finn walked slowly along its banks, their water bottles dangling from their hands. They'd slathered themselves with sunscreen and Marley had insisted Finn wear a hat to avoid heatstroke. He hadn't packed one, but she'd found an old one of Hayden's in the very back of her cupboard. A sweat-stained, white wide-brim hat emblazoned with the words "Darnee Devils" that had been part of his cricket uniform in high school. Finn had obediently put it on despite wrinkling his nose when he saw it.

The cicadas were loud in their ears and the heat was stifling as they headed for the church. Marley planned on speaking to Father Curtis after midday mass was finished. She wasn't entirely sure what she would say to him. She felt torn between thanking him for using the place to help Rosemary, and wanting to choke him for having the audacity to think he could just waltz in and commandeer her house, changing the locks without so much as an attempt to contact her.

But Marley's mind was mostly on Finn. Since she'd snapped at him that morning, the air between them had been staticky. They were being extremely polite and reserved with one another, and the ease that she had loved about their friendship so far seemed to have disappeared with the coffee grounds he'd tossed out. She wracked her brain to think of how she could fix it, but the more she worried, the more she clammed up.

"Did you swim here as a kid?" he asked.

She wrinkled her nose. "No. Other kids did, I hated not being able to see what was at the bottom. Although, it was a lot better then than it is now."

"Is there some kind of plan to rehabilitate it?"

"I honestly don't know. Our local councilman has been a bit of a good-for-nothing his whole career. But no one challenges him, and no one's taken the river on as a cause. Everyone just kind of accepts things around here."

Finn nodded. "It must have been pretty isolating to grow up here. If you didn't feel like you fit in."

There was a lump in Marley's throat and she grabbed a low-hanging branch of a red gum as they passed it, plucking a cluster of flower buds from it. These were her favourite trees. She loved the way the layers of bark peeled off to reveal a palette of soft earthy pinks, yellows and browns. You could aim a camera at a red gum trunk and shoot randomly, and still come away with art. When she was young, she'd picked the delicate creamy-yellow spiky flowers and gifted them to GamGam, who had always made a fuss over them despite, Marley learned years later, being allergic.

As she and Finn walked, Marley pulled the buds off the cluster, tossing them into the river one by one.

"I always had GamGam," she said finally. "She was

everything. And she was enough." She smiled tightly at Finn. His eyes were shaded with prescription sunglasses against the glare of the day, but their intensity still burned through. "And then I had Hayden," she laughed dryly. "Or so I thought."

"He wasn't a good husband?"

She paused, tossing the remaining buds into the brown water. "He was never truly mine. He was in love with Susie Baker the whole time we were married. Their affair never stopped."

"The one the cop mentioned last night? The real estate agent?" Marley nodded. Finn puffed out a sharp breath. "If you don't mind me asking, is that why you didn't have kids with Hayden?"

Marley gulped, then shook her head. "The thing is, I didn't even really care about his affairs. I realised now that's probably a sign I never truly loved him. I thought I did, but … I found his affairs more embarrassing than heart breaking. Anyway, GamGam made me promise to wait a year before getting pregnant. She knew Hayden wouldn't make a good father. She could call his alcoholism for what it was. After that year, I waited a little longer. I kept waiting for any sign that it would be okay to bring a child into the family. That sign never came."

Finn stopped walking, staring at her earnestly. "What a huge sacrifice, Marley. One that you were never going to be rewarded for." He shook his head. "I … you're amazing. You're going to make an incredible mother."

Marley stared out over the water, trying to get her emotions under control.

"Thank you," she whispered. She tried not to think about the fact that it was the first time since losing GamGam that she felt truly *seen*. Before she knew what she was doing, she stepped towards him and he wrapped his arms tightly around her. She leaned her head on his broad chest and after a moment, slipped her arms around his waist. They stayed that way for a long moment, until the embrace changed and became electric. Marley pulled away as her breathing grew unsteady.

She turned on the church steps to face Finn. "Are you sure you don't mind waiting?"

"I'm sure," he answered, glancing around at the bare churchyard as a bead of sweat slipped down his forehead. "But are *you* sure you don't want me to come in with you?"

Marley shook her head. "I won't be long. I just need to do this by myself."

She pulled open the heavy, rounded wooden door to the church and slipped inside. It smelled of sweat and incense and old wood. It was also so cool and dark, such a welcome relief from the heat outside, that Marley wondered whether some folk didn't just come for the reprieve. Not many people in the town had air-conditioning, although Marley's place did, and Darnee had neither a cinema nor a shopping mall. Maybe this was the town's equivalent, and that's why they always had a healthy turnout for mass. Maybe people here weren't God-fearing, they were simply boiling to death.

Marley walked down the middle of the church, towards the white draped altar. She passed rows and rows of hard wooden pews, watched the large statue of a weeping, crucified Jesus coming into focus. Out of habit, she genuflected as she reached the altar.

Father Curtis hadn't heard her. He was folding his vestment and wiping out the chalice with a starched cloth, making every movement in a studied, ritualistic way.

"Father Curtis," she said quietly, and he spun to look in her direction. He squinted, and then took several steps towards her. The hairs that had previously sprouted from his ears and nose were gone, trimmed. As were his unruly eyebrows. Other than that obvious change, he hadn't aged a lot in the two years since she'd last seen him. Perhaps a tad more grey around the temples, perhaps a slight stoop in his shoulders. The same haughty expression.

"Lena. So the rumours are true."

"You know they are. I found your set of keys outside my house this morning."

He coloured and wouldn't meet her eyes. "Uh, yes. I want to apologise for that."

Marley studied him a moment, struggling with her emotions. Part of her wanted to scream at him. She felt sorry for the naive young girl who had come to him expecting some kind of help with Hayden, only to be dismissed again and again. But she knew she was also angry at herself for believing the priest could do something. She felt like Father Curtis had Hayden's blood on his hands. But then, there was a part of her that thought she did too. Before she could stop herself, the words were out.

"Are you apologising for using my house without my permission, or for ignoring my warnings about Hayden all those years?"

Father Curtis fell silent and looked down at the shiny tips of the loafers peeking out from under his cassock. "Lena, there's no question. I failed him. I failed *you*."

Marley was taken aback. She swallowed. She hadn't been expecting an outright admission. "What?"

He sighed, and she saw remorse written in the grey depths of his eyes. "I should have done more. I hold myself more responsible than you'll ever know." Father Curtis looked weary. "Lena. You have my humblest and most sincere apologies. For *both* those things," he added, holding up a hand when she opened her mouth.

"Thank you. I won't press charges." He blanched, as though he hadn't considered the possibility. "But I came to talk about the house," she continued. "I want to sell it. I like what you did with it. But I can't just *give* my house to the church. Are you willing to make an offer?"

Father Curtis looked regretful. "If we could, I'd have bought something else to use instead of … *borrowing* your house. Besides, I have a feeling it wouldn't work over the longer term. It's difficult to keep secrets in this town."

Marley pondered. "You're right. It's a shame. People in danger should have somewhere safe to go. Maybe it doesn't need to be secret if it's properly protected and registered as a refuge."

"Yes, I have been considering something like that. Thankfully we haven't had need since that young family moved on, but perhaps we'd discover there were people just waiting for somewhere safe to go. It will take a while. I've been discussing it with Susie Baker." After he'd said her name, Father Curtis flinched, remembering. When he spoke again his voice was slightly unsteady. "We'd probably require something larger than your place."

"Yes, I suppose you would." Marley let out an exhale. "I guess I'm going to have to speak to her as well."

He bowed his head in assent and gestured back to the altar, to the partially folded vestment. They nodded their farewells. Marley was almost at the door when he called out to her.

"I am sorry, Lena. Truly. I am."

She paused for a moment, and then pushed the heavy door and went back out into the heat.

CHAPTER TWENTY-SIX

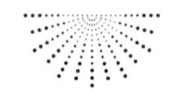

She found Finn in the graveyard, standing respectfully in front of her family plot. She took a moment to admire his tall, athletic build—staring at him until her breath came quicker. Then she realised he was hugging the shade of the myrtle tree and that his water bottle was empty. There were fresh sweat stains on Hayden's ridiculous cricket hat. Poor Finn.

Marley wondered whether she should be annoyed with him for having sought out her family's plot. This was a kind of prying after all, a kind of nosing around. Then again, he was in a public place. Everyone was free to wander through and visit graves if they wanted and it wasn't like he was dancing on them, or blowing party whistles.

She just hated that this was the only way he could ever meet her family. Standing in front of a huge tombstone.

"Shall we go?" she called, and he turned to her.

"Do you want to—" He gestured hesitantly to the grave.

She shook her head. She'd come back later, of course, to tidy it up, wipe down the stone and place fresh flowers in the holders. But she would do it alone.

They fell into step together, heading in silence back towards the house by way of the river. Marley handed Finn her water bottle and he took a grateful swig.

"I did some asking around while I was at the grocery store. Not about the curse!" he added quickly. "About good restaurants round here."

"I'm sure that was a short conversation."

"Well, not if we're willing to drive into Silton Town. There's apparently a killer Japanese place that recently opened up."

"In *Silton Town?*" He nodded. "Are you sure?"

"Yes. Phoebe was raving about it," he said.

"Oh, well if *Phoebe* thinks it's good ..."

He grinned. "She said it was authentic. A Japanese chef fell in love with a woman from Silton and opened up a restaurant after his visa came through."

"It seems highly unlikely. But I suppose the alternative is you cooking me a lavish feast. So it's your call."

"Great, because I already made a reservation. I hope you brought nice clothes."

Marley elbowed him. "I only have nice clothes!"

Finn snorted. "I remember the first day I ever saw you. You were wearing this brightly-coloured jumpsuit. It was like a rainbow had walked into the clinic."

"The Hawaiian print? I love that!" Marley cried. "It's actually incredibly comfy."

"But you know you don't dress like anyone else, right?"

"Is that weird?"

"No! It's ... I like it." He sounded almost shy and Marley fell silent, smiling.

Finn stopped next to a flowering shrub along the river bank. "What's this one?" He poked a finger at the silver-green fronds and small slipper-like purple flowers.

"Silky emu bush."

He leaned to pluck some of it. "This would be nice in a vase—"

"Finn, stop!" Marley caught his hand and gestured to the clusters of tiny insects on it. "It's full of thrips."

He screwed his nose up. "I thought you could only catch thrips from public toilet seats."

Marley laughed and they started walking again. He hadn't let go of her hand, and she hadn't let go either. Her heart was thudding and she avoided eye contact. She noticed something else too. Something she didn't want to examine too closely. It felt completely and utterly natural to hold Finn Mayberry's hand.

"I can't believe you still remember what I was wearing that day," she said after a moment. They left the river and turned into her street.

"I remember everything about it," Finn said gently, stealing a sideward glance at her that she didn't dare meet. "I thought, 'what the heck is this beautiful woman doing in those insanely weird clothes?'"

Marley burst out laughing, but her mind stuck on the word "beautiful". She remembered the strange feeling she'd had on that first day. As though something had clicked into place when she saw him up close.

A notification pinged on her phone and Marley pulled it out of her pocket as they neared the house. It was a text from Dr Trish Brenner's office in Silton Town. They'd received Marley's paperwork from MacArthur, and she was booked in for the ultrasound and bloodwork needed to ensure the medication was working properly ahead of her insemination appointment.

At the thought of it, she pulled her hand abruptly back from Finn's. He didn't say anything.

"I need a shower and probably a nap before dinner," Marley said, realising she was talking too fast. "And I need to ring around every single real estate agency in the neighbouring towns and see if there's any way to avoid Susie Baker."

Finn nodded as Marley slipped the new key into the door. Without turning to look at him, she headed straight for the bathroom.

She'd always loved the shower. GamGam had splurged on a big shower head, which she used even when restrictions were in place. "We'll just have to shower a lot quicker," she'd say. "But I'd rather have a short, indulgent shower than a longer, miserable one!"

Marley smiled as she turned the water to a cool temperature, stepping under the spray and almost sighing with pleasure at the chill. She decided to wash her hair, having found bottles of apple-scented shampoo and conditioner in the old wooden cupboard under the sink. It was the cheap stuff she was familiar with from Super Saver Mart, and her heart wrenched thinking about Rosemary Wilson and her kids staying here, fleeing from their husband and father by hiding in plain sight and having cut-price supplies smuggled in from the mart.

Marley liked the idea of the town having a safe house, but it was true what Father Curtis had said—it wouldn't stay a secret for long. Plus, her place was too small. Marley briefly wondered about the plans Father Curtis had mentioned he and Susie were working on. Her stomach knotted as she thought about seeing the other woman. It had been four years. Maybe longer. Susie had disappeared just days after Hayden's death. She hadn't even attended the funeral. Marley had been glad. She wouldn't have made a fuss if Susie had appeared, but at the same time she hadn't wanted the final indignity of her husband's mistress attending his small and intimate farewell.

Marley mentally made a list of things she needed to do, including search for real estate agents. Her upcoming appointment with Dr Brenner brought her thoughts back to Finn. She shouldn't have held his hand like that, especially after hugging him on the way into town. She had to be careful. She didn't want to get used to having him around. Besides, she'd been so catastrophically wrong about Hayden —she simply couldn't afford another mistake like that. Not when there was going to be a child involved. And when the child wouldn't be Finn's.

Even if they did have feelings for one another, he wouldn't be ready to have a baby with her next week and neither would she with him. And she didn't want to wait anymore. The brief time she'd spent with Rebecca's son Walter had just reinforced it for her. She wanted a baby, so badly. And she was ready *now*.

She'd just have to try extra hard to force distance between the two of them. It wasn't going to be easy, considering they were sharing a house for the rest of the week and were about to head into town for dinner.

Finn was dozing on the sofa when Marley emerged from the shower. His glasses were folded neatly on the floor, beside a huge empty water glass. He must have been dying of thirst. She sincerely hoped he didn't have heat stroke—she knew how treacherous the Darnee heat could be.

She suddenly remembered the air-conditioning and spotted the remote on the TV stand. She clicked and the unit sputtered to life. For a second she worried there'd be a horrible stench, that perhaps something had crawled in there and died with the years of disuse. Then she remembered it *had* been used, and sure enough, the air came out smelling fresh and cool.

Finn stirred. "Is it my turn? I'll be quick, I know it's my second shower and there isn't a surplus of water around here."

"The reservoir level is okay at the moment," she said. "I checked online. *Yes,* we have that information online. No restrictions in place right now. Are you feeling okay?"

He sat up, smiling. "Yeah, I'm fine. The heat just makes me lethargic, that's all." She nodded. "I'll get ready and then we can head in. It doesn't stay open late, so it's an early dinner. I hope that's okay."

"Totally fine." Marley smiled. "To be honest, I still don't think it actually exists. I think it's Phoebe trying to haze some newbie to the town."

Finn grinned. "Yeah? Darnee gets *so* many tourists that you need to send them away on a prank? I find that hard to believe!"

CHAPTER TWENTY-SEVEN

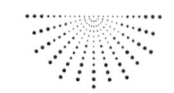

The restaurant was a pleasant surprise, an oasis in the middle of the staid shop fronts along Silton Town's quiet Main Street. But then, even that was a step up from the Darnee Main Street. And Silton Town itself looked much more lively and cosmopolitan than Marley remembered. Cute boutiques and vintage bookstores and even a juice bar peppered the arterial roads heading to Main Street. Marley saw teenagers dressed in Sydney fashion, rather than the farmer-chic popular in Darnee. Darnee had always felt like Silton Town's poor cousin, but the difference was much more pronounced now.

They were greeted at the door by a bubbly blonde woman of about fifty—Nelissa Nobiyaki, the woman who'd managed to snag a Japanese chef while they were both on holiday in Thailand. It seemed like a very unlikely match to Marley, until she saw Chef Nobiyaki himself. He looked like a Japanese Father Christmas, with his round belly, rosy cheeks and jovial smile. The restaurant was chic and modern, with surprisingly life-like silk cherry blossom branches festooning the ceiling, sleek birch furniture, a long bank down the centre of the space for people who wanted to eat with a more communal feel, and an open kitchen.

"I thought all chefs were Gordon Ramsay hard-nose types," she whispered to Finn, as Nelissa guided them to a cosy corner table.

"He looks far less terrifying," Finn agreed.

"Georgia will be serving you tonight," Nelissa said, gesturing to a tall, shapely redhead whose back was turned to them as she served another table. "We're *so* glad you decided to dine here tonight. Are you local?"

"Ex-Darnee," Marley said, smiling politely. Nelissa nodded, not even the hint of a wrinkle in her nose. Marley had grown up being looked down on by Silton Town folk so Nelissa's lack of reaction was a pleasant surprise.

"Hiro and I are glad to serve you and we hope you enjoy your meal. Georgia will be with you in just a moment. You need anything, give me or her a shout."

Finn and Marley smiled at one another as Nelissa moved to the front to greet another couple entering. The restaurant was already half-full, with a surprising amount of guests opting for the communal bench. The menus were printed on crisp parchment and Marley's mouth watered as she read through. Tempura vegetables, salmon sashimi, wasabi edamame … she was already mentally selecting a few courses. She still couldn't believe a place like this existed, let alone thrived, in Silton Town.

"Thanks for bringing me here," she said to Finn. In the warm lighting, his eyes looked deeper than usual, his lashes casting shadows on the planes of his tanned, smooth face. He smelled of apple shampoo, just like she did—his midnight-coloured hair so shiny and thick that she longed to push her hands through it. She swallowed and looked back down at her menu.

"You're welcome," he said, and there was something in his

tone that stopped her from looking up. A tenderness she was afraid to see reflected in his eyes.

"Hi, I'm your waitress, Georgia."

Marley gazed up at a set of sea-green eyes framed by impossibly long lashes and a set of dimples that curved below the waitress's high full cheekbones. Her silky, coppery hair was pulled up into a bouncy ponytail, wisps framing her face, and she smiled to reveal perfectly straight white teeth cocooned between pillowy lips. She looked like an off-duty sports car model.

"Hi," Marley said, realising she was staring at the other woman. It didn't matter, Georgia couldn't take her eyes off an oblivious Finn, whose gaze was on the menu.

"Are you two here on a date tonight?" Georgia asked in a light tone.

Finn looked at Marley and opened his mouth but she beat him to it. "No," she said quickly, shaking her head. "Just friends."

Georgia didn't even bother to hide her delight. She waved away a busboy who was reverently heading towards their table with a tee light in a tall red glass. "Can I start you off with some drinks? On the house," she added, shifting closer to Finn's side of the table.

"I'll have a beer," Finn said, finally looking up at Georgia. Marley waited to see his pupils dilate, or his nostrils flare, or some other indication that he'd taken in Georgia's breath-taking beauty. Nothing. Not even a flicker. "You're okay to drive, right?" He turned back to Marley.

"Of course."

Georgia leaned forward, her head close to Finn's as she led him through the beer menu. "So, we usually recommend something like a Kirin or a Sapporo, but it depends on what you're planning to order. Have you seen anything you like yet?" Her last sentence dripped with innuendo and Marley fought the urge to roll her eyes and shove Georgia backwards away from Finn.

"Still looking, but I'll go with a Kirin for now. Marley, what do you want?" He held her gaze, seemingly unaware that Georgia still crouched beside him.

"Uh, I'll have a sparkling water with some fresh lemon."

Georgia bounced perkily to her feet. "You got it. I'll be right back, and then I can talk you through the menu and tell you about our specials tonight."

"Oh my God, Finn," Marley said, breaking into a grin as soon as Georgia was out of earshot. "What the hell was that?"

"What was what?"

"Are you kidding? That waitress was all over you!"

"No she wasn't," he scoffed. "She's just being friendly. It's her job."

"Have you seen anything you like?" Marley repeated, batting her lashes and mocking Georgia's coy tone.

Finn grinned. "She meant on the menu, weirdo."

"Well, unless she's legally blind, she didn't need to get that close to show you the menu."

Finn tilted his head at her. "Wait, are you *jealous?*"

"Oh, stop it," she said, flapping her hand at him as colour rose to her cheeks. "Of course not! If you're interested in her, go for it! I'm sure she can drive you back to Darnee tomorrow morning."

His smile flickered, then steadied. "Really? If I want to go home with her, I can? No hard feelings?"

Marley swallowed and stared down at the menu. "None at all," she said with forced lightness. "I couldn't care less."

"Couldn't care less," he repeated.

"That's right." She cleared her throat. "What are you leaning towards? Want to get anything to share? I definitely want the tempura vegetables."

"They do sound excellent. What if we get all the smaller dishes and share them?"

A warm glow lit Marley's tummy at those words. "Sure," she said casually. "That sounds like a good way to do it."

She set the menu down just as Georgia came back with their drinks. Georgia stood tightly beside Finn's chair, reaching to hand Marley her water glass from that side of the table. Then she crouched down beside Finn, her arm brushing his as she lifted his menu from the table.

"I'll talk you through everything now. The specials tonight are wagyu carpaccio, salt and pepper ika which is basically squid, and baked crab."

Marley waited for Finn to tell Georgia they'd already settled on their orders, but he leaned his head in towards her slightly, gazing over the menu. "Could you tell me a bit more about the signature sushi?" He rested his finger beside hers on the menu, looking up at her.

Georgia beamed. "That's Chef Nobiyaki's house sushi platter. It's a mix of tuna and salmon, and it pairs well with this here." She leaned further towards him, pressing her finger firmly against his and blushing prettily.

Marley's breath stalled when she realised what Finn was doing. He was taking her at her word and trying to get Georgia to go home with him. She was actually going to have to sit here and watch them flirt. Her heart started pounding wildly against her ribcage, but she vowed not to give anything away and instead looked at them both with a pleasant smile.

"You were asking about the soft shell crab too, Finn. Did you want to check on that with Georgia?"

"I'd happily explain," she said, eyes crinkling with happiness.

Finn looked at Marley with an expression she couldn't

read. "Please do," he said, inching his chair almost imperceptibly towards Georgia. "It sounds amazing."

"So, the crab is locally sourced. Although not from the river in Darnee," she added with a little laugh, "but rather from fresh, clean waters. It's cooked only with salt and water, but comes with a special sauce. Chef Nobiyaki brought the recipe with him from Japan."

"That sounds amazing, Marley, doesn't it?" Finn looked up at her, his smile wide.

Marley showed her teeth. What she really wanted to do was fling her drink in Georgia's face. Her fingers were itching to do it and she laced them tightly together in her lap. "It sounds incredible," she forced herself to say. "*Especially* since it's not from Darnee. Why don't you get that, Finn? I'm thinking of getting the wagyu Georgia mentioned. Georgia, what drinks would you recommend Finn pair with the soft shell crab or the sushi platter?"

As Georgia launched into a long spiel about the different types of beer, her ponytail fell forward over her shoulder, the russet strands gently brushing Finn's hands. He didn't move away.

He raised his gaze and locked eyes with Marley. She saw her own steely determination mirrored in his glance.

They drove the whole way back to Marley's place in silence until she shut the engine off outside her house. She leaned to open her door but Finn caught her hand.

"Wait. Are we going to talk about this?" he asked.

"About what? I told you you could go home with the waitress. You said you didn't want to. There's nothing else to say. I'm sure you got her number. Maybe you can meet up tomorrow."

"Marley," Finn waited until she looked at him. His expression was earnest, the depth of his eyes visible in the front porch light coming over the fence. Marley's body responded, her pulse rate spiking. "Why can't you admit you have feelings for me?"

"Because I don't." She shrugged. He pressed his lips together and held her gaze. She took a deep breath and bit her lip. "Okay. Okay, Finn. I'm attracted to you. A lot, as I'm pretty sure you already know. But there's no point to it. I don't want a relationship right now. I want to concentrate on my plan. You don't understand what it's like to wait your whole life for something." She choked up slightly and paused before continuing. "I'm right on the brink of making it happen. And even though you're probably the best man I've ever met, I won't throw that away and I won't risk starting something with you and realising it's a mistake. I'm sorry."

Finn's chest rose and fell roughly. His eyes had widened as she spoke. Her hand was still in his and Marley could feel the heat tingling out from where they touched, in a radius that included the pit of her stomach. She wished he wouldn't look at her like that. It just made everything so much harder.

"From the moment you walked into the clinic, I knew there was something special about you," he began, his voice thick with emotion. "And the more I got to know the more sure I was. You are amazing. What you've been through, what you're doing, who you are. I think we could be something if you'd give us a chance."

Marley swallowed audibly and looked down at their hands. For a while, the only sound in the car was their ragged breathing. Then Marley withdrew her hand from his, trying to steady her heart rate.

"Goodnight, Finn."

She slipped out of the car and a moment later, he followed. Marley went straight to her bedroom and closed the door.

Marley lay flat on her back, staring at the ceiling in the bedroom as the air-conditioning vent hummed softly. How many nights had she lain awake staring at it during her marriage to Hayden? For a while, it had seemed like that would be her whole life—staring at the ceiling like she was already in her tomb, either trying to drown out Hayden's drunken snoring or wondering where he was.

Finn was nothing like her ex-husband, she knew that. And the feelings she had for Finn were completely new to her. It was a revelation to feel the way her body responded to something as simple as holding his hand. It made her painfully aware of how much she'd been lacking in her marriage, even though she'd believed herself in love with Hayden to start with.

For a moment, Marley let herself imagine what it would be like if she skipped her insemination appointment and took a leap of faith with Finn. He was wonderful, no question about that. Funny, smart, kind and ridiculously good-looking. And being with him felt more natural than she knew it was possible to feel.

A moment later, she sighed and rolled over as reality broke back in. There was no point in daydreaming about a relationship with Finn. She wanted a baby—that had never changed and it would never change. And she'd waited as long as she was willing to wait. She wouldn't risk getting together with Finn and waiting a year or two until they felt ready to get pregnant as a couple, only to find out they never felt ready or that they didn't work that way. Or worse still, rushing into it and then being stuck co-parenting with someone who'd turned out to be a fling or simply lust and not love.

The best thing she could do would be to forget Finn had said anything. Forget the admissions they'd made to one another.

She flicked on her phone to find her group chat with Amy and Lyra exploding with text messages she hadn't yet answered. They were mostly just the usual kinds of observations and memes they shared in the group, but there were a couple asking her how things were going.

All fine here, she texted. *Well, actually, not really.*

She filled them in on what had happened with Finn in the car. Marley half-expected them to tell her she was crazy for passing him up, that she should march into the living room right that moment and do something involving the eggplant emoji.

To her surprise, they completely understood. They reassured her that she was doing the right thing in trusting her gut—that she could appreciate Finn and at the same time want to move ahead with her plan.

In all her time in Darnee, she'd never found her people. She always stuck out. She was too tall for a girl, she was pretty but in a weird way, she was dating Hayden, her parents were dead, she was cursed. But in Sydney, on one of her first nights, she'd met Amy. And everything had changed.

When she finally fell asleep, it was with both a frown and a smile on her face.

CHAPTER TWENTY-EIGHT

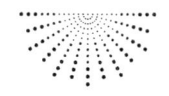

Marley started working her way through her list of to-dos with Olympic-level fervour the next morning. She'd been up with the kookaburras, padding around the house and trying not to wake a sleeping Finn. She'd appraised every inch of the house with a microscope, looking for anything that needed to be mended or improved in order to get the house up for sale. She had to admit, there wasn't a lot to do. Perhaps a fresh lick of paint in some of the rooms, some small repairs to the back deck which could also do with a coat of varnish, a leaking tap in the laundry that needed fixing, and one fly screen that had a few holes in it. Perhaps the oven could also be replaced, but that was nit-picking.

She checked every single real estate agency that serviced Darnee and the surrounding areas. She kept coming up with the same thing. Susie Baker had the industry sewn up. There was no way to buy or sell anything without her real estate firm. Marley bit her lip as she studied the other woman's photo on her website. Susie had never been particularly beautiful. She'd aged a lot in the four-odd years since Marley had seen her. Her black hair was streaked with grey and crow's feet folded at the corner of her eyes. Her smile was professional in the picture, her suit crisp. She looked competent.

Marley contemplated putting the house up for sale on her own. Would it be possible? She could ask Father Curtis to take the key back and see whether he'd be willing to show prospective buyers around. But she'd have to come back to Darnee to finalise things, maybe check up if progress was slow. It seemed best just to let a pro deal with it. And she had to face up to the fact that it would be Susie.

She gently closed the door of her bedroom and dialled the real estate office line. It was early still, only 8:30, but perhaps someone would be there. The call seemed to be diverted, clicking through to a second number with a different ringtone.

"Susie Baker, Baker Real Estate. How can I help you?"

Marley paused, her heart hammering. She contemplated hanging up, but her number would have shown on screen. Susie would simply call her back, figuring they'd been disconnected. She took a deep breath.

"Susie? It's Lena Phelps-was-Gibbons. Was Phelps," she added, and then cringed. She sounded like an idiot. There was silence on the other end of the line. "Hello?"

"I'm listening," Susie said cautiously.

"I need to talk to you about selling my house."

"Do you want me gone?" Finn asked.

Marley had filled him in on the full history with Susie, his eyes widening as he sat on the sofa after breakfast and sipped his coffee in silence, listening. Neither of them had mentioned the conversation from the previous night, and Marley was relieved that Finn was acting normally. He wasn't making this difficult for her at all. She might even have believed they'd never had the conversation, if it wasn't for the fact that every word he'd said to her last night was burned into her brain.

She shook her head now. "No, please stay. If I murder her, I'm going to need help with the body."

Finn grinned. "I would totally bury a body with you. And actually, I don't think it would be that hard in this town."

Marley smiled. Finn's hair stuck up at odd angles from his sleep, and it was unbearably cute. "I might hold you to that," she said.

He set his mug down and stood up to fold his blanket. "What do we need to do to get the place ready?"

"If we can just stuff some of our things away into our duffels to tidy up, I'll clean the kitchen while you shower. Is the sofa honestly comfortable, by the way? I have a horrible conscience about you sleeping out here. I should have kept the second bedroom as a guest room instead of clearing everything out. Then they wouldn't have needed to add the kid's beds. Maybe we can go buy an inflatable mattress today and put it in there."

"No, it's fine. The sofa's comfy. You go do the kitchen. I'll straighten up in here and then jump in the shower."

In the kitchen, Marley started rinsing off their breakfast plates. She had an appointment at Dr Brenner's the day after next. When she thought about it, there was a knot in the pit of her stomach. A knot she could trace back to her discussion with Finn in the car the previous night.

A few minutes later, she heard the water start up in the shower and she tried hard not to think about the fact that Finn was naked, in this very house, separated from her only by some thin walls.

She started whistling to distract herself, staring out into

the empty backyard as she washed the frying pan and coffee pot.

When she was younger, GamGam had installed a shed and Marley had used it as a kind of cubby house. She'd loved that place—it had been her own little castle. She hadn't even shared it with Hayden, she'd told him GamGam kept her gardening supplies in there.

After school, Marley would line her stuffed toys up along the wall, and write a lesson on the A-frame chalkboard. But the role plays didn't mimic real life scenarios she'd encountered that day. Instead, these were her fantasies. The stuffed toys would fight over who could sit near her, they'd clamber to be her friend, eat lunch with her. She was never isolated, never ignored, never picked on. She just had a normal life.

Hayden had changed things for her, in a way that she had never really admitted to herself. His devotion to her when they were teenagers had changed her from tragic to mysterious. Changed her from an outcast to someone a bit *above*.

Girls still hadn't liked her, they were too jealous of Hayden's affection for that, but their teasing shifted. It no longer crossed a line. They were too afraid of getting Hayden offside, of becoming the focus of one of his famously cutting remarks. In a way, the town had made Marley feel grateful to be chosen by Hayden. They'd made her feel that she should count herself lucky. It didn't matter that he already showed alcoholic tendencies, or that she was a promising student from a good background.

Hayden had chosen her.

But none of that mattered now. What mattered was keeping it together when Susie visited. She didn't want to scream at the other woman and risk looking like a psycho in front of Finn.

Finn. She should not think about Finn in the shower. *Definitely* not think about Finn. Naked. In the shower...

An hour later, Susie Baker pulled up in a sleek silver Mercedes Benz C-class cabriolet, the windows tinted so dark Marley could only see the fence railings reflected in them. It sounded as though she left the engine running and Marley wondered whether she was preparing for a quick getaway.

Marley surveyed Susie as she walked through the gate and across the yard. She was bone-thin, her face more weathered in the harsh midday sun than Marley remembered, and with more grey in her hair than in her website portrait. Her tailored pants suit and the clipboard under her arm gave her an official air, while the designer sunglasses and heels, as well as the gold dripping from her ears, neck and wrists, made it clear she had money.

Marley opened the door before Susie could knock and the two women stood for a long time, staring at one another. Susie flipped her sunglasses to the top of her head, and Marley could see the pain in her eyes. She drew a deep breath and vowed to remain calm.

"Hi, Susie, it's ... thanks for coming." She had been about to say it was nice to see her, but that wouldn't have been the truth.

"You're welcome. I'll make it quick." She slipped out of her shoes and arranged them neatly by the door. Based on the name emblazoned in the arch, they cost more than Marley made in a month.

Susie blinked as her eyes adjusted to the relative darkness inside. Marley propped the front door open, closing only the screen door to let more light filter in.

"So, I'll just conduct a short appraisal and then give you my best estimate of what this place would fetch in the current market. I can also highlight some areas that you might want to pay attention to to bump that up."

Marley nodded, glad the other woman was sticking purely to the professional. "This is Finn, by the way," she said, as he wandered in with another cup of coffee, smelling shower-fresh. Susie's eyes widened ever so slightly as she shook his hand. Marley wondered what Susie was thinking, and a part of her hoped she assumed Finn was her boyfriend. It would be nice to have the shoe on the other foot for once.

"Are these the original floorboards?" Susie pulled her clipboard from under her arm and poised her pen over a form.

"Yes. I meant to have them polished, but … "

"They're still in fine condition. But we will need them polished before we show. And I see you have air-conditioning. Definite plus, as you can imagine."

Finn and Marley trailed Susie through the house, as she delivered curt but wise assessments. Her list more or less tallied with the one Marley had mentally drawn up that morning, but she had other suggestions as well. Finn noted them down all diligently on his phone.

"We can do a drive to the hardware store later," he said. "Pick up some supplies."

"Oh, I was just thinking I'd pay someone?"

"Don't be silly. I can do most of this stuff. You don't need to spend more money on it."

Susie smiled tightly at the conversation, pulling back the shower curtain in the bathroom. "That's a lovely shower head, but you need to bear in mind the restrictions we often have."

"I usually just take shorter showers when the restrictions are on. But if you think we should change it …"

Susie tapped her pen on her chin. "I'd suggest adding a handheld one as a second. An alternative they can use when restrictions are in place. Don't get rid of the existing one, it adds a bit of luxury." She leaned forward. "Looks like all the fasteners are already there. You'd just have to screw in a mount and connect the second to the supply."

In the main bedroom, Susie's eyes scanned the walls, over the closet and seemingly everywhere but the bed. She cleared her throat. "The room's a decent size. It could do with a bit more styling, but we can talk about that when the time comes. My fee includes full staging of the house, as well as professional photography. But this place has great bones. It just needs the small touches we've discussed and I think you'll get a good price for it. Darnee property isn't exactly booming, but it's starting to pick up as Silton Town grows."

"It's not too small?" Marley asked hesitantly. "I mean, the block of land? Most places around here have a couple of acres at least."

Susie shook her head. "Believe it or not, that's an advantage. Especially if the buyers are either elderly or a young family. It's good to have a fenced in space where you don't need to worry much about maintenance, or the safety of little kids. You could easily fit a swing set or a cubby out there."

They'd arrived back at the living room and Susie peered out the side window, scribbling some notes on her clipboard.

"Mummy?" A tentative voice at the door made them all turn. A boy of about four stood in the doorway, his face pressed into the fly screen. His blond curls hung over his eyes as he looked mournfully at Susie, who had drained of all colour. "Mummy, I know you said to stay in the car but I need to wee. Sorry."

Susie's expression softened and she cleared her throat. "Come in, baby. Marley, this is my son, Benedict. Is it ... do you mind if he uses your ..." She trailed off, catching the expression on Marley's face.

Marley's heart had stopped in her chest. She felt as though she were looking at a ghost. In a way, she *was* looking at a ghost. Benedict looked exactly like Hayden. He was Hayden's child. Marley raised her eyes to Susie's. The other woman blushed, but there was something else in her expression—a plea. She was begging Marley not to say anything in front of Benedict.

Marley took a long breath and smiled warmly at the child. "It's the last door on the left. Do you already know your left from right?" she asked gently. Benedict beamed and held up his left hand, nodding. "That's pretty advanced."

Benedict skittered gaily down the hall, leaving the two women staring at each other.

"Would anyone like a cup of tea?" Finn asked, trying to break the tension. "Or should I clear out?"

"Don't go anywhere," Marley said tensely.

"Look, Lena. I can explain."

"That you had a *kid* with my husband?" Marley hissed in a low voice. "I'm pretty clear on how that happened. Not much left to explain."

Susie pressed her temples, letting out a long slow breath. "I'm sorry. My mum was supposed to babysit but she had a thing. Listen, could we go for a coffee? Maybe in Silton Town? I can drive. I'd like to talk to you somewhere private."

"What can you *possibly* have to say to me? Unless there are a bunch more kids waiting in the car. Did you guys have triplets? Just tell me now."

Susie shook her head. "It's just Benedict." She glanced at Finn, as though trying to assess whether he'd be friendly to her cause. "Please, Lena. I'd like the chance to explain some things. And I also have an idea for the house."

Marley was silent. She looked to Finn, who raised his shoulders and eyebrows in a gesture that said, "hear her out?"

"The day after tomorrow," Marley agreed tightly. "In Silton Town. I have an appointment there anyway."

They fell silent as Benedict reappeared. Susie hoisted him up onto her hip, though he looked heavy. "Come on baby, Mummy was just finishing up. Say goodbye."

"Bye-bye," Benedict said, waving happily. He leaned into Susie and it was obvious they shared a strong bond. "Mummy, can we get ice-cream now?" he asked in a low voice. "You promised if I stayed in the car, but it was only because I had to wee."

"Oh, okay. You twisted my arm." Benedict giggled. "We'll go past on the way home. You can have a little scoop."

Marley closed the door gently behind them as they left, waving at Benedict until the last minute so he wouldn't suspect anything was wrong. She resisted the urge to slam the door—hard—when Susie looked back.

Once she shut the door, Marley leaned her back against it and let out a long, slow breath. Tears threatened.

Finn hesitated, then stepped towards her. "Are you okay?"

"No." She shook her head, biting her lip to stop the tears flowing. "No, I'm really not."

And for the second time, she fell into Finn's waiting arms.

CHAPTER TWENTY-NINE

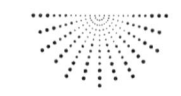

"Marley. The hammer is upside down."

"Oh." She sighed and wiped sweat from her brow, leaning into a squat on the back deck they were fixing. It wasn't as though she didn't know how to use a hammer. She'd been GamGam's handy-person for a lot of her teenage years. She was distracted because she couldn't stop thinking about Benedict and Susie.

She'd been unable to sleep the previous night, haunted by visions of Benedict, and his eyes. *Hayden's* eyes. It was as though her dead husband had been staring at her from beyond, reproaching her for having another man in the house they'd shared. Or for not having given him a child.

She knew it was ridiculous, of course. Not least because the eyes belonged to a child that had come into existence through Hayden's cheating. He could hardly point fingers about a guy sleeping on the sofa in the next room. In the morning, she'd been annoyed at herself for letting the strange thoughts steal her sleep. Her appointment at MacArthur was fast approaching and she wanted to be stress-free and well-rested on the day, to give her body the best possible chance of getting pregnant.

But she was exhausted. And it didn't help that Finn was shooting sympathetic glances at her. She hated that he'd been witness to it all. That he knew how long she'd let her marriage go on, while her husband busily impregnated women behind her back. She felt pathetic. But Finn didn't seem judgemental. He seemed to understand, and somehow … that made it worse.

"Why don't you let me finish the deck?" he said now. "You can go and get started painting the dining room."

"You need to come inside soon," she said. "It's getting too hot to be working. We can keep doing this part later, when it cools off a bit in the evening."

"We've got a lot to get done in a couple of days. Besides, it's not too bad right now."

She had the feeling he was lying, since she could see damp sweat patches forming under his arms and around his chest. He wore Hayden's cricket hat and his forearms were slathered in sunscreen. They glistened as he sawed off the end of a plank of wood to replace the rotten one. Marley found it difficult to take her eyes off the play of his muscles, glad she was wearing sunglasses.

"Okay," she sighed. "I'll get some lunch ready for us, and some cool drinks. I'll force you to come inside in about half an hour."

He grunted, the saw biting easily through the wood under the force of his movements. Something about the scene made Marley light-headed.

It was bliss to step back into the air-conditioned cold and she angled herself at the kitchen window so that she could still see Finn working as she sliced up cucumbers, smeared bread with butter and layered cheese over it. GamGam used to make her own iced tea, a taste Marley remembered with fondness from her childhood. But she'd never been able to replicate it, and GamGam hadn't left a recipe. So Marley had settled on buying a few pre-mixed bottles from the Super Saver Mart. She smashed up ice-cubes with the meat tenderiser and topped up two glasses with the store-bought tea.

Now Finn was fixing the new plank into place. It should have been her job, but she'd apparently forgotten how to hold a hammer, so she wasn't much use. At least a paintbrush would be easier to figure out. She'd get started in the dining room once they'd finished lunch.

They'd driven to the hardware store after Susie's visit, heaping supplies into the trolley and checking them off their list at a cracking pace. Marley had been hoping to avoid running into anyone she knew, but in Darnee that was a near impossibility.

Two people had stopped her under the pretence of asking how she was, but they'd been not-so-subtly checking Finn out as they did so. No doubt his presence was keeping the gossip mill well-fed.

Marley's phone lit up with a video call from Amy. She swiped to answer it and found both her best friends crowded into the camera.

"Marley Phelps, you haven't video called us. We miss you!" Lyra said.

Marley grinned. "I'm so sorry! It's just a bit weird here."

Her eyes ran over their faces. She'd missed them so much in the days she'd been gone. Lyra with her hair up in a messy bun, dark shadows bruised like thumbprints under her eyes. Amy with her hair in a thick fabric Alice band that perfectly matched her orangey-red lipstick.

"Why are you two together in the middle of the day?" she asked.

"Mental health day," they said in unison, laughing.

"No, just kidding," Amy said. "I'm on a long lunch break—"

"And I thought I'd get more inspiration outside on a day like today," Lyra added, grinning. "It was too pretty a day to be stuck inside!"

"It's a scorcher over here," Marley said. "Not a cloud in the sky, check it out."

She tilted the phone out the window, and they spotted Finn.

"Jesus Christ," Amy whispered, as Lyra sucked in a breath. "Are you freaking kidding me?"

Marley quickly turned the phone back to face her.

"Okay, I'm changing all the advice I gave you the other night!" Lyra whispered.

"Uh, me too!" Amy added.

Marley shook her head, but couldn't keep from smiling. "You guys ... stop! I'll be home three days from now. We have two more full days, then we're driving back on the third. Let's have a proper chat after that."

"Okay, but we are planning a girls' night literally the *second* you get back to civilisation." Amy pointed a finger into the camera. "You have a lot to 'fess up!"

"And we are going to discuss that work of art on your back porch," Lyra added.

"The signal's breaking up!" Marley said, laughing.

"Marley, we can see you perfectly, we know you're—"

"Bad reception. Sorry! Talk soon." Marley hung up the call, smiling to herself and shaking her head. She hoped Finn hadn't heard any of that. Her phone pipped, and about one hundred flame emojis appeared in the message preview screen in their group chat. She flipped the phone face-down.

Finn came in a few moments later, making a noise of pleasure as the cold air hit him. Marley flushed, and busied herself cutting up the sandwiches and setting the table. Finn pulled off his hat and switched his sunglasses for his regular ones, mopping sweat from his brow.

She took a seat at the dining table and he pulled out a chair opposite.

"Did you make *cucumber* sandwiches?" His grin crinkled the corners of his eyes, and Marley couldn't help but notice that physical exertion suited him. His tan had deepened even in the few days they'd been in Darnee and it made the black of his hair and the blue of his eyes even richer and more striking. There was a ruddiness to his cheeks that made her think about different kinds of physical exertion ... Even the way he tore up the sandwich with his slightly calloused hands triggered indecent thoughts. What was wrong with her? She needed to snap out of it. Maybe the hormones were skewing her thoughts. That must be it.

"Did you wash those filthy hands?" she asked, heat tingling her cheeks. "And yes, I made cucumber sandwiches. Well, cucumber and cheese. Is that not good enough for his majesty?"

He stood and washed his hands at the kitchen sink, shaking his head. "Uh, I'm pretty sure royalty isn't treated this way. And cucumber is fine, it's just not the kind of reward I expected after slaving away in the hot sun for a few hours."

"Deck looks great, by the way. My ploy of pretending not to know how to use a hammer is paying off." He swatted her lightly as he returned to his seat. "I was thinking tonight we could go get some of Darnee's famous fish and chips?" she said. "Maybe have a picnic on the living room floor or something ... since we're going to have to move the table and chairs out of here to paint the walls." Her chest tightened as she asked him. She couldn't shake the feeling that it was like suggesting a date.

Finn grinned at her, his cucumber sandwich back in his hands. "So Dungaree *is* famous for something?"

"Lots of things, actually. Hot springs, the big rock."

He slipped a piece of cucumber out of his sandwich and flicked it at her. It glued with a slap to her forehead before falling off and landing on her plate. Finn's eyes widened in alarm, as though he was unsure what her reaction would be. "Oh my God! I'm so sorry." He couldn't completely stop a grin from spreading across his face.

She slowly reached down and lifted the cucumber with one hand and while he was distracted, flung her glass of iced tea at him. It soaked his chest and he instantly leapt up, gasping at the shock of the icy liquid.

"Right, that is *it*. You're going to get it now."

"No!" she squealed, springing up from her chair, the table between them. He lunged around to his right, grinning, and she ran in the same direction, keeping the table between them. "Stop it!" she laughed, "I get weird and anxious when I'm being chased!"

He nodded and pretended to stop, then lunged again, and this time kept chasing her as she squealed, running from the dining room and out into the living room with him at her heels. He caught her easily, of course. She wasn't exactly difficult prey when she was laughing so hard. He wrapped his arms around her waist and lifted her effortlessly off the ground as she kicked and laughed.

"Oh God, Finn you're tickling me. You're tickling me!"

He set her down and she twisted to face him, but he didn't release his arms from her waist. They stood, pressed together, laughter slowly dying as they stared at one another. The intensity in his blue eyes took her by surprise, and her reaction was swift. Before she could stop herself, she slipped a hand behind his head and pulled his mouth to hers.

For a split second, he seemed startled. His body stiffened and she felt his breath hitch. Then he groaned in a way that made her feel weak and kissed her back, hungrily. Her hands were in his hair and his powerful grasp clenched tighter around her waist as their kiss deepened. He pushed her, just this side of roughly, up against the living room wall and she gasped, taking her mouth off his for a second to stare at him. His eyes were black, his hair mussed from her hands and his breath was hot on her face. She should end it ... she should really end it. But her thoughts were scrambled by the look of desire in his eyes, and the ache of longing filling her. He smelled of fresh sweat and iced tea and Finn. Slowly, very slowly, she moved her lips back towards his.

"Do you want to stop?" he rasped, as their lips grazed. "I'll stop ... I can stop."

"We should, shouldn't we?" she whispered back. "This is absolutely a bad idea."

"The worst ..." His voice was a rumble in her ear, and he was shaking with the effort of restraint.

"It's just, your t-shirt is wet and I don't want you to catch a cold ..." She reached her fingers up under the fabric, tracing them lightly over the rippling muscles above his hip bone.

He sucked in a hard breath. "You're right. Maybe I should take it off."

"You really should."

Then they were kissing again, ravenously. A moment later, he lifted her up, pressing her firmly against the wall. All thoughts of ending it were gone.

CHAPTER THIRTY

The enormity of what they'd done only sank in to Marley when they reached the fish and chip shop later that day. It was jammed. Before they even entered, they could see a crowd three people deep, shoulder-to-shoulder in front of the counter. An unflappable, red-faced woman shouted the waiting orders over the din, in a voice that carried out into the street.

"Four battered fish, scallops, four bucks worth of chips! Two grilled fish, onion rings!"

Marley and Finn exchanged looks, hesitating outside.

"Is it *that* good?" Finn asked.

Marley nodded. "It's incredibly fresh. The fishermen don't get it from the river, don't worry. GamGam's friend Lucas used to supply here, and sneak us some as well. It was always amazing."

Finn shrugged one shoulder and they pushed through the greasy plastic strip curtain and into the fray. The air was hot and thick with frying fat and Finn wrinkled his nose.

"This better be worth it."

"You'll see."

It was a long wait to get to the front of the line, where they were barked at by the same woman shouting the orders. She had an uncanny knack for knowing exactly who was next to be served, and wasn't remotely put off by the men and women shouting for her attention, or huffily claiming they'd been overlooked. Marley and Finn were pressed closer and closer together the nearer they got to the counter. Despite the surroundings, she was very conscious of the places where his smooth, warm skin touched hers.

Oh God. She'd *slept* with Finn Mayberry. She'd slept with *Finn Mayberry*. She'd done the one thing she'd vowed not to do. It had been stupid and dangerous, not to mention unfair. She didn't want a relationship with Finn.

Her plan had been perfect, it had been clean. A donor father, her own child, a small family unit that she could control and no messy, doomed relationship connected to it. For a moment, she felt something like a flash of irritation at Finn for having messed everything up for her. She quickly realised how unfair that was. After all, she'd been the one to start it ... and continue it.

They hadn't discussed it. Nothing at all had been said. But as they lay on the living room floor afterwards, their limbs tangled together and their heart rates slowly returning to normal, Marley had only been thinking of one thing. How right it had felt. How well they had fit together, how naturally they seemed to understand one another's bodies, how her feelings had gone dangerously beyond the physical already. And how she could add bodily perfection to the list of Finn's attributes.

"What can I get you, darl?" the woman asked when they finally reached the front of the line.

"Two pieces of grilled fish, five dollars worth of chips and four scallops."

Marley hadn't consulted Finn on the order and he leaned

over to her now. "I like it when you just take charge," he whispered in her ear.

Her body thrilled but she squirmed slightly away from him, afraid she was going to lose control and start making out with him in the fish and chip shop, scandalising the whole of Darnee. Again.

He noticed her discomfort and his smile dropped. "Sorry," he said in a louder voice, standing straight.

And that was the thing. She was petrified of him being near her and making her lose control, and equally terrified she'd never get to be near him that way again. They had to talk about it. She'd raise it once they were back at the house, and she'd tell him it had been a one time thing only. A moment of madness. And that it couldn't mean anything.

Most of all, it couldn't happen again.

Once they were settled, cross-legged atop a slightly musty picnic blanket on the living room floor with the parcel of fish unwrapped between them, Marley poured two glasses of iced tea and carefully avoided Finn's eye.

"Cheers," he said, as their glasses chinked. She lifted her eyes and found him watching her, a crooked smile on his face. Her heart thudded in response and she gulped her drink to avoid saying anything. He cleared his throat. "So, are we going to talk about—"

"You know, I realised something," she said quickly, setting her glass down and wiping her mouth. He looked at her quizzically. "I don't know the story of Finn. Like, at all. It's weird because in some ways I feel as though I've always known you. But then I realised I wouldn't be able to answer even simple questions about your life. Do you have brothers and sisters? Are your parents still together? That kind of stuff. So, fill me in. Please. If you want." She stopped talking, taking a deep breath. She wasn't used to feeling flustered. She wasn't used to feeling a lot of things she felt with Finn.

He nodded slowly, smiling with half his mouth and looking at her as though he could see through her. "Okay. The story of Finn. I warn you that it's not nearly as interesting as the story of Marley/Lena."

"Few things are," she replied archly.

"Careful. I'll slap another cucumber on your forehead."

They laughed, and Marley's body throbbed with the memory of what that slice of cucumber had led to. Finn turned thoughtful as he ate a bite of fish. "I have one older sister, and she's a pain in the butt. I love her, don't get me wrong. But she's very, uh, she can be a little overwhelming."

"How much older?"

"Six years."

"Oh, that's a lot."

"Yeah." He nodded. "It meant I was pretty defenceless when she wanted to dress me up as her baby doll when I was small."

"Photos or it didn't happen."

"Oh, there are photos. Believe you *me*, there are photos. And they've so far been wheeled out at my twelfth, eighteenth, twenty-first and thirtieth birthday parties." He ticked them off on his fingers and Marley couldn't help laughing.

"How old are you?" she asked.

"Thirty one. A year younger than you."

"I *really* hope I'm invited to your fortieth."

"You think I'm having a party ever again?" Finn sipped his tea and shook his head. "By the way, this fish is *good*. I can see why it's famous."

"Right? Although technically I guess it's not truly from

Darnee. But still, it's something about the way they prepare it. And the chips are amazing."

"We've only got two more full days. We should get this again tomorrow."

Marley popped a chip in her mouth. "Oh yeah? You don't want to have a chat to Phoebe about the hottest new restaurant?"

"Turns out Pheebes is a one-trick pony. Nobikyaki, Nobiyaki." He mimed a blabbering mouth with his hand and they laughed. Finn switched the cross of his legs, rubbing his shins and then rolling out his shoulders.

"So, did you always dream of being a physio?" Marley asked, trying to tear her eyes off the golden skin of his calves.

He shook his head. "Nah, not always. I don't even think I knew what that was when I was younger. I suppose in a way I always wanted to do stuff to help people. I dreamed of being a superhero, a firefighter, a doctor. The typical stuff."

"I don't think it's that typical anymore," Marley said, straightening the edge on the picnic blanket. "I read that kids these days all want to be vloggers and influencers."

"Oh God." Finn rolled his eyes. "My kids are going to be raised Amish. They won't even find out YouTube exists until they move out of home."

Marley looked down, tearing off the edge of a scallop. She kept her voice light as she asked, "So, you want to have kids?"

"Oh yeah," Finn nodded enthusiastically. "Yes. I want to open my own practice *and* I want kids. I want them close in age, so no child has to suffer what I went through when as a kid." He gave her a mock-haunted look and she laughed.

"It must have been nice to have a sibling though. Being an only child got lonely sometimes. I often dreamed about having a brother or sister."

"I can imagine." He gave her a sympathetic look. "I suppose she's okay. She's come into her own now. Plus, I get to play with her kids. And she took the pressure off me a bit by having them. And I'll get to play with them even more now."

"Why?" Marley frowned. "Did they move closer or something?"

Finn cleared his throat, dabbing some grease from the corner of his mouth with a serviette. "Uh, Bess kind of hates kids."

"Whoa," Marley laughed. "She's in the wrong job." When Finn didn't answer, she tilted her head. "But she'd agreed to have them with you? You'd planned it?"

He shook his head. "Actually … we constantly argued about having kids. When we first got together she was a bit indifferent to it, but not dead against. The proposal kind of brought it all to a head. She thought I'd change my mind, and," his mouth twisted, "I stupidly thought she'd change hers. That's why we'd been a bit unsteady for a while. Well, that plus the clinic stuff."

He still wants them. And I still don't. He's not going to change his mind and neither am I. Marley had a sudden flashback to the conversation she'd overheard at Icebergs, when she'd been trapped by the sinks with Bess in the foyer on the phone to her mother. She must have been talking about children.

Marley felt a rush of affection for Finn. She knew how it felt to pine for a baby, better than most people. She hoped his next partner was someone who had similar goals to him. She chose to ignore the sickening lurch of her stomach when she thought about Finn with anyone else.

"Still, it's kind of ironic when she runs a fertility clinic, isn't it?"

Finn smiled, sadness tinging the corners of it. "I guess. She's got a strong head for business and she has a high success rate. She's a typical type A perfectionist. She likes the process. Her business partner is the much more gentle one. He has kids himself, and he's genuinely in it to help people make the families they want."

Marley nodded. "If you don't mind me saying so, you and Bess sound like you were kind of an odd couple."

"Ah, that Marley tact." He tried unsuccessfully to hide a grin. "It never seemed that way in the beginning. If anything, I kind of liked the way she was so hard to please. I felt like it pushed me to be better, trying to impress her. I probably realised I never could, but there was something about the striving that felt—" He shrugged. "I don't know. I believed for a while that's how relationships were supposed to be."

Marley thoughtfully chewed a chip. "That's not what I want. I think partnerships should be more about you accepting one another and cheering one another on and having one another's backs." She flushed. "Not that I want anything right now."

Finn cleared his throat. "Well, I've realised that's what a good relationship should feel like." He tore a scallop in two, keeping his eyes fixed on it. "You have your tests tomorrow, right?"

"Mmh," Marley said, looking down and fussing with the corner of the picnic blanket again. "Yeah. So, are your mum and dad still together?"

"Marley," Finn said gently after a moment. "We can talk about your appointment, it's okay."

She raised her eyes to his, nodding slowly. "I didn't mean to avoid it, I just—it kind of feels weird to talk to you about it."

"This is how we met, remember?"

"Yes, but that was then."

He tilted his head at her. "This can still be 'then' if you want." He flushed slightly, "I don't regret what happened earlier, but I understand that it was just a moment of madness for you …" He gulped. "I hope you don't feel like I took advantage."

Marley pressed her lips together. The thing was, she'd never felt more sane than at that moment she'd kissed him. And if anything, *she'd* taken advantage of him. But letting Finn believe she might regret it, or at least not want to repeat it, would be a good idea. It would be safest for them both.

"You didn't take advantage. Not in *any* way. But, yeah," she said finally, her voice almost level. "A moment of madness. That's all. I saw Susie's kid and I … forgot how to think rationally."

They studied one another's faces. Finn's jaw was tight and his smile was lopsided. She could tell he believed her, and she wished it hadn't been so easy to convince him. She tore her eyes from him and they went back to their meal.

CHAPTER THIRTY-ONE

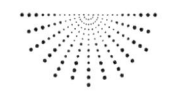

The next day, Marley drove to the cafe Susie had chosen for their meeting. It was understated and elegant and it marked the second time Marley had been pleasantly surprised by the hidden gastronomical delights of Silton Town. Rose's Cafe reminded her of something she might see in a quaint English drama. Frothy white curtains tied up with sashes at the windows, plush pastel seating, waiters and waitresses in delicate white aprons. The clientele seemed well-to-do: older ladies with twinsets and pearls, men with pressed linen shirts unbuttoned just so. Everyone had shiny hair and held their conversations in muted tones. Basically the complete opposite of the fish and chip shop.

Susie was stirring a pot of tea and Marley watched as a waitress set down a scone on a delicate china plate, surrounded by dipping pots of jam and clotted cream.

"Thanks for agreeing to meet me," Susie said as Marley took a seat opposite her.

"I don't have long. I'm due at Dr Brenner's in an hour. So start talking."

Susie flinched. "You don't need to speak to me that way,

Lena. I had always understood that you knew about Hayden and I. You never asked him to stop—"

"I'm sorry. Should I have *had* to?"

Susie frowned, studying Marley's face. "I honestly didn't think …" She bit her lip. "Never mind."

"Honestly what? This isn't the time for 'never minds', Susie. I saw your child. *Hayden's* child. You said there was something you wanted to explain. Well, I'm listening."

Susie fiddled with her napkin, then laid it down. "It's just that honestly I didn't think you loved him anyway. He made it seem that way."

Marley's mouth hung open. "You genuinely didn't think I loved the man I married and stayed married to for almost ten years?" They paused as a smiling, round-faced young waitress approached the table. "Sparkling water, please. And one of those scones." Marley pointed to Susie's plate. The waitress nodded pleasantly and moved towards the kitchen.

"Actually, no. I didn't. Hayden—" Susie shook her head, puffing out a long breath. "I think half our relationship was him crying to me about you."

"Why the hell did he think I married him then?" Marley's voice rose an octave, and several nearby diners cast irritated glances their way. She lowered her voice, frowning at Susie's ashen face. "You believed it too? I suppose it was better for you to think that was the truth. Convenient for Hayden, as well. He could carry on without a bad conscience if he told himself that story enough times to believe it."

"Lena, I honestly don't know what to say. When I heard you were back in town, I was prepared to throw certain things in your face. Especially when I found out you'd moved on." She meant Finn. Marley opened her mouth to object, but Susie continued. "Then … I saw the way you looked at Benedict. And I wondered if maybe I could have been wrong this whole time."

Marley looked down at her lap and swallowed. "The feelings are long gone, but they did exist once." She let out a breath. "Benedict just looks so much like him."

Susie looked down at her scone, eyes welling. "It's like a punch to the stomach sometimes. Hayden, he was all I ever wanted." She stirred her tea in a slow, hypnotic motion. "I was in love with him from the moment I first laid eyes on him in primary school. I never stopped loving him. I love him now. I—" She trailed off, her voice shaking as a fat tear slid down her cheek.

Marley found something about Susie's grief heartbreaking—didn't like watching a woman who looked so pulled-together and professional crumple. After years and years of seeing Susie only as an enemy, Marley suddenly saw her as a fallible, flawed human. She softened just the smallest bit.

"Why did he marry me, if the two of you were in love?" she asked. "It would have spared a lot of agony on all our parts."

Susie pressed her lips together, her eyes darkening. She shook her head. "I don't think he ever truly loved me. I was a convenient side piece who forgave everything, took what she could get and always made him feel better about himself." Susie fought the words out, her face flushing with shame. But she held her chin up, as though she'd faced the facts about who and what she was. "He wouldn't leave you, and believe me, I asked. I'm sorry, but it's the truth. You've no idea how hard it was. Loving him so much and watching him pine for you when you couldn't care less."

Marley frowned, her heart racing. She'd always assumed she was being ridiculed by the other woman for the duration of her marriage. She'd felt like a laughing stock, like the affair made a mockery of her marriage. But for Susie, maybe it had even been even worse. To want someone so badly, and only ever have a small piece of them. And to think that the bigger piece was being repeatedly offered to someone indifferent to it.

"I think I can sort of understand." Marley surprised herself as the words came out.

Susie stared at her, then exhaled sharply. "I wouldn't, if I were you."

"I didn't during our marriage, that's for sure. But it can't have been easy on you either. I never realised that until now." They sat silently for a moment. "Did Hayden know about your pregnancy?" Marley asked gently.

Susie nodded, wiping her nose brusquely with a tissue. "He was excited about it at first. He said you wouldn't—you wouldn't give him a baby." Marley clenched her jaw tightly, but couldn't bring herself to answer, though Susie looked searchingly at her face. "And I thought maybe it would change something. That he'd want to be with me and the baby when it came. But instead, he was just worried about you finding out. That was the only thing he cared about, after the initial excitement wore off. That his precious Lena would catch wind of it."

Marley struggled to keep her breathing even. Susie was showing her a parallel universe. The whole time Marley had been taking the pill and dreaming of a child, sacrificing her own happiness, there'd been another woman prepared to give Hayden a baby under any circumstances.

"How long was this before he died?" Marley asked.

Susie blinked, as though Marley had used too harsh a word. "Two and a half months. We'd had an argument the night he," she gulped, "the night he passed."

"About me?" Marley whispered.

Susie nodded. "I'd asked him again to leave you again. He'd said it was out of the question, and told me the baby couldn't have his name. That it couldn't be a Gibbons."

Marley let out a noise. A soft, sympathetic noise that seemed to surprise Susie. The other woman eyed her suspiciously.

"I'm not saying it doesn't hurt to hear this stuff," Marley said. "This plotting and discussing behind my back. But the truth is, by that stage, I'd more or less given up on Hayden and I. So ... it doesn't hurt as much as you might think."

Susie's eyes narrowed. "So you *didn't* love him."

Marley waited until the waitress had set down her order, and then she looked at Susie and held her eye. "Not by the end. No. And I don't think you of all people can blame me for that."

Susie's chin crumpled. "Why didn't you tell him?" she whispered. "It might have made all the difference. Maybe Benedict would have a father, and ..." she broke off, her eyes welling.

Marley reached her hand across the table, cupped it over the top of Susie's. "Because I had absolutely no idea. My whole life I've just thought you were heartless, or just—" She groped for the right word. "Amoral? Maybe if you'd come to me. Or if he'd have mentioned it. Or if gossip had reached me ..."

Susie shook her head fiercely. "No one knew. I made sure of it. That's why I left town before I was showing."

"All I'm saying is, I might have understood. Maybe. Hayden was right, I wouldn't give him a child. But it wasn't because I didn't want one. I did. I *do*. Desperately. It was because I thought he'd make a terrible father. If I'd have known there was a child with someone else, if I'd have known there would be a future Benedict, I might have done things differently. I'm sorry, Susie. I'm sorry for you and your son."

Susie swallowed audibly, the sound almost like a squeak as she struggled with her emotions. "All this time I thought you were the enemy. You always acted so much better than us all—"

"What? You all ostracised me!" People turned again and Marley lowered her voice. She pulled her hand back from Susie's and took a long drink before continuing. "I was never part of this community, not even after having spent my whole life here."

Susie studied her, as though weighing up whether or not to say something. She shrugged as if deciding for it. "You know we were jealous, right? We all wanted to be you. Beautiful, tragic Lena. Always top of the class, always so clean and well put-together. You got to go home every day to Petunia, who loved you so much it hurt to watch, when most of the rest of us went home to junkyards and a hiding."

"You were always close with your mum, I thought?" Marley couldn't hide her surprise at this alternate version of her history. She had always assumed there was something wrong with her, for her not to fit in. Never that there was something wrong with her peers. Never that she had something they wanted.

"Mum, yes. She's an angel. Dad, no. I think I can count on one hand the number of honestly happy families in Darnee. Certainly no others in our grade at school."

Marley shook her head, staring unseeingly down at her scone. "This is ... a revelation."

"You really had no idea?"

"Of course not! I had a mum and dad buried in the town graveyard, I was being raised by an elderly woman, we never had much money. I was being cheated on by my boyfriend and then husband. I felt like I did everything right, and nothing ever worked out for me. What was there to be jealous of?"

Susie started to laugh. Just a little at first, and then it grew louder and more uncontrollable, with a slightly hysterical edge to it. She stuffed a knuckle into her mouth as Marley looked around, alarmed. They were definitely turning heads with this outing.

"What is it?" she finally whispered, as Susie dabbed tears of laughter from her eyes with the napkin.

"If only we'd spoken." Susie said, getting her laughter under control. She took a sip of her tea, and set the cup back down with a shaking hand. "My God, if *only* we'd spoken."

Marley raised her eyebrows. "It might have changed a few things, I agree." Marley wanted the conversation to be over. She felt exhausted, and she had a lot to process. She also wasn't sure how many more bombshells she could handle, or how much more she could bear to look into Susie's mournful, lovesick eyes. She discreetly checked her watch. "I've got to go soon. Would you like to tell me about your idea for the house?"

Susie straightened and cleared her throat. It was as though a switch had been flicked and she instantly became the polished professional Marley had seen two days earlier.

"I heard from Father C that you liked the idea of women in need of refuge having a place to go."

"Yes. Of course, I don't think anyone in their right mind could object to that. But he seemed to think it would be an issue—that it couldn't be kept quiet."

"I think I can help get it started. At least, by donating a larger property for use than your house."

Marley looked up, her mouth full of scone. She wiped a speck of cream from the side of her lips. "What's the catch?"

Susie paused for just a second, then held Marley's gaze. "I want to buy your place. I've made a *lot* of money over the past couple of years. The house I bought, it's too big for Benedict and I. I want something smaller for the two of us. Something less ... palatial and cold. I think it would be fitting for it to be the house Hayden last lived in."

For a moment, Marley was stunned into silence. Then she vigorously shook her head. "Absolutely not. I'm sorry, I'm not okay with that. That place was mine and GamGam's, and it was never truly Hayden's home. I've said I can kind of find peace with what was happening between you and him, but I find the thought of selling that place to my husband's mistress a bit hard to swallow."

Susie's jaw clenched but her expression remained defiant. "I understand you don't want to commit to anything just yet. But I'm prepared to offer above market for it. And my place, the house I currently live in, I'd donate that. Well, I'd retain the deeds, but I'd offer it for use rent free, for women in need."

Marley heaved a sigh. "Jesus, Susie."

"You never know who you're going to get as a buyer, Lena. This way you know it's going to a loving mother and son. We'll take good care of it. It's a perfect place for the two of us."

Marley stared down at her scone, her appetite gone. "I'm sorry, I have to get to my appointment." She gulped down more of her water, then stood, tossing some notes on the table.

"I'll give you a couple of days, then I'll call you," Susie said.

"You're wasting your time." Marley grabbed her handbag and turned to leave.

"If not for me, for Benedict. And for anyone in danger around here."

Marley paused but didn't turn back.

CHAPTER THIRTY-TWO

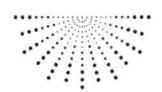

"Either she lives here with her ghost, or you keep it forever because of yours," Finn said, as he and Marley sat at the kitchen table that evening, sipping glasses of iced tea. They were both splattered with paint, a huge glob of it drying on Finn's cheek, his hair flecked with white. He'd spent the whole day painting, and Marley had joined in to help finish once she returned from her appointment with Dr Brenner. She'd felt guilty leaving Finn to do the work, but he assured her he didn't mind. The living and dining rooms were now finished, and Finn had cooked a light dinner of stir-fried greens and beef.

"I hadn't thought of it like that. Though I do think GamGam would have *hated* the idea." Marley traced a finger down the condensation on her glass. She had come to love these evenings with Finn. The quiet time after sunset, nothing but them and the hum of the air-conditioner, their conversation filling the air. It made the house seem alive in a way it hadn't since she'd lost GamGam.

"Maybe she wouldn't, if she'd had all the facts," Finn said gently. "That's the horrible thing when someone dies.

They're frozen in your memory the way they were, with the opinions they held. If they were still here, things might change. Maybe if you could explain to her what you've learned about Susie in the meantime, maybe she'd understand."

Marley nodded, seeing the truth of his words. "I don't care what anyone says, you can be wise, Finn Mayberry."

"What anyone says? Phoebe been trashing me again?"

"Like you wouldn't believe." She grinned, loving that they had these private jokes now. The evening held a bittersweet note—it marked their second-to-last before they headed back on the long drive home to Sydney.

Marley was excited to get home, of course. Her scan had gone well today, and Dr Brenner would email her the ultrasound images and the bloodwork results the following day. Marley would send them straight through to Dr Coleman and wait for the final green light for her insemination appointment.

"Maybe I should think about it then? It's just a bit galling to think of Susie living here."

"Is it though? She seemed like a loving mother." He held up a finger. "Don't get me wrong. Horrible person, obviously, for what she did. But her kid was sweet, and this *is* a great house for a child to grow up in. I realise he's your illegitimate step-son or something," Marley couldn't help but laugh at that, "but I honestly think you should consider it. I mean, you'd be responsible for a women's shelter in a way. Not to mention said she was going to offer above market?"

"You're clearly just thinking about your practice," Marley said, nudging his hand.

"Oh, I'm only here for the moolah. I saw dollar signs the instant I met you. I think it was your sophisticated outfits."

"Stop it!" Marley laughed.

He held up his hands. "I like your wild outfits, I already admitted that."

She grinned. "You're the only one who's ever said they like them."

Finn nodded, pleased. "That's why you love me." He'd meant it as a joke, but the atmosphere between them instantly changed, turned electric. Marley peered into her iced tea and coughed, her blood pumping fast. She could sense Finn's discomfort. "I didn't mean—"

"Shall we put up that additional shower head now?" she asked, quickly, checking her watch. "Or do you think it's too late?"

Finn's face tinged with colour, but he recovered swiftly. "Marley, your nearest neighbour is about six hundred metres away and approximately one hundred years old. I think we can use a power tool after nine."

"Do you know what you're doing with that drill though?"

He wiggled his eyebrows. "Always."

He stood up and grabbed the toolbox on the way to the bathroom. Marley caught sight of herself in the reflection of the dining room sliding door. The curtains were pulled back and she could see herself with crystal clarity. She was grinning like an idiot.

"But the instructions said to disconnect the water first."

"Yeah, yeah." Finn waved his hand. "They always say that."

"Probably because it's sensible?"

"Pssht. Hand me that wall plug."

"The …" Marley scanned the scattered pieces of the shower head set that were spread over the tiled floor. They'd tucked the curtain up over the shower rail and Finn was crouched in the recess with a measuring tape.

"The tube-type thingo. The plastic one."

Marley handed it to him, their fingertips brushing. Her heart skittered in response and she had a sudden flashback to the moment Finn had pushed her up against the living room wall. She willed herself to concentrate on something else. The toilet, for instance. The small crack in one of the bathroom floor tiles that bloomed with a hint of mould.

Finn turned on the drill, the shrieking noise almost unbearable as he sank it into the shower tiles at high speed. Marley put her hands over her ears until he finished.

"Hammer," he commanded, hand held out. He pushed the wall plug into the hole and tapped it gently into place. "So, you actually never told me about the donor you chose," he said casually. "And I was thinking maybe you wanted to talk about it?"

"What with you?" Marley's tone was teasing, but she gulped—mentally weighing it up. She supposed it couldn't hurt to tell Finn about it. Maybe it would even help keep them apart. Which she needed right now, because all she could focus on was the way his tongue poked out to the side of his lips when he was concentrating. Not necessarily the gesture itself, although she found it endearing. It was more the thought of that tongue on her body. She shivered slightly. *Mould, Marley. Toilets.*

"Yeah. Talk about the donor with me," he said. "Pencil."

She handed it to him and he pulled out the measuring tape from his back pocket with the other hand.

She took a deep breath. "Okay, well, his name's Tim, and—"

"*Tim?*" He blinked at her, his eyes deep in the warm tungsten light of the bathroom.

"Obviously I don't know his real name, but I called him Tim."

"Why the heck would you choose the name Tim when you could choose anything! Why not, I don't know, Fabio or something?"

"*Fabio?*" They snickered. "Do you think I chose a beefy, long-haired Italian?"

"Is the real Fabio Italian?"

"Actually, I don't know," Marley admitted.

"I thought he was Polish. Or maybe Hungarian? But I can definitely see Italian."

"In any case, I'm almost certain he's not the donor."

"But Tim is," Finn said, keeping his eyes trained on the spot he marked for the next drill hole.

"Tim is. Or will be."

Finn started up the drill, and Marley wasn't sure whether she imagined it, but he plunged it in with much more force than the previous time. "I'm honestly happy for you," he said, as the drill whined down.

She swallowed. "Thanks, yeah. I'm happy too."

He tapped in the wall plug and turned to her. "Really, I am. I know you've wanted this for a long time, and you deserve it. You sacrificed a lot. It's your time to be a mother, and like I said before, you'll be awesome at it."

Marley was suddenly overcome with emotion. "You'll make a great dad, too," she whispered.

He gave her a tight smile and turned back to the shower wall. "I hope so. One day. Okay, hand me the mount. The long metal thingo."

Once it was installed, they stood back to admire Finn's handiwork.

"I definitely thought it would look weird with the two showers. But Susie was right," Marley said. "It works."

"It does." Finn nodded in agreement. "Let me just test it." He stepped back into the recess.

"You know, when you didn't turn the water off, I was worried you were going to—aaaah!" Marley screamed and raised her hands as a cold jet of water soaked her. "Oh my *GOD!*"

Finn doubled over with laughter, shutting the tap off as Marley stood dripping, her mouth open in shock.

"And now we're even," he said gleefully.

"No! Gimme that!" She lunged at him and tried to wrestle the shower head off him. His grasp was firm and he was far stronger than her. She tried twisting it from him, but he wrenched it toward himself and she flew forward. For a moment, their bodies were pressed together again, the shower head wedged between them. The memory of the previous day shocked through Marley like electricity and she quickly held up her hands and stepped back, almost slipping on the slick tiles.

"Finn, the floor is *soaked*!"

"Okay, sorry. Truce?" His tone was gruff, and when Marley looked up, she could see that he was trying valiantly not to stare at the outline of her body through her wet clothes. "I'll just, I'll hang this back up," he stammered, fumbling with the shower head, "and I'll, uh, you can ... you shower and then me, I'll—"

They moved awkwardly around one another, trying to give each other a wide berth as Finn stepped out of the recess and headed for the door. Marley crossed her arms over her chest, and inched backward. They still brushed against one another lightly and the contact made her heart pound.

She stepped into the recess once he'd closed the door, and flipped the shower curtain down, drawing it across. She stripped, shivering slightly, but still set the water temperature to cold. She had a feeling she needed it.

CHAPTER THIRTY-THREE

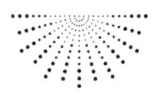

"Okay, it's your last full day in God's country, Finn. The day before we head back to the big smoke. What would you like to do?"

Finn grinned at her from the dining table where he sat nursing his coffee. Marley was buttering their toast and flipping eggs on the hob.

"What can I choose from?"

"Mmh, good question. We don't have anything left to do to the house. Ah! Aside from the leaky laundry tap. I'll run a load of towels and peg them out, and then," she heaved a sigh, "I'll give Susie a call."

Finn raised an eyebrow. "You decided?"

Marley nodded, licking a smear of butter from her thumb. She put her hands on the counter and faced him. "Yeah. I'm glad her place can be used as a refuge. That was a huge deciding factor. I'm not sure I'm one *hundred* percent okay with her living here. But, more money is more money, and she's right. I have no way of controlling who buys the place anyway. This way, I can just give her the keys, and she can sort all the details out. We can do the official paperwork and all that by post, and," Marley looked around the room, "I can say farewell to this house knowing it's going to someone who really wants it. Plus, Benedict was pretty cute."

Finn nodded, a hint of pride in his expression. "I think it's the right thing. And I think it's big of you at the same time. Well done, Marley."

"Thanks." She smiled and switched off the hob, levering the eggs onto their plates and bringing them over to join him at the table. "I thought about it a lot last night and it feels right. For the most part."

She didn't mention she'd thought about *him* a lot last night too. About being in the living room with him ... about the situation in the bathroom before bed, about his hair, his eyes, his voice, his company. About how much she would miss being in the same house as him. There had even been a terrifying moment where she'd convinced herself she should ask him to come sleep in the bed with her. She'd reasoned that it was impolite to let him sleep on the sofa, and that surely nothing would happen between them. She'd gotten halfway down the hall before she'd come back to her senses and admitted there was one reason she wanted him in that bed and one reason only. And it had nothing to do with etiquette. Or sleep.

"Benedict is going to be happy here, I'm sure," Finn said.

Marley smiled, thinking of the little boy who looked so much like Hayden. "I want to go visit my family at the cemetery. Alone if that's okay for you?" She shot him a quick look through her lashes and he nodded solemnly. "But then, we could either take a walk along the river—"

"In this heat?"

"Or go for a swim in the river. Your tetanus shot is up to date, right?" She bit into her toast, an innocent expression on her face.

He grinned. "I would not touch that water with someone else's toe."

She giggled. "We could drive into Silton Town and check out the antique store."

"Actually, I find antique stores kind of spooky," Finn admitted sheepishly.

"That's a real phobia, you know."

"Epiplaphobia," he nodded. "Yeah, I don't have that. I just don't like the stores themselves. I tend to get sneezing fits.'"

Marley chuckled. "We could go back to Nobiyaki's restaurant?"

Something flickered across Finn's face, too fast for Marley to read it. "I'm good," he said finally.

She threw her hands up in mock-exasperation. "I don't know what to do with you then. You seem determined not to have any fun. Oh, church!" Marley said triumphantly. "You can attend Father Curtis's midday mass ... if it's on. I forget the days."

"*Finally,*" Finn said, slapping his hand on the table. "A decent activity." They grinned at each other. "Nah, don't worry about me. I'll just hang around here, start packing my stuff up, play on my phone. Waste a bit of time. Do you get TV signal here?"

"Ooh, yes. Regional TV is ... I don't even have a word."

"I'll check it out."

Marley nodded. "I'll bring some fish and chips home for lunch."

"Get battered this time."

"You get battered," she joked.

He snickered as he cut up his eggs. Marley felt her face grow hot, even just watching the way his hands worked his cutlery. Good God, there was something wrong with her. In some ways, she couldn't get home fast enough. Being around

Finn Mayberry was a minefield. And it had already exploded once.

Marley pushed open the wood and glass door to the florist, a bell tinkling to announce her arrival. She stopped just inside the door, taking a deep breath of the damp, sweet, earthen smell. Darnee's only florist was smartly positioned equidistant from the cemetery and The Blushing Bride. It had been run all Marley's life by a warm, kindly woman named Nancy, who was currently nowhere to be seen.

"Be with you in a moment!" Marley heard her call from a room behind the scoured wood counter. The same till Marley had seen her whole life still stood atop it, alongside a pair of secateurs, bunches of greenery and assorted ribbons.

Nancy came out, dusting her hands off on her overalls and Marley was pleased to see she still sported the same hairstyle. She'd kept it over the years, even as her hair had changed from chestnut to salt-and-pepper to purest white.

Nancy finally looked up, her eyes widening. "Why, *Lena!*" She beamed and hurried around the counter to wrap Marley in a warm hug. "It's wonderful to see you." Nancy held Marley at arm's length, examining her face. "You look well. Really well. That makes me happy."

"Thank you, Nancy. It's so lovely to see you."

"It's been what, two years?"

"A little longer now. Near two and a half?"

"Well, I never. Why don't you tell me about the big city while you look around?"

Marley glanced at her, wondering how she knew where she'd been the last few years. Nancy caught the look and smiled. "Crystal Norman was by here the other day with her girl, the sweet poppet. We couldn't help but discuss it."

Marley smiled and nodded, trailing her fingertips over buckets of billy buttons and roses. "I'm sorry I didn't say anything before I left. There were people I wanted to tell. You were one of them."

"I know. You came in to buy a bouquet the day before you left. I figured that was kind of a farewell. Also, Lacey told me she saw you in a bar in Sydney."

Marley flicked her head up, heart pounding. Nancy's daughter Lacey had recognised her at the Whistle Stop one night and approached her in front of Amy and Lyra, using her old name. Marley had brushed her off, pretending she had no idea who Lacey was.

Nancy shook her head, smiling. "You needn't worry that you offended her. I told her you probably just didn't want to be recognised."

Marley bowed her head. "Please tell her I'm sorry," she said when she finally looked up. Nancy nodded kindly.

Marley stopped by a bucket of brightly-coloured, open-faced flowers.

"Petunia always loved gerberas," Nancy said. "She liked the orange ones best. Wish I had some of those in for you. Ironically, she was never a fan of petunias."

"Did … did my mum have a favourite flower type, do you know?" Marley trained her eyes on the gerberas, selecting the brightest and healthiest looking from the bucket, their stems dripping water over the raw concrete floor as she pulled them out.

Nancy shot her a sympathetic look. "I'm sorry, honey. I don't remember. I wish I did. I know your father bought her flowers now and again. Always looked so happy doing it too."

Marley set the bundle of flowers on the counter, and

Nancy got to work arranging them and edging the bouquet with greenery.

"You going over to visit them all now?" Nancy asked. Marley nodded. "I won't put paper round them then. You can set them straight into the container." She wrapped all the stems together with twine, setting the bouquet down gently on the old scoured work surface.

"Twenty-two dollars," she said gently.

Marley pulled her purse out and set some crumpled notes on the counter. She stared at them, unable to slide them over to Nancy.

"That doesn't seem like enough, does it?" she asked. "GamGam should be getting flowers all the time. They all should. Not one bunch for twenty-two dollars every couple of years."

Marley looked down at the bouquet, her chin quivering. Nancy reached across the counter and laid a palm on Marley's hand, keeping it there for a moment as Marley struggled with her emotions.

"We do have a service you might be interested in. Not trying to push you into buying anything, but I can lay something simple out there once a week. A bright posy with whatever's good that day. I can text you a picture as well. Don't do that part for anyone else, but for you I would."

Marley smiled up at the other woman, her eyes bleary with tears. It was a long moment before she trusted herself to speak. "Actually, I'd like that a lot. Thank you, Nancy."

A figure stood at the graveside, slightly stooped and wearing an almost ludicrously wide-brimmed hat against the midday sun. The cicadas were deafening as Marley approached, the brittle brown grass crunching beneath her feet. The figure turned to her, and Marley sucked in a breath, recognising Miss Grenville.

Old Miss Grenville. The familiar words started up in Marley's mind and she willed them to stop, smiling as she reached the other woman.

"Good afternoon, Miss Grenville."

"Hello, Lena." Miss Grenville smiled. Up close, Marley was surprised at the smoothness of her skin, the plump lines of her still-red lips. Miss Grenville had aged well. *Very* well. Had she always been attractive and Marley had simply never noticed? In her mind, Miss Grenville had been perpetually old. A spinster. A reject.

The woman before her looked nothing of the sort.

They chatted for a few moments, Miss Grenville sharing a couple of stories about GamGam when they were schoolgirls. Marley hadn't heard them before and soaked them up, storing each precious detail away to examine carefully later. The stories were gifts and Marley tentatively asked whether she could phone Miss Grenville now and again to hear more. The old lady eagerly agreed.

Marley swallowed. "Miss Grenville, there's also something I want to apologise for."

"Hmm?"

"The rhymes we sang as kids. They must have been so hurtful and—"

Marley broke off as the older woman burst out laughing. It was a rich, throaty sound and Marley couldn't help but smile, even though she didn't get the joke.

"Oh, Lena. Thank you, dear." Miss Grenville patted her arm, almost patronisingly. "But you have absolutely nothing to apologise for."

"I know it wasn't just me, but—"

"I found that rhyme funny."

"You did?"

"Oh yes. Smells like a hen-ville? Come on, that's hilarious."

Marley shook her head, not certain she had heard right. "It didn't offend you?"

"Oh, dear me no. Lena, if you let a bunch of children get under your skin, you've got bigger problems than a rhyme. Besides, I chose to be a *spinster*, although I'm fairly certain we don't use that word anymore."

"You chose it?"

"Darling, there seems to be an echo in the graveyard, can you hear it?"

Marley blushed. Or she would have, if her face hadn't already been beet-red from the heat. "I'm sorry! I'm just so surprised. This whole time, I thought you must have been in pain from the things that were said about you."

Miss Grenville put one hand on her hip and leaned back, considering Marley. "Let me tell you something, Lena. When I was growing up here, there was *one* way to do things. And that was to get a husband and have kids. I always knew I didn't want kids, so it stood to reason I didn't need a husband either. And you know what?"

"What?"

"I had *so* much more freedom than anyone else my age. If I wanted to go into Silton Town and get drunk with a strange man and bring him home, I could. I just went ahead and did it." She waved her arm in the air as though scattering fairy dust. "If I wanted to go bathing naked in the river, I could. Wouldn't do it now, mind you. Infections can kill at my age. I had a job, I earned good money that I could spend on whatever I pleased. Squander it if I wanted to—there was no one to confess to. I could fall asleep with a tub of ice-cream on my lap if the whim took me. Still do."

Marley stared at Miss Grenville, a grin spreading slowly over her face. "Oh my God. You beat the system."

"I beat the system," she repeated with a grin. "And I have had the time of my life. I loved Darnee, never wanted to be anywhere else. And those songs, those rhymes, they actually helped me. People left me alone. *Men* left me alone, and," she shook her head as though incredulous at the wonder of the world, "I couldn't have been happier."

"Wow." Marley breathed. "Just wow."

Miss Grenville nodded, her face still split wide in a grin, and turned back to Marley's family plot. "Of course," she added, "it's not like that anymore."

"What do you mean?"

"Well, now that people don't *have* to get married, I find it horribly romantic when they do. Maybe I'd even do it, if I had my time again. There were one or two that almost broke me."

"Lucas?" Marley asked suddenly.

Miss Grenville spun back to face her. "Well how on *earth* could you know that?"

Marley shook her head. "It just suddenly made sense. That he'd never married. I don't know. There aren't that many people in the town, I guess."

Miss Grenville laughed. "Well, maybe we'd have been something now. Now that people can take their time to choose. They can pick someone they truly love. And most importantly, that they can try before they buy, so to speak." Miss Grenville nudged Marley with her elbow, and Marley's face grew heated as she thought about Finn. "Anyway, dear. I'm heading off. Those are beautiful flowers by the way. Petunia would have loved them."

Miss Grenville turned and gave her a brief hug, almost taking Marley's eyes out with the brim of her hat, before wandering contentedly in the direction of the graveyard gates.

Marley shook her head, watching after her for a moment

before turning back to the family tombstone. She squatted to gently lay the flowers down and pulled a small microfibre cloth from her pocket. She dipped a bit of water onto it from her bottle and started polishing the dusty stone.

"Did you hear that, GamGam?" she whispered. "Turns out Miss Grenville was something else." She stopped and pressed her hand to the stone, bringing her grandmother's face to mind. "This town was full of remarkable women the whole time." She polished the stone again, then sat staring at it. "I hate the thought that you're stuck here, GamGam. But I don't think you are. I think you're wherever you want to be. Maybe you're finally seeing the beach. And I know you'd be happy. I know you'd be happy I made it out."

She stayed almost an hour. Sometimes sitting and letting memories wash over her, sometimes weeping softly, sometimes talking in a low voice. She finally stood up to leave when her legs were numb and a heat headache began to throb in her temples.

She kissed her fingers and touched them tenderly to the stone, saying farewell to her family as she promised to be back before too long. Then she started the walk home. She did not stop at Hayden's grave.

CHAPTER THIRTY-FOUR

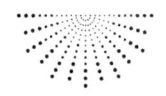

"Marley, these people are racing lawnmowers!" Finn turned gleefully to her as she walked back in the front door. He was sitting on the sofa, an open beer in his hand, the TV tuned to a local channel. She could hear the commentator's familiar voice over the whine of the engines on-screen.

"Oh yeah." She took a moment to close her eyes and savour the cool before coming to sit beside him, moving a packet of potato chips out of the way to do so. "Is this the semis already?"

"The sem—" He turned to her. "You *know* about this?"

She clicked her tongue. "Do I know about the Fifty-fifth Annual Inland New South Wales Inter-diocesan Lawnmower Derby brought to you by Bill Quomeran's Mowers and Lawn Service for all your yard needs? Is that a *joke*? Who's winning? Let me guess. Boob Todd."

He stared at her, open-mouthed. "Yes!" he said finally. "Boob Todd *is* winning! Although I was pretty sure I heard the name wrong."

"Oh no. It's not his real name, of course. His real name is

Jeremy, or Jebedy or something. He's just always been called Boob." She shrugged and took a chip from his packet. "Pretty much unbeatable, although it shouldn't be too much longer before someone steals his crown. He's getting a bit long in the tooth."

Finn burst out laughing. "This is the most ridiculous thing I've ever seen in my life and you're not only sitting here like it's totally normal, you know everything about it!"

She chuckled. "You saw all Darnee had to offer in about forty-five seconds. Can you truly be surprised at the ways we've invented to entertain ourselves?"

"I just have one question."

"What?"

"Why the *hell* aren't we at this thing?"

"Finn, Finn, Finn." She shook her head, mock-disappointed. "Tickets to this sold out a year ago. At least."

He looked back and forth between her and the TV, a grin spreading over his face. "You have to get us tickets for next year. You *have* to."

"I'm afraid that's impossible."

"Why?"

"Because next year is a leap year and traditionally, the women of Darnee will present their beaus the gift of two tickets to the Derby on a leap year as a way of proposing."

"They let women propose out here?"

"Only once every four years. And only the whores do it, of course," she joked. He chuckled. "You accept the tickets, you're as good as married."

"So, let me get this straight." He raised his eyebrows at her. "You would need to propose to me for us to go to the Derby next year?"

"You see why it's impossible."

"I accept your proposal."

She gasped and clutched her heart. "Finn, it's bad luck to

accept without the tickets in front of you. The woman could be bluffing! How could you not know that?"

They stared at one another until Marley could no longer keep a straight face.

"Oh my *God.*" He slapped the sofa. "You made all of that up?"

"Everything except the bad luck about the tickets. The rest, unfortunately, is true." She stood. "I need a quick shower. What did you make us for lunch?"

"You said you were getting fish and chips!" Finn called as she walked down the hall.

"Ah, crap. We can go get them when I get out."

They lay on their backs in the grass late that afternoon, arms hooked behind their heads, looking up at the sky as storm clouds gathered. The southerly wind brought cool relief and Marley felt a pleasant nostalgia. She couldn't possibly count the number of times she'd lain here in this grass as a girl, making shapes out of the clouds and wondering how big the incoming storm might be. GamGam would be watching her through the window, making dinner or maybe playing bridge with her friends. If they caught eyes, they'd smile and wave at one another. No matter what was going on, that smile and wave would make life seem pretty perfect.

She was glad she'd come back to Darnee, glad Finn had been here with her. She felt as though this time she'd be leaving on the right terms. Not running from anything. It would be strange not having GamGam's house to come back to when she wanted to visit. But it made her happy to think of the new lease of life it would get from Susie and Benedict moving in.

Susie had been delighted when Marley had called to tell her, thanking Marley profusely and promising to get everything sorted out as quickly as possible. Marley told her there was no rush. She felt genuinely happy that Susie was happy—something she never thought she'd be able to say.

Everything felt right with the world. And in just a couple of days' time she'd be in Dr Coleman's office, about to start the next phase of her life. Finally.

"Thanks for coming with me, Finn." She turned her head to look at him. "Really. Thank you."

He twisted his head to look at her and she felt the familiar lurch in her heart at the sight of him. The sweep of his lashes and the coal-black of his hair and the shock of his eyes.

"You're welcome," he smiled. "It was good for me too. I needed to get out of Sydney for a bit. Might not have chosen Armpit River on my own, but I had fun. It's gone quickly."

She looked back up at the sky. "Yeah. It has. Time flies when you're having fun, I guess."

Her fingers brushed against Finn's in the grass. Slowly, he cupped her hand in his. She resisted the urge to pull it away. She resisted the urge to lean into him. She just looked up at the sky, her fingers threaded with his, and enjoyed the perfect moment.

"Oh, I almost forgot!" She sprang to her feet sometime later, unwinding her hand from Finn's. "Wait right there."

She slid open the door to the dining room and grabbed what she needed. Finn sat up in the grass, a few blades sticking out of his hair and a smile of anticipation on his face.

"Let's head out through the gate," she said. "But we'll need to be pretty quiet."

"Why do you have a bag of grass clippings?"

"Trust me." She touched her finger to her lips and beckoned him. They slipped through the side gate, into the vast open area behind her house. A few wallabies were grazing in the middle distance, their forms hazy in the slowly fading light. "They're usually here around dusk," she said, keeping her voice low.

Finn's eyes widened as he looked at her. "You've kept this from me the whole time?"

Marley grinned. "I only just remembered. Sorry! Here." She opened the bag of alfalfa hay and thrust a large clump into Finn's hand. "Approach them slowly. Keep low. No sudden movements. They're pretty tame so they should eat right out of your hand."

A smile spread across Finn's face as he looked back and forth between Marley and the wallabies. Then they slowly approached the animals, pausing now and again so as not to frighten them.

They were as tame as Marley remembered, assessing the humans inquisitively and watching them placidly with intelligent black-brown eyes. As one cautiously approached Finn, he instinctively got down low and held his palm flat. After a few sniffs, the wallaby tilted its head and delicately nibbled the hay from his palm.

Finn's face lit up and Marley felt as though something was switching on inside her as well. Something huge and illuminating and almost frighteningly powerful. The golden afternoon sun glanced off Finn's hair and set off the warmth of his tan. When he looked up at her, they locked eyes and stayed that way for a long, lingering moment—perfectly quiet as the fine-featured wallabies devoured their snack.

CHAPTER THIRTY-FIVE

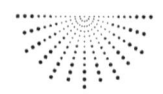

"This isn't the right exit?" Finn sat up straighter and Marley glanced at him in amusement.

They'd been on the road half the day, having bundled up their things at dawn and made a quick breakfast out of the leftovers in the fridge. Finn had taken out the garbage and vacuumed while Marley ran the dishwasher and folded towels. Then she'd taken her time slowly meandering through the house, saying farewell to her grandmother and a lifetime of memories. Finally, she'd left the key under the front mat for Susie and Finn had taken the first driving shift while she wept quietly for the best part of an hour before taking over the wheel.

"Why do you still think I'm going to kill you?" she asked. "I would definitely have done it in Darnee if I was."

"That is an excellent point."

"There's just a nice lookout off this exit, but I should have asked whether you're in a rush to get back."

"Unemployment doesn't just happen on its own, Marley."

"You're right. I'm *so* sorry." She grinned and navigated the turn off the highway onto a narrower two-lane road. "I swear, the detour is worth it though. If we're lucky, they'll still have a kiosk there."

Ten minutes later, they were unwrapping Cornettos and gazing over the railing into the deep gorge. Below them stretched a vast reddish-orange rock and dirt expanse, patchy with low, dark green scrub. A thin river twisted through, bleaching the area along the bank to a dusty pink. Opposite the lookout, almost a kilometre away, the other side of the gorge rose grandly upwards, the layers of sedimentary rock shifting through gold and copper to deepest red.

"Wow," Finn breathed. "It's incredible."

Marley nodded, scanning the scene with the same awe she felt every time she saw it. The moment was somewhat ruined when her elbow was jostled by a plump man who'd come to stand unnecessarily close to her. Her Cornetto smooshed slightly into her face and Finn chortled.

"I'm sorry." He held his hands up as she pretended to glare at him. "I have a tissue if you want it?"

She nodded and wiped her mouth, tempted to nudge the man back as he lifted his own ice-cream to his lips. She hadn't expected the lookout to be this crowded. But at this time of day, the view was spectacular.

They stayed until they'd finished their ice-creams, pointing out oddly-shaped trees, or marvelling at how the cloud shadows rushed over the landscape and altered the colours. Marley spotted a pair of kangaroos stooping over the water to drink and Finn lamented not having brought his binoculars.

"Why do you need binoculars when you live in the city?" Marley asked, as they climbed back in the car.

Finn took the driver's seat. "Oh, just bird watching," he said quickly, feigning nervousness and she giggled as they slammed the doors.

The car was hot and Finn turned the engine on, blasting the air-conditioning. He put the car into reverse and then froze, staring out the windscreen at the parts of the gorge they could see.

"What? What is it?" she asked.

He said nothing.

"Finn? Are you having a neurological event?"

"Marley, I need to tell you something."

A knot twisted itself into the pit of Marley's stomach. A premonition.

"Let's just get going," she said quickly.

"No, I need to say this, even though …" He kept his eyes trained out the windscreen, not turning to look at her. His jaw was clenched, face tinged with red. "Don't do it."

She paused, wanting to be sure she understood him right. "Don't do what?"

"Don't go to your appointment." He turned to look at her and her breath stopped.

"Why not?" she whispered.

"I don't want you to do it."

"Finn, we already talked about this." She could barely hear her own voice.

He looked back out the window and time slowed for Marley. She could hear air rushing through the vents, the low hum of the engine, her own blood in her ears. The world had narrowed to this lookout, this car, this conversation.

"You got married at *nineteen*," he began softly. "Of course it was a mistake. I see how that town is. How," he groped for the words as she watched him silently, "small and how cloying and how restrictive. It was probably always going to be a mistake to marry someone from there. Especially that young."

"Finn—"

He held up his hand to stop her. "I know you have your

perfect plan figured out. I know you wanted a donor because you don't want anyone else involved. I know you're afraid of rushing into a mistake again, and I know you don't want to wait any longer. But ..." He turned to her again, his eyes earnest and hot. "I just don't want you to go."

She could feel her body rocking slightly as her pulse throbbed. "You're the one who got me that appointment."

"I know." He gulped. "I know. I'm just asking that you consider what I'm saying. From the moment I met you, I knew something was different about you. I knew I had to make big changes."

She should stop him. He'd tried to tell her this once before, when they'd spent time with Rebecca and Walter at Lilac Bay. She should stop him now before he said it, before she'd never be able to unhear the words.

"Finn—"

"Because I never," he swallowed. "I never felt about anyone the way I did about you from an *embarrassingly* short time after I met you. I realised Bess was never truly serious about me, and I thought I had been serious about her, but ..." He shook his head. "Then there was you."

She closed her eyes and leaned her head back against the car seat. His words hung in the air for a long time. Her chest felt squeezed, her body torn. She wanted to cup his face in her hands and pull him to her and kiss him. And she wanted to scream at him.

He knew what he was asking of her and yet he was still asking it. He knew she had feelings for him, but she'd already explained there was no point to them. She shouldn't have slept with him. She shouldn't have hugged him, held his hand, kissed him. She'd made a huge mistake. A series of them. And she knew this time it was different. The conversation they'd had coming back from Nobiyaki's restaurant where he'd flirted with the waitress—that hadn't been like this. This was big. If she pushed him away now, she knew they might not be able to come back from it. She might lose him altogether.

She closed her eyes and brought to mind an image of herself carrying a child. Her child. That was the most important thing. Nothing could be allowed to interfere with that. Not when she'd waited so long, and not when she was so close.

She opened her eyes, staring straight ahead while she steadied her breath. Then she turned to him. "Finn, please don't say things like that ever again."

His head reeled back—the slightest motion, like he'd received a tiny, invisible blow.

"Yes, I have feelings for you," she continued. "Strong feelings. I feel more for you already than I've ever felt for anyone. Even my husband. I think you're ..." She puffed out a breath, holding her palms up. "You're everything. But I'm going to my appointment. I want a baby, Finn. You know that. You know how long I've waited. I'm not getting younger, and I don't know how many years I'll get with my child. But I don't want to waste another single one waiting."

"I'm not—"

"You're asking me to try something with you. And believe me, I'd love to. This past week has been incredible." She threw up her hands. "More than incredible. Easy and comfortable and *fun* and right. But we just met. You were almost engaged to someone else until basically five minutes ago."

"No, I wasn't—"

"We aren't ready to have a baby together, not by a long shot. And I'm not prepared to wait." He pressed his lips together, nodding slowly and not meeting her eye. "Not even for someone as amazing as you," she finished in a whisper.

She looked at him, traced the lines of his face with her eyes and fought the urge to cry.

He studied her back for a long moment, then turned to look out the window. He nodded slowly. "I understand," he said finally, his voice tense but not unkind. "Don't worry. I won't mention it again."

He started the engine and they drove the last few hours home in relative silence.

They hugged briefly and awkwardly in the glow of the street lamp outside Marley's apartment block. Finn attempted a smile. Marley looked down, unable to bear either the pain in his eyes or the thought that she had broken everything between them.

She reached the front door to her block and turned back to find him watching her. "See you soon?" she called.

"Of course," he said softly, smiling. He picked up his duffel and waved once. Marley tried to believe he wasn't lying.

Her apartment felt strange. Lonely and quiet and not like home anymore. She'd adjust within a few hours, she was sure. Right now, she probably just needed a sandwich and a shower and a nap. Not necessarily in that order.

She groaned when she realised the fridge was empty—she'd cleaned it out before her trip. She picked up her phone to order takeaway and noticed a string of messages from the girls, demanding to know whether she'd arrived home safely and whether Finn was with her. She sent a quick voice note, thanking them for their concern and letting them know she was okay and would call them properly the following day.

It was thankfully still early enough that she could place a delivery order with her local Thai restaurant. Then she switched her phone off and threw it on the kitchen table, determined not to look at it for the rest of the evening. Maybe even the whole of tomorrow.

Over Yam Nua and a reality TV show, Marley tried to slow her thoughts.

Finn's request in the car had played over in her head their whole drive back. She'd given him a straight answer, but that was the problem ... the answer wasn't straight and her mind wasn't as clear as she'd made out.

Her plan had been perfect. It was neat, it ticked all her boxes, it would make her a mother and she had removed romance from the whole equation—just like Rebecca had said to her that day at Lilac Bay. Marley had never been so sure of any plan in her life, and the fact that she'd put everything in motion like clockwork, starting on the night Hayden had died, had just made her even more certain. Her decision was crystal clear, it was comforting, it was exciting.

And then she'd met Finn. And he'd thrown a big muddy rock into the calm pond of her plans. She knew that wasn't exactly a fair way to think of it, since he hadn't done anything besides exist and be ridiculously attractive and sweet and thoughtful and funny and—

"Stop it!" she said out loud to the empty room, setting down her food with a clack on the coffee table.

She tried to think of what her grandmother would tell her to do in a situation like this. Instantly, the answer came to her. A list. A pros and cons list of everything. Of all possible options and outcomes.

Feeling calmer already, Marley went to her kitchen drawer and pulled out a notepad and pen. She switched the TV off and sat at the dining room table. For the next two hours, she drew columns and added items, scratching them back out and moving them from one row to another and then back again.

At the end, she was none the wiser, but at least she was thoroughly exhausted. And one thing was startlingly clear—it wasn't an easy decision. Her feelings for Finn ran loudly through every column, ruining the perfect symmetry of her path. It was evident from the marks on the paper and the squeeze in her heart that she was in love with Finn.

As she prepared herself for bed, she stared at her reflection in the mirror. It felt strange to be going about her evening rituals without hearing Finn in another room, without knowing he was there with her.

Okay, so she loved him. Big deal. Marley was nothing if not practical, and love was just a hurdle she could overcome. She'd overcome so much before. And she was no longer the kind of person who let love win over everything else.

CHAPTER THIRTY-SIX

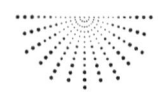

"Thank God you're back," Dr Martelle said to Marley, practically pouncing on her as she opened the door.

Marley startled and put a hand to her heart. She'd been expecting the office to be dark and empty, the way it usually was. Since she'd started working there, she couldn't remember a time Dr Martelle had beaten her in.

"Great to be back," Marley said, recovering herself. "You're in early. Is everything okay?"

"Yes. Yesyesyes. Yeees." Dr Martelle made a noise that could have been mistaken for a giggle and trailed Marley to her reception desk. "It's just that one Monday without you was *more* than enough. I swear, people save it all up over the weekend just so they can bombard me once work starts again."

"But you had Tilda, right?" Marley asked in alarm.

"Yes. Which reminds me. You may or may not need to manually add some appointments into the system."

"She couldn't get the hang of it?" Dr Martelle shook her head. "Okay. But you put *your* notes straight into the database right?"

"If the appointment was in there, yes."

"Oh God." Marley groaned. "So I have notes to add in as well. We *really* need to look into hiring someone else." She set her satchel down in the cupboard and turned to her desk. "Or at least signing a contract with a temp agency or something. Oh, speaking of which," she added, booting the computer up, "I need tomorrow off." She winced, sure Dr Martelle would make a fuss.

Dr Coleman from MacArthur Fertility had messaged her early that morning to tell her everything looked great for her appointment Tuesday. Marley's stomach had fluttered with a mix of anticipation and anxiety all the way into work, and only as she arrived at the building did she remember she hadn't yet asked for the day off. She'd been afraid of jinxing everything.

"Of course! Of course," Dr Martelle flapped her hand like it was no big deal.

Marley was slightly taken aback. "Really? You're okay with it? So soon after I got back? I'm sorry I forgot to mention it earlier. It's a specialist appointment so it would be difficult to move it, but I didn't expect you to be so …"

"Honestly. *Totally* fine." Dr Martelle grinned widely at her. Marley had the distinct impression something was up, but she had no idea what it could be, and she didn't have the capacity to try and puzzle it out at the moment. Not with everything else going on in her mind.

"Okay, great. Thanks." Marley cleared her throat and looked pointedly at her computer screen, but Dr Martelle continued to stand awkwardly on the other side of the desk.

"And you're right about the temp agency. Why don't you look for one this morning? I'll sign off on everything you want."

Marley's hand froze on the mouse and she frowned at the other woman. "Are you sure everything's okay?"

"Yes! Yes of course, what a silly question. Hahaha." Dr Martelle grabbed a random stack of files from the desk—probably leftover from the previous week—and tapped them into an orderly pile. "Okay, so just send in the first patient when he or she gets here?"

"You mean like ... I always do? You mean do my job?"

Dr Martelle burst out laughing as though Marley had said the funniest thing in the world. Then she turned on her heel and walked abruptly to her office. Marley couldn't be sure, but she thought she heard the other woman say, "smooth, Elizabeth", as she closed her office door. Marley stared in that direction for a moment, then shrugged and got on with her day.

Which passed painfully slowly. It was as though the universe knew Marley couldn't wait for her Tuesday appointment, so it was doing everything it could to teach her the value of living in the present moment. None of the things that usually passed a day quickly happened. They didn't have a lot of patients. No one fainted or threw up. No one came in and loudly gave Marley an unprompted and inappropriately detailed history of their medical complaints. The printer didn't jam. Even teeing things up with a temp agency went a lot faster than Marley expected. The first place that claimed to have trained medical receptionists on their books had very reasonable rates, a few sample blind CVs that perfectly fit the bill, and a very uncomplicated contract process.

So Marley was free to think. And her thoughts kept running in circles that involved Finn Mayberry and her future child.

She already missed Finn, it was no use pretending otherwise. She missed his sense of humour, the gentle way he had of teasing her, his looks ... his mouth. She cleared her throat to stop her brain from racing down that track again. The one that was apparently now a super-highway in her brain. The one that ended with her being held against the living room wall.

At lunch, she wandered aimlessly around the neighbourhood, unable to sit at her desk a moment longer. She grabbed a sandwich to go from a bakery and passed by the same boutique store she'd stepped into the first day she'd met Finn at the Greek. The day she'd bought the bracelets for herself and her future baby. They were still wrapped in the soft tissue paper, still tucked into a pocket of her satchel. Marley walked to the tiny park a block from her office and sat on a wooden bench beneath a spreading fig tree. Only one area of the bench was free of bird-droppings, so she sat perched on the very edge with one-and-a-third buttock cheeks. Biting into her sandwich, she fished the tissue paper package out of her satchel with the other hand.

She hadn't undone the tape since she'd bought them, but now she carefully unwrapped the paper and stared at the two circlets of tumbled stones. They were prettier than she had remembered. She held her sandwich in her teeth as she rubbed the stones between her fingers, a slow smile breaking over her face.

"Marley?"

In one motion, she looked up, dropped her sandwich out of her mouth and tipped sideways off the bench. "Oof."

"Oh my God!" Finn hurried towards her. "Sorry!"

"I'm fine!" She sprang up, abandoning her sandwich but collecting the bracelets from the ground. "I was sitting a bit awkwardly, that's all."

She discreetly tucked the bracelets into her pocket as she dusted off her skirt, then looked up into his concerned eyes. Barely two days since she'd seen him and her body was responding as though it had been starved for months of his company. She felt full of flames.

"It's so good to see you," she managed to get out.

"Yes, you too." Now that the initial flush of meeting up had passed, he seemed slightly awkward.

"What are you doing around here?" she asked.

"Oh, uh. I have a meeting." He gestured vaguely in another direction.

"Oh cool. About a job?"

"Mmh." He looked down.

"You know you won't need it long. Once the house sale goes through ... Unless it's already to be a physio?"

He shook his head and cleared his throat. "You know I can't take your money."

"I can make you," Marley challenged, and their eyes held for a moment before they both quickly looked away.

"Are you—you're all set for tomorrow?" he asked.

"Uh-huh." It was her turn to feel awkward.

He looked at her for a moment, then nodded. "Great. You can just give me a call if you need anything, okay?"

"Oh, that's nice of you." She felt as though they were both stuck in a terrible movie, and had been given lines that didn't work. "I, uh, I should probably get back to the—"

"Yeah, me too," he said.

He stuck his hand out to shake hers at the same time as she leaned in to hug him.

"Sorry!" She tried to laugh, moving back from the hug and patting him weirdly on the back.

He smiled as they stepped away from each other. "Have a good day, Marley."

"Thanks. You too."

Marley sat shakily back down on the bench, letting out a long exhale as he walked away. She watched his form recede and couldn't help feeling like it was an ending for them. She hated the idea of such uncomfortable exchanges if they ran into one another. Even worse was the idea that they might not run into one another at all.

She felt into her pocket for the bracelets and pulled them out again, closing her fingers over the cold stones. They felt solid and real, and made her future child seem real too. She pictured herself slipping the smallest one onto a chubby little wrist.

She just wished the picture felt as perfectly complete as it had only a few weeks ago.

CHAPTER THIRTY-SEVEN

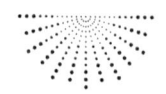

On autopilot, Marley headed out through the MacArthur clinic doors the next morning, waving a half-hearted goodbye to the young woman at reception as she passed her. She was full of big emotions and needed a hug. A hug, an entire box of chocolates and maybe a room where she could scream at the top of her lungs. But the girls were both at work and she didn't know of any padded cells that could be rented by the hour. Chocolate would have to do.

Calling Finn was … not a good idea right now. She needed time to process everything. He'd texted her that morning. A simple, *Good luck today*, but she had felt his unspoken pain between the lines. In a way, though she'd answered him on the day, the question he'd asked her at the lookout still hung in the air, affecting their former ease. Marley wondered whether they'd ever be able to get it back. She knew Finn would try, no matter how bruised his feelings were. And that was heart-breaking.

She found herself in front of a cute cafe a block from the clinic. It was still mid-morning and the place had a chalkboard out with a brunch menu. Her stomach growled—she hadn't been able to eat before her appointment and wasn't sure she'd be able to eat now.

Taking a seat at a small street-side table, she smiled distractedly at the waiter who came out to serve her. After staring blankly at the menu for a moment, she ordered some eggs, hash browns and freshly squeezed juice.

While she waited for the food to arrive, she stared unseeingly out at the road. Had she made the right decision? It had been the biggest decision of her life and the most frustrating part of it all was that she would never know for certain whether she'd done the right thing. Never know if another path would have been better.

If only GamGam was alive. Marley would give anything to talk to her, even just for the duration of a breakfast. She heaved a sigh. The loss of her was something Marley would never truly get over. Until she'd met Amy and Lyra, GamGam's death had left her completely alone in the world. Hayden hadn't filled the void, and Marley had been stupid to expect he would. But there had never been anyone else ... until Finn. The girls had long felt like family, but Marley had been taken by surprise at how quickly she'd also felt close to Finn, in a way she never had with Hayden. It was all painfully confusing.

She took out her phone, briefly messaged the girls an update and invited them both over for Thursday night. She hoped to also spend time with them over the weekend, though she knew they'd likely already have plans with Alex and Rick. At least Thursday gave her something to look forward to. If nothing else, it would distract her for an evening.

Her food arrived and she toyed with the eggs, breaking open the yolk with her fork as she stared into space. She thought of Finn. About how wonderful it had been to spend that week with him in Darnee. How natural and comfortable she felt with him, how safe. It was nothing like being with Hayden, but still ... there was no way of knowing.

She drew a shaky breath, trying to make peace with the fact that everything was uncertain. That she'd never know whether she'd made the right decision. In a way, she was choosing for both their futures, hers and Finn's, and that was a lot to take on. She'd have to tell him, have to text him back about her morning. Just not now. Not today.

Today was for freaking out.

Marley stared at the message on her phone the next morning. She'd been staring at it for twenty minutes already. The sleepless night she'd spent definitely wasn't helping, but every time she read the message, it hit her all over again. The fierce jab to the solar plexus, the winded feeling, the blood rushing in her ears.

Hi Marley. I hope it all went well yesterday. I just wanted to let you know Bess and I have come to an agreement. Back together, it looks like! I'll tell you more about it when I see you next. Thought you should know. :)

He was back with Bess. He'd come to an agreement with her after Marley had pushed him away on the drive home. A fresh wave of nausea flipped her stomach.

She was already in the office, though neither Dr Martelle nor any patients had yet arrived. Theoretically, she could make a run for it. Text Dr Martelle that she was feeling ill, run home while praying she didn't bump into the doc along the way, and hide under her covers for at least the rest of the year. Amy and Lyra would definitely bring her food and check her mail.

But she didn't want to be at home alone, and her girlfriends would both be working.

A thought hit her that almost made her laugh. She felt like talking to Finn. He'd know what to say, he'd know how to comfort her. Or so she had thought. It was going to take her mind a while to accept the fact that she'd made another huge misjudgment where men were concerned.

Her body put the escape plan into action before her mind had a chance to object, and she was at the door, satchel over her shoulder, when she collided with a patient.

"Oh, I'm so sorry, dear," the elderly woman said, putting her hand on Marley's arm to steady herself. "Was that my fault?"

"Not at all, Mrs Liddle," Marley said unevenly. "Did you, uh, how can I help you?"

Mrs Liddle blinked. "Well, I want to see the doctor, of course. What a question!"

"Okay, and you—you have an appointment?"

"Well now you're being silly," Mrs Liddle guided Marley back towards her desk, Marley shooting a longing look at the door over her shoulder on the way. "It's about that strange pattern on my tongue. It's changed again and I'd like Dr Martelle to have another look at it."

"I see. It's just that I was—" Marley made one last attempt to extricate herself from Mrs Liddle's surprisingly firm grasp.

"L-I-D-D-L-E," the old lady said pointedly, crooking a finger at Marley's computer. "Do you need my Medicare card?"

Marley stifled a sigh and took her place back behind the desk. The computer was still on, she hadn't remembered to shut it down before making a break for it. She clicked into the calendar, found the appointment and marked Mrs Liddle as in attendance.

"Please take a seat in the waiting room, Mrs Liddle. The doctor will be with you shortly."

Marley sat glumly at her desk and put her phone beside the keyboard, open to Finn's message. She forced herself to read it over and over, in the hope she'd become desensitised to it.

She was struggling against tears when Dr Martelle rushed in a few moments later, smiling warmly at Marley as she reached the reception desk. Marley tried, but couldn't muster a smile back.

"How is my favourite office manager this morning?"

"Mrs Liddle is already here. You have a busy morning."

"Okay," Dr Martelle said slowly, collecting the file Marley proffered. She tapped it against her other hand as Marley stared back at her screen. "Did you have a relaxing night's sleep? Eat a healthy breakfast and everything?"

"Huh?" Marley looked up, confused. "Liddle. It's about her tongue again."

The corners of Dr Martelle's mouth turned down slightly and Marley thought her shoulders slumped. "Send her in a few minutes, please," she said finally, her voice low.

Marley gave a curt nod and returned her attention to her phone. *Back together, it looks like!* Why had she ever gone back to that clinic, once she'd met Finn? She'd known from the beginning she might develop feelings for him. That strange click she'd felt inside when she'd looked at him closely the first day they'd spoken, that should have been her signal to run. She'd thought she was so smart—that she could stay one step ahead of her own heart. That purely because it was impractical to fall for Finn, she wouldn't. If only he hadn't ended things with Bess. She could pinpoint that as the moment her troubles truly began. With a sigh, she shut her phone off. There was nothing she could achieve right now.

She was chained to her desk for the rest of the day. And the day was sure to last six hundred years.

Just before lunch, Dr Martelle came out and loitered around Marley's desk for a moment.

"Are you looking for a patient file?" Marley asked, noting with annoyance that her voice sounded more gruff than she'd intended. She needed to pull herself together or her attitude would get her fired.

"I wondered whether you had any interesting plans any night this week?"

Marley frowned. Dr Martelle never asked such blatantly personal questions. Never really asked questions at all. Marley wondered what she was getting at. Maybe Dr Martelle thought she'd been staying out late. But why would that matter?

"Am I doing something wrong?" she asked finally.

"Oh, no! Not at all." Dr Martelle's rush to reassure Marley was even more puzzling.

"Then I don't understand the question, I'm sorry?"

"Never mind." Dr Martelle shook her head, a flash of irritation crossing her face. Marley got the distinct sense the irritation was aimed at the doctor herself. "Who's up next?"

"Brad Finger," Marley said automatically, sticking the file out.

The two of them had a tradition that whenever Mr Finger, who was something of a hypochondriac, paid a visit, Marley would help Dr Martelle get her giggles out before going to collect him for his appointment. It had begun when Mr Finger had accidentally set fire to a pair of gloves while barbecuing in winter. He'd been wearing them at the time. Dr Martelle, distracted, had called into the waiting room for a "Bad Finger" and Mr Finger had thought she was laughing at the expense of his wounded hand. It had caused all sorts of trouble, made much worse by the fact Dr Martelle couldn't stop giggling through the entire ordeal.

"Okay, are you going to help me?"

Marley stood. "Sorry, I need the bathroom."

She could feel Dr Martelle's eyes on her as she walked away. When the day was finally over, Dr Martelle poked her head out from her office. "You can head off any time, Marley. I'll close up."

Marley stood wearily, her head pounding. "Thank you," she said, her voice barely above a whisper.

A couple of blocks from home, she heard her name called. She looked up to see Don Hamlet jogging towards her, a grin on his face.

"Hey, Marley."

"Oh, hi, Don." Marley gave a brief wave and tried to keep walking. She felt minutes away from crying and didn't want to do it right there in the street.

"Are you going home after work?"

"Yes. I'm kind of in a rush so—"

"Would you have dinner with me?" he asked. "Maybe some time this week? Or early next week?"

She glanced up at him in surprise. He was biting his lip, his handsome face clouded with worry.

"Oh, Don. I don't think that's such a great idea."

He brought his hands together in an unconscious plea gesture. "Can't I convince you? I have something I urgently need to talk to you about."

Marley bit back a sigh. "What is it?"

He shook his head, glancing awkwardly around as though he suspected they were being watched. "I don't want to talk here. It could be a quick dinner. We can just go to that restaurant on Cresthill Road. Sushi Jam. I'll pay."

Marley knew the place well. It was overcrowded and noisy, the tables squished together so closely that people struggled to get in and out of them—certainly not the kind of place where a besotted waiter would keep plying them with free goods. She didn't have the energy to argue, and whatever it was Don wanted to tell her, she was sure she could just nod and smile for the duration of a speedy single course. It wasn't lost on her that she had an objectively gorgeous man practically begging to go out with her. She just wished it made her feel anything but panicky.

"Next week. Tuesday night?" She deliberately picked the least romantic of all the nights.

"Great! I'll see you there at 7:30?"

Marley nodded once and patted Don's arm in a quick goodbye before he started up with a rhyme.

When she finally made it home, she locked and dead bolted the door behind her, and fell face first on her bed to cry.

CHAPTER THIRTY-EIGHT

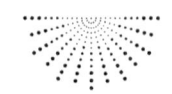

"I just don't think Finn would do a smiley face at the end if he meant he was back with Bess *romantically*," Amy said, handing the phone back to Marley with a shrug of one shoulder.

The three girls sat crowded onto Marley's sofa that Thursday night, the coffee table crammed with half-empty containers of beef shawarma, flatbread, baba ghanouge and garlic dip, falafel and cabbage rolls. Marley had ordered the Lebanese with a growling stomach, but had barely touched a bite once the food was actually in front of her. She was glad the girls had tucked in and enjoyed the feast. And she'd have leftovers for whenever her appetite decided to return.

"Why not?" Marley asked Amy. "He thinks I'm not interested. He probably thinks that will make me happy to hear."

"But he's not a psycho," Amy said calmly. "You never told him you didn't have feelings for him, just that you wouldn't act on them. I don't think he'd rub it in your face like this."

"What else could he mean?"

Amy spread her hands. "I have no idea. But not that. I really think not that."

Lyra twisted her mouth. "Also, Marley, I think there's a different question we should be asking here." Her voice was low and kind. She'd hugged Marley tightly when she'd seen her, sympathy etched on her features.

Marley knew she looked rough. She'd barely slept and hadn't been able to eat much either. She was intermittently furious at herself for having told Finn she couldn't be with him, angry at him for having asked even though he knew how she felt, alert for signs of pregnancy, heartsick that he was back with Bess and simply exhausted that she'd let herself fall for the wrong guy again.

"What?" Marley asked, slightly cross as she took the phone back from Amy and examined the message once more, though she knew every word by heart. She still hadn't responded to Finn's text. She'd gone to plenty of times, both in her dreams—waking with panic at the admissions she'd typed there—and in real life. She just hadn't actually managed to hit send on anything.

"Why *did* you refuse to act on your feelings?" Lyra asked.

Marley gave her a sharp look. "Really? You know everything that happened in my life, Lyra. And you're asking me that?"

Lyra stood and for a moment Marley was worried she'd upset her. But she simply walked to the floor cushion and sat opposite Amy and Marley.

"Sorry, my neck is getting craned like that. Plus, I'm so stuffed from that food I'm expanding in real time." She locked eyes with Marley. "You were a *girl* when you made the mistake with Hayden. It's not like you have fundamentally flawed taste in men, or that you have a 'type' and you keep picking destructive, damaged men. You got supremely unlucky with him. That's it. That's the story."

Amy nodded slowly beside Marley, sipping on the red wine she'd brought over to share with Lyra. "I agree," she said.

Marley felt a flicker of annoyance and gestured to her phone. "But here's proof I've done it again! I can't be trusted. And soon, I might not have just myself to worry about. Besides, you can't just dismiss my concerns like that. They're real. Just because you don't feel the same way doesn't mean they aren't valid."

Lyra's eyes widened. "Of course they're valid. I'm only saying, I think it could work with you two. Finn seems incredibly sweet and he's clearly very interested and from what you've told us … I'm sorry to tell you this but it sounds like you've already fallen for him."

"I know that," Marley snapped petulantly. She toyed with the cushion that had been supporting Lyra's back. "But now he's back with his ex anyway, so this is all pointless and I feel stupid."

"I don't think he is though," Lyra insisted. "Amy's right. I don't think he'd do that."

"But Lyra, you always just want people to get together. Remember when Rick flat out lied to Amy and you were still totally in support of him?"

Amy sucked a breath in and set her wine down as Lyra made a 'yikes' face. Marley instantly felt horrible having so flippantly brought up a sensitive episode in Rick and Amy's history. Especially since Rick had been guilty of an omission of truth, rather than a lie.

"We're not talking about Rick now," Amy said, surprisingly calmly. Marley shot her an apologetic look and Amy patted her arm reassuringly. "And I agree, Lyra does tend to see the best in people. But I think there's only the best to see in Finn."

"And it's not like you believe that silly curse thing, is it?" Lyra asked. "You didn't push him away because of that."

Marley shook her head. "No. That's just a horrible set of coincidences or whatever, but no. I don't think there's a plague on my house. But …" She looked at each of the girls in turn. "Ugh. It's pointless discussing this because he's back with Bess."

They both looked at her ruefully.

"You're only going to know that for sure if you actually communicate with him," Lyra said tentatively. "Remember what a big mistake I made with Alex? Just *call* him."

Marley clearly remembered Lyra's own omission—one that had almost cost her her fledgling relationship with Alex. It was a wound that had healed over for the couple, but still, Marley's eyes pooled with tears. "I will. I will. Just not now. I don't want to know how big of an idiot I am yet."

"When can you do a pregnancy test?" Amy asked, reaching for Marley's hand.

"Next week," she said with a sigh. "It's absolute torture waiting so long."

"We'll come over," Lyra said resolutely. "You can take it with us here, and we can all … process the news together afterwards. If you want," she added hastily.

Marley sniffed. "I would love that. Thank you."

Amy held a finger up, her eyes glittering. "I have the *perfect* way to distract us for a moment."

"What?" Lyra asked, grinning. Amy's enthusiasm was contagious.

"Come on, come on," she ordered, hauling them both up by the hands. "Follow me!"

They trailed her into Marley's bedroom, where she flung open the wardrobe doors and beamed over her shoulder at the other girls. "Ta-da!"

Marley tilted her head. "I don't get it?"

Amy held up a finger. "First, I have one question. How much of this stuff do you *actually* enjoy wearing?" She gestured like a TV host across Marley's cluttered closet, jammed with a tangle of coloured clothing in absolutely no order. "Like, feel confident in, feel like yourself in and get joy out of wearing?"

Marley considered. "Ninety percent?"

It was clear that wasn't the answer Amy had been expecting. She shot Lyra a surprised glance and then quickly changed tack. "Okay, so we're going to organise this space properly."

"Ooh," Lyra said, bringing her hands together. "Can we do like a rainbow of colours? I've seen that on TV on those home design shows. It looks so pretty."

"I like that idea," Marley said, nodding encouragingly.

"Then that's what we'll do!" Amy said. "Lyra, get in here."

They reached into the wardrobe and started grabbing fistfuls of clothes on hangers, tossing them onto the bed.

"Finn told me he likes my outfits, by the way," Marley said, perching on her bed and watching the girls as they emptied her wardrobe.

Lyra grinned. "That is a smitten man!"

"She's just kidding," Amy said, giving Lyra an admonishing look. "We're not trying to change you. The outfits can be as wild as you like, as long as you *really* like them. When I look at the state of this wardrobe, I have to admit I'm surprised you're so organised with the doctor."

"I think I use it all up at work and then I have nothing left when I get home," Marley said, smiling. She felt a flicker of excitement and was grateful for Amy's idea. This would definitely take her mind off things for a while.

"Let's do this!" Amy lifted her arm as though it was a battle cry and Marley couldn't help but laugh.

CHAPTER THIRTY-NINE

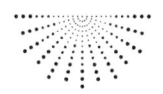

"You look nice," Don said, as Marley approached him out the front of Sushi Jam for their meeting. Marley refused to think of it as anything other than a meeting. She had no idea what Don thought was so important that he had to tell her face-to-face and wasn't in a hurry to find out. Not to mention it seemed odd he wouldn't have said it on the street but felt comfortable saying it in a busy restaurant.

"Thank you," she said, leaning back ever so slightly as he dipped his head to peck her cheek. He withdrew, embarrassed. "Shall we go in?"

"Yes." He rubbed his stomach, then closed his eyes. "He was so hungry he could eat a horse / instead he decided just to eat a course. Or two / At Sushi Jam, with Marley yes ma'am—"

"Don?" He opened his eyes. "Shall we head in?"

He smiled and they entered the restaurant. Marley instantly regretted having agreed to go out. Sushi Jam was living up to its name. The tables were closer together than she had remembered, the din louder, the waitstaff more harried. It was too late to back out now though and she stifled a sigh as they were led to their small two-seater table along the restaurant's front window, one of the last available in the place.

"Would you like to sit facing the window or facing into the restaurant?" Don asked politely.

"Restaurant, I guess." Marley shrugged and wriggled herself awkwardly between the tables to take the seat with her back to the window. There were two women sitting beside them and Don smiled apologetically at them as Marley sat down.

"A bit crowded in here," he said.

"Don't worry about it, it's fine," the women said, their pupils dilated and their fingers busily twirling tendrils of hair.

A young waitress thumped a carafe of water and two glasses onto their table. "Orders?" she asked, eyes glued to her notepad.

"Oh. I'm so sorry. Did we forget to pick up a menu somewhere?" Don craned his neck to look at her.

Marley could pinpoint the exact moment the waitress clocked his looks. She heard the hiss of intaken breath, saw her jaw slacken slightly, noticed the tiny involuntary step forward she took.

"Totally my fault," she said, palming her forehead. "I'll be right back."

"Oh, he can just have ours," said one of the women from the neighbouring table. She leaned over before the waitress could answer and helpfully placed the menu directly into Don's hands.

He smiled and passed it to Marley. "We still need one more."

The waitress spun on her heel and all but mowed down a couple walking to their seats in her haste to get Don a menu.

Don smiled anxiously at Marley. "I'm so glad they have

actual menus and not those QR codes that are so popular now. I can never get those to work."

"Oh, I hate those as well," Marley agreed, relaxing slightly. It wasn't like Don was terrible company after all. She just hoped he didn't launch into too many more poems. "So, what did you want to talk about?"

He drew in a deep breath, then seemed to change his mind, shaking his head. "Let's wait till our food arrives. What do you fancy?"

"Uh, okay." Marley scanned the menu in her hand. "I'll get the tempura vegetables I think. I'm not particularly hungry. Or maybe some honey prawns."

"I think they have great sashimi here," he said. Marley wrinkled her nose and Don laughed. "Okay, I'll get that on my own then."

The waitress returned with a second menu, leaning indecently far over Don's shoulder to hand it to him. Marley flashed back to her dinner with Finn at Nobiyaki's Restaurant in Silton Town. The situations were similar—waitresses flirting shamelessly with her male dining companions. Except watching Finn with Georgia had made her almost feral with jealousy. Now, she didn't feel the slightest twinge at this server's over-the-top attention to Don.

Once they'd placed their orders, Don excused himself for a quick bathroom break. He seemed nervous and Marley briefly wondered whether it was related to whatever he wanted to tell her.

As he left the table, Marley's view of her surroundings widened, and her eyes landed on Finn, seemingly alone at a table on the other side of the restaurant. Her body responded by bowling her heart against her ribcage. He was staring down at his phone and the small smile on his face as he looked at the screen made her glow. His shiny black hair was flopping slightly over his forehead in a way that made Marley's fingers ache to brush it back. Her phone pinged with a message but she barely registered it, unable to peel her eyes from Finn.

A moment later, he looked around and his gaze locked with hers. His face lit up and he raised his hand uncertainly. She slowly raised hers and was considering getting up to go and speak to him when she spotted Bess walking from the bathrooms back towards Finn's table. *Bess.*

So it was true. She'd been right. They were back together and were out on a date. She immediately dropped her gaze to the table, willing back the tears that threatened, trying to ignore the cricket bat to her stomach. Her pulse was in her throat and she felt sick. Quickly, she reached for her phone, ignored every other alert and scrolled straight to her group chat with Lyra and Amy. She texted the girls under the table.

At a restaurant and just saw Finn. With Bess. ON A DATE.

From her peripheral vision, she could see Finn trying to catch her attention. She stared determinedly down at her screen, hoping the girls would text her something to keep her sane. She scanned the restaurant for Don, studiously avoiding Finn and Bess's table. She planned to tell Don she suddenly felt ill, and make a getaway. She spotted him across the restaurant, smiling at her as he approached their table. Finn was watching him too. He couldn't have missed Don if he'd been trying—the restaurant practically stood still to watch the man walk. Finn paled and his jaw tensed as he realised Don was there with Marley. The last thing she saw before Don blocked her view was Finn's stricken face.

Well *good*, Marley thought. For a split second, she was glad he might think she was on a date. It would certainly make her feel less like an idiot than she did in that moment having seen him there with Bess. A second later, she was sickened by the thought Finn might mistake this for something romantic.

She tried to smile at Don as he took his seat, but she wasn't entirely sure her features were cooperating. She felt detached from reality, itchy to get out of there. "Don, I'm so sorry to do this, but I suddenly don't feel well. At all. Can we take a rain check?"

Don's face fell with concern. "Of course. Oh my goodness, are you okay? Let's get you out of here." He gestured a waitress over. "Unfortunately we're going to need to go home."

"We do hope you'll come back again very soon," the waitress said, almost tearfully.

Don stood, and Marley moved to get up as well. Across the room, she spotted Bess and Finn finalising their bill. Bess gathered up her blazer and designer handbag from the back of her chair while Finn discreetly tried to get a view of Marley and Don's table. Marley dropped back into her seat.

"Uh, I don't feel well enough to stand," she said desperately, hoping Don would sit back down until Finn and Bess were gone. Instead, he surveyed her worriedly for a moment, and then stood and pushed his way between the tables, his shapely buttocks caressing the arms of the women sitting beside them—much to their delight.

Marley gasped as she realised what he was about to do. "No, Don, don't!" she whispered urgently.

"I shouldn't have brought you to such a crowded place," he said, frowning and reaching his arms out. "I'm really sorry. You don't look well at all. But don't worry, I'll get you out of here."

"Oh God."

In a single swift movement, Don leaned forward and plucked Marley out of her chair, cradling her in both arms like a new bride. He swept her over the top of their table, her foot knocking a carafe and a glass onto the floor. Despite Marley's hissed protests, Don carried her through the restaurant, drawing the eyes and ire of every woman and half the men present.

Finn watched open-mouthed as they paraded out, and a table full of older women broke into a smattering of applause as they passed.

"Oh, I think that's Don the Bard from YouTube!" Marley heard one of them say, to a round of cooing.

Once they were on the street, Marley kicked out of Don's arms, her face flushed. "What on earth did you do that for?" she demanded saltily, adjusting her top.

Don paled. "I honestly thought you were going to pass out. I didn't even think, I just did it. I'm so sorry."

Marley drew a deep breath. "It's okay," she said shakily, trying to see into the restaurant to catch Finn's eye. He and Bess were blocked from her view. "Don, I just need to get home. Do you want to quickly tell me whatever it was you wanted to tell me, or shall we do it another time?"

Don hesitated. "You look much better now we're out of there, but you still don't look great."

"I'm absolutely fine, I just need some rest. So?"

"I'll just get it over and done with quickly." He drew a breath and closed his eyes, speaking rapidly. "When they met he couldn't forget / her eyes so green as she stared at her screen."

"Don—" Marley shifted her weight from foot to foot impatiently, willing him to speed up so it would all be over and done with.

"They went on a date, which he thought went great / but then she went away, he didn't see her for days."

"Don."

He held up a finger, a harried frown on his face. "Then Liz came along and his heart was a song / she makes him float on air and she'll always be there. And that's why, though it's hard, he let down his guard / now Liz is the final queen of his heart. So to Marley he says, with a sorrowful gaze / I'm leaving you now, though I hate to part ways—"

"Don!" Marley interrupted, frustrated.

He opened his eyes, thrown. "What?"

"I don't get what you're trying to say? Can you say it in prose?"

Finn and Bess pushed through the doors out of the restaurant and Marley was furious at herself for having stayed outside so long. She couldn't bear the idea that she might see Finn and Bess link arms, or kiss. The very thought made her insides heave. Why had she lingered? She hadn't wanted to be rude to Don, but she should have jumped in a cab and told him to text her whatever he was on about.

Finn frowned in confusion as his gaze caught Marley's, looking back and forth between her and Don. Bess noticed and, without acknowledging Marley at all, pulled on Finn's arm, guiding him in the opposite direction.

"Come on, Finley. Let's grab that drink."

He was rooted to the spot, staring at Marley. Reluctantly, he let Bess pull him away.

"Marley, I just need to let you know I'm seeing someone else," Don said finally.

Marley could tell from the way Finn's footsteps faltered that he'd heard Don clearly. Her mouth dropped open and she yanked Don by the arm further from the entrance, away from earshot of Finn and Bess. "What do you mean someone *else?* We weren't dating!" she hissed.

"I met someone and I just want to be completely upfront about it all. I mean, because of the situation."

"What situation?" Marley demanded.

"Because it's *Liz.*"

Finn glanced back over his shoulder at Marley and the

pain on his face made her worry for a second that she would genuinely be sick, right there in the street. Finn was with Bess and he thought she was with Don and the whole thing was a huge mess and she wasn't even entirely sure how it had happened.

She'd call Finn once she got home. Even though he'd probably be tangled in the sheets with Bess by then, she didn't want him thinking she'd secretly been with Don while they were in Darnee.

"Fine, Don. It's fine. I wish you and this Liz the very, very best of luck. This could have been a text though. Actually, scrap that. It didn't need to be anything at all."

Don looked flustered. "I just didn't want it to be awkward."

Marley felt a flicker of shame and hung her head. "I'm sorry, Don," she whispered. "This isn't your fault. Things are just … I'm not in the right headspace at the moment." She looked up, and his grey-green eyes cleared. She put a hand on his arm. "I sincerely, genuinely wish you and Liz all the best. You deserve to be happy, Don."

He beamed. "Thank you, Marley. I wish all the best for you as well."

———

Marley three-way video-called the girls the instant she walked in her front door. They'd been on full alert after her desperate text message, and she'd frantically updated them with more texts during her short cab ride home. She'd never been so glad she had them in her life.

"I cannot believe he *carried* you out of the restaurant!" Amy said as soon as she answered, clapping a hand to her heart. Marley would have known Amy was at her own flat in

Bondi even if the background hadn't been visible—Amy wore the sapphire silk bonnet she used when she was doing a hair treatment.

Lyra lay stretched out in bed in the flat she shared with Alex, her eyelids drooping as she struggled valiantly to stay awake for her friend.

"It's the weirdest thing that's ever happened to me. But ... you guys. *Finn. Bess.*" Marley dropped onto her sofa, letting tears run down her cheeks.

Lyra made a soft clicking noise with her tongue. "There's *got* to be an explanation, Marley. Why don't you just call him now? You can ring us right back. "

"I can't! He's probably in bed with her as we speak." The idea of it brought a fresh twist of pain to her heart.

"Marley, you're never going to know if you don't just at least text him," Amy said. "There could be a thousand reasons they were there together. Maybe they're divvying up stuff in their apartment or they have some boring paperwork to do and thought they'd may as well get it done over dinner."

Marley shook her head, sniffing and wiping her eyes. "Sorry I'm crying. I *hate* crying. But I just don't see how that would be the case. He said Bess was making his life difficult when they broke up. I overheard part of their conversation in the car on the way to Darnee. They were on pretty crappy terms."

"Well, you were there with Don and it wasn't a date. And you think he might have heard Don saying he was breaking up with you. What's he supposed to think?" Amy said. "You're worried he might be on a date, he almost definitely thinks you were."

Marley sighed, shaking her head. "We have to admit it. I've made a huge mistake. Again. I'm an idiot. And now there's nothing I can do."

Both girls would be coming over in two days' time for

Marley's pregnancy test. She wasn't sure how she was supposed to cope without them until then.

Lyra's eyes widened. "Yes, there is. You can just talk to him! Oh, if I wasn't so exhausted, I would come over there and shake you."

"Were you at the studio?" Amy asked Lyra.

Lyra grunted, her eyes sinking back to half-mast.

"Do you want to talk about it?" Marley asked, trying to be polite although all she wanted was to talk about Finn.

"I'm fine," Lyra said tiredly. "Just a long day."

They talked around in circles for another few moments, both girls encouraging her to call Finn, Marley adamant she couldn't. Finally, Marley changed the subject to wedding planning. "When are we going dress shopping?"

Amy pressed her lips together, eyes twinkling. "We should probably wait until after your test, right?"

Marley clapped a hand over her mouth. "My dress! Amy, I'm sorry!"

Amy chuckled. "Yes, it was very inconsiderate of you to potentially get pregnant before consulting me on my nuptials. Come on," she said, tilting her head as she took pity on Marley. "We'll just buy you a bridesmaid dress with a ton of pleats and pray you don't break your waters in front of the celebrant. You are permitted to either attend with a newborn, or dance yourself into labour a respectable amount of time after we say 'I do'."

"Or I'm not pregnant at all," Marley added, her heart slumping as she said the words.

Amy shook her head. "Positive thoughts only."

In the background of Lyra's chat window, Alex entered the bedroom. Lyra's eyes had closed and her breathing had deepened. Alex walked over to the phone and gently plucked it out of her hand, raising a finger to his lips as he looked at the girls onscreen. He walked out of the bedroom and shut off the light, quietly closing the door.

"Is she okay?" Marley asked.

Alex sighed. "She's been working like crazy. Selena and the producer are both psychopaths if you ask me. But, of course I don't tell her that. This is her dream."

"Can she say no at all?" Amy asked.

Alex shrugged. "I honestly don't think she wants to. I know she finds it physically demanding, but she lights up whenever she talks about it. Plus, she has the contract and the albums coming out and the tour coming up. I just wish they weren't working her to the bone. I feel like she might end up getting burnt out."

"Thank God she has you to look after her," Amy said.

"I wish we could do more for her as well," Marley added sadly.

"You guys are her besties, she knows you'd do anything for her."

"Good, because we would." Marley's voice was fierce and Amy nodded in agreement.

They all signed off from the call and for a split second, with the phone in her hand and the silence of her flat so pronounced after hearing their friendly voices, Marley contemplated messaging Finn.

But as her finger hovered over his name in her contact list, she pictured Bess guiding him away by the arm.

She couldn't do it. Not tonight. Not yet.

CHAPTER FORTY

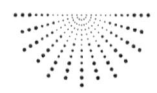

"Hi, Mrs Wiśniewska," Marley said, greeting the older woman warmly as she inched slowly towards the reception desk with her walking frame. Her last patient for the day. "How's Pavel?"

"Fat," she huffed. "He's too fat."

"Did you try walking him like we discussed?"

Mrs Wiśniewska glared at her. "You can see me moving here, can't you? You think that dog will lose any weight when he's with me?"

She continued her glacial approach and Marley managed a smile. Her insides still felt as though they'd been torn out, but the old lady could always bring a bit of joy to Marley's day.

"Then what about the diet?"

"Pssht," the older woman scoffed. "You can just put a knife in my heart this minute if we two can't have treats. Pavel and treats. That's all I have."

"*You* don't have to go on a diet. But maybe Pavel should if you want him around for as long as you're around. Which I think will be a while yet."

Mrs Wiśniewska stopped and squinted at Marley. "What's different about you?"

Marley shook her head, shrugging. "Nothing, I don't think?"

"Nah, nah," Mrs Wiśniewska frowned and continued her appraisal from her spot three metres away from Marley. "It's your clothes? You aren't dressed like such a *błaznować* anymore."

"A what?"

She waved her hand in the air, searching for the word. "Buffoon."

"Oh," Marley grinned and looked down at her outfit—a simple navy A-line skirt and a rust-coloured blouse. After the girls colour-coded her wardrobe, Marley found herself reaching for tamer outfit choices for work.

Mrs Wiśniewska screwed her mouth up. "But, no. That isn't it."

"If you can just keep moving forward, I'll take your Medicare card. Or you can head straight into the waiting room and I'll grab it from you."

"You're taking my nothing!" She recoiled as though Marley had tried to mug her. "But what is it? Your hair? That's also less …"

"I'm growing it," Marley said quickly, before she could hurl another insult.

"*Nie*. It's not that either." The old lady shook her head in frustration.

Dr Martelle poked her head out from her office door and beckoned Marley over. "Would you have a couple of minutes to stay behind and talk this afternoon?" she asked in a low voice once Marley reached her.

Marley frowned. "Is everything okay?"

"Yes, yes." The doctor nodded vigorously. "I just … I'd like to clear some things up. You didn't answer my text message last night."

Marley had switched off her phone after the video call with the girls and hadn't switched it back on. She didn't have it with her.

"Why did you text me? Why wouldn't you just talk to me at work?"

Dr Martelle coloured. "Never mind, I'll explain it all this afternoon."

"If it's about the pay rise—"

"It's not."

"Okay," Marley said slowly, her heart pounding. "Sure, I can stay."

"Great, thank you. And send in …" Dr Martelle lowered her voice and gestured vaguely at Mrs Wiśniewska. "Send *her* in when you're ready."

Marley closed the front door behind Mrs Wiśniewska with shaking hands and knocked tentatively on Dr Martelle's door.

"Come in."

Dr Martelle was staring out her window into the street, toying absently with the clunky model kidney that usually sat on her shelves. When she turned to look at Marley, her face was contorted with worry.

"What's wrong?" Marley asked.

Dr Martelle took a deep breath. "You're the best thing that ever happened to this practice, Marley."

When she didn't elaborate, Marley tilted her head. "Okay?"

"I just don't want to lose you. I've come to think of you as a friend. Or, well, at least an acquaintance I like. But that's saying a lot for me." She smiled. "So I've really been struggling about the awkwardness between us, and I wanted to get everything out in the open."

"The awkwardness?" Marley asked blankly.

Dr Martelle gave her a sceptical look. "Come on, Marley. We've both noticed it. I'm offering you a chance to have it out. You get a free shot at me. What I did was underhanded, and I feel ashamed of myself. I'd rather you just yell at me and we get back to the way things were."

Marley's eyes were round. "Dr Martelle, I have absolutely no idea what you're talking about. What did you do that was underhanded?"

"You know."

Marley held her palms up. "I'm the most confused I've ever been. And I've been a bit confused lately," she added with a humourless laugh, as a picture of Finn came to mind and made her whole body ache.

Dr Martelle scrutinised her. "You don't know? He said he told you."

"Who said he told me what?"

Dr Martelle pulled her head back, realising Marley was genuine. "Don."

"Don? Who's ..." Marley gasped as she put the pieces together. "*You're* the Liz that Don Hamlet is dating?"

"*Yes*. He didn't mention it was me?"

"No!" Marley started to laugh. "No, he didn't. Well, he said Liz but I didn't think anything of it. And you were worried that I—?" She pointed to her chest.

"I knew the two of you were dating and I felt absolutely rotten about it." Dr Martelle brought her fingers to her temples. "I thought that's why you were giving me the cold shoulder. I texted you last night because I just couldn't bear it any longer. When you didn't reply ..."

"No, no, no." Marley shook her head. "I haven't been

giving you the cold shoulder! At least not intentionally. And Dr Martelle, Don and I were *never* dating. We went on a single date that to be honest didn't go that well. I said I'd rather not see him again romantically."

Dr Martelle looked dumbstruck. She set the kidney down with a clunk. "That man, that *god* asked to see you again and you said no?"

Marley nodded, grinning. "And honestly, I'm slightly surprised that you two hit it off."

"Oh, the poetry?" Dr Martelle waved her hand. "It's shocking. But I couldn't care less. I actually find it kind of sweet."

Marley puffed out a short breath. "What on earth do you two talk about?"

Dr Martelle averted her eyes. "We haven't done a *lot* of talking. But it's not just physical. I'm so used to dating men who want to outdo me, you know? They're specialists and they consider dating a GP to be slumming it. Or they're in academia and they look down on me for other reasons. Or they're bankers and they love to rub my nose in how much more money they make, throw it around. Or they're none of those things but they're intimidated that I'm a doctor or by how much I make." She shook her head wearily. "I cannot tell you how *over* all that I am. Don is …" Her face softened, became wistful. "He's gentle and kind and he's in awe of me and he is a *genius* in the sack and he cooks me breakfast and he lays my slippers out and," she took a breath, "he's quite frankly exactly what I want and need."

Marley's eyes were sparkling. "It sounds perfect. I'm … wow."

"He wanted to make sure he told you face to face, to save any awkwardness between you and I. It's so Don." She sighed, clearly smitten.

Marley shook her head in amazement. "How on earth did you two get together?"

Dr Martelle pursed her lips. "Well, that's the thing. The week you were away, he stopped by with some flowers for you. He told me he'd asked you out and I assumed ... but we got to talking, one thing led to another and we ended up having dinner and drinks that night."

Marley puffed her cheeks out, wondering why on earth Don had thought she'd want flowers from him.

"Oh, Marley, I can't tell you how stressed I've been," Dr Martelle continued, putting two hands on her desk and practically slumping over it in relief. "I was ready to offer you just about anything to get you to stay." She looked Marley in the eye. "You know you're irreplaceable, right?"

Marley smiled. "I love working here, don't worry. I'm sorry if I've seemed off, I've just had ... some stuff going on. I'm not irreplaceable, especially now we have the temp agency set up. You won't have to deal with Tilda when I'm away, unless you want to. But thank you for saying it."

"Did you get everything done that you needed to in your hometown, by the way?"

Marley nodded, swallowing. She found it difficult to think about that week in Darnee without picturing Finn. She drew a deep breath. "Actually, if you are considering doing something for me, I know what I would want that to be."

Dr Martelle cocked her head. "We've established I don't need to do anything."

"Well, have we?" Marley asked. "You did steal my boyfriend, after all."

Dr Martelle grinned. "Alright. I'll hear you out at least. That's all I'm guaranteeing."

"That's all I ask."

CHAPTER FORTY-ONE

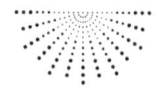

Just before Amy and Lyra arrived on the day of Marley's pregnancy test, she worked up the nerve to switch her phone back on. Keeping it off had meant she wouldn't be tempted to call Finn. She was terrified she'd end up in tears, being pathetic on the phone.

Despite what the girls had said, she was still afraid he was back with Bess. She kept replaying the conversation they'd had during their living room picnic in Darnee, when Finn had told her that he liked the fact Bess pushed him and was impossible to please. Yes, he'd said he didn't want that anymore, but what if he'd changed his mind again? What if Bess had realised that she did want kids, once they'd broken up? A million things could have happened and Marley was haunted by them all. She'd broken all her own rules about falling for someone with Finn and then he'd promptly turned around and got back together with Bess.

She sighed and looked at her phone again. His was the first name she scrolled to, and she felt a flicker of anticipation when she realised there was an unread message in the thread.

Hey stranger. I miss you. And don't tell anyone, but I *kind* of miss Dungaree. Hope it's okay to tell you stuff like that. Let me know if not. But anyway, we need to catch up. You haven't even told me if Tim's going to be a dad ...

Marley blinked, staring at the timestamp. Tuesday night. When she was in the restaurant. She remembered the secret little smile on his face as he'd stared down at his screen. The smile had been for her.

Her doorbell rang and the girls filed in, both looking as anxious as Marley felt. Marley didn't let the phone out of her hand.

"Sorry I fell asleep on the call the other night," Lyra said, hugging Marley as she kicked her sneakers off. Amy stepped gracefully out of her patent leather pumps, the height of the heels making Marley's feet ache just to look at.

"Oh, don't be," Marley reassured her, leading them both to the living room. "Alex took the phone and we yakked it up for hours."

"Had a ball," Amy added smoothly, her cherry-lacquered lips breaking into a grin.

"Ha-ha. You're both hilarious."

They trooped into the living room, Amy sitting beside Marley on the sofa and Lyra pulling the floor cushion over to sit near them. There was a large pharmacy bag on top of the coffee table and Marley saw them both glance at it.

"I need to show you something," Marley said. She held her phone out with Finn's last message on it. "He sent me that when he was at the restaurant with Bess. I didn't read it until now."

Amy squinted into the phone, then pulled back and clapped. "See, I *told* you he wasn't back with her!"

"Show me," Lyra demanded and Marley pointed the phone in her direction. "Yes!"

Marley shook her head. "It doesn't prove anything, does it?"

"Well, yes it does. It proves he was thinking of you when he was there with her. That means it really wasn't a date," Lyra said.

"But he could have just meant it in a friendly way. Like, 'hey, I'm here with my girlfriend, but I spared a thought for my old chum Marley.'"

Amy frowned. "Does he use the word *chum*?"

"No," Marley said, managing a smile. "But you know what I mean."

"Come on, he *definitely* didn't mean it that way," Lyra said. "Why are you so determined to believe they're back together?"

Marley let out a long breath. "I guess because it would hurt, but ... I don't know. It's less scary than the idea I should have tried something with him. Relationships are terrifying. I knew I didn't want one. Or ... I thought I knew. And then there's this ..." She gestured to the coffee table and bit her lip. "It's all mixed up in my head. Also, if he's back with Bess, then I got between two people who were supposed to be together. What kind of woman would that make me?" She stared at her hands. "I'd be no better than Susie."

"Oh my God, that's *completely* different!" Amy shouted.

"You didn't do anything wrong, Marley," Lyra said firmly. "You didn't touch him until long after they'd broken up."

"But I knew I was attracted to him," she said mournfully. "I should have just never gone back to that clinic."

"The city is peppered with hotties," Lyra said. "We couldn't go anywhere if that was the rule."

Amy side-hugged Marley. "You're not the same as Susie at all. And I understand that relationships are terrifying, but when they turn out to be worth the risk ..." Her face went dreamy for a moment, clearly thinking of Rick. Then she snapped back. "Do you feel up to taking the pregnancy test? That will give us a lot more answers and help decide next steps."

Lyra peeped into the bag and her eyes widened.

"I got eight," Marley explained. "Do you think that's enough?"

"I think if you can pee on eight test sticks in one go, you have a future in some kind of circus," Amy said.

"And it's probably not one children can attend," Lyra added.

"Right." Marley nodded resolutely, but couldn't get up.

"We'll walk you to the bathroom," Amy said. "Unless you're not ready to do it yet? We can keep talking, and we can keep explaining to you why you're not like Susie and Finn isn't like Hayden."

"I want to know but ... I'm too scared to know." Marley bit her nail as they nodded sympathetically. "You guys. This is everything."

They both nodded. After a moment, Lyra wordlessly held out her hand and Marley took it, grabbing the bag of tests. Together, the three of them walked down the corridor to the bathroom.

"Okay," Marley said, squaring her shoulders. "This is it." She opened the door, then changed her mind and brushed past the girls to walk quickly back to the living room.

"You're not going to do it in the bathroom?" Lyra asked, panicked.

"Yes!" Marley said, sitting down on the sofa and staring up at them as they filed back in after her. "I'm just not quite ready. I'm not ready to know."

"Do you have any feelings yet?" Amy asked, sitting beside her and taking her hand.

"I don't know. I mean, my boobs are kind of sore, but that could be anything."

"Could it?" Lyra asked, frowning.

"Well, it's not conclusive."

"That's what eight tests are for," Amy said, smiling.

Marley exhaled slowly. "What if I'm pregnant? What if it's really happening? Did I do the right thing, not waiting for a nuclear family? Will I mess the kid up?"

The girls immediately and vehemently shook their heads.

"Look at us three. We all come from broken or somehow different families," Lyra said a moment later. "My mum's gone, my dad disowned us. And I turned out fine. More or less. We started off nuclear. That doesn't guarantee a thing."

"Same here. My dad gambled away our family home and went to prison, and my mum often can't stand the sight of me," Amy added with a shrug. "I'm pretty fine, too."

"And you have your story," Lyra added, reaching to smooth Marley's hair back from her face. It was such a gentle gesture, no one had done that since GamGam was alive. Marley felt her chin quiver. "The point is," Lyra continued, "if you're pregnant, your baby already has a family. A kind of patchwork, odd, definitely not nuclear family. But it has one. And more importantly than anything else, it is *surrounded* by love. Plus, it'll have the best mum ever."

Marley squeezed her eyes, trying to keep her breathing steady.

"It's aunties are going to embarrass the hell out of it and have so much doing it," Amy added.

"And don't you even *try* to discipline that child," Lyra said, mock seriously. "If you deny it anything, you better know its aunts are going to go right out and get it for them."

Marley laughed. "This kid is going to be so spoiled."

"Yeah, it is," Amy said firmly.

"Okay," Marley steeled herself, put her hands resolutely on her thighs and stood. "I'm ready."

They went in a procession towards the bathroom.

Halfway there, Marley turned to them. "Don't come any closer. I won't be able to do it with you standing outside."

"We'll wait in the living room," Amy said, quickly backing up. "But bring it out as *soon* as you're done. I want to watch the lines appear."

Marley nodded, eyes wide. They both hugged her quickly and she went into the bathroom, closing the door.

A moment later, she brought out the stick and set it on the coffee table. All three of them leaned in to watch, holding hands as the solution reacted and spread over the display window.

And as the result became clear, Marley started to cry.

CHAPTER FORTY-TWO

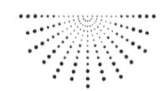

Marley was almost as nervous as she'd been the first time she'd walked into ReproJoy. Except this time when she walked in, she knew Finn would be there. She'd texted him with a brief, *I have something to give you. Can I see you?* that morning.

He'd replied saying he was at ReproJoy, and her heart had started racing as she read the message. Why was he there? Was he there just randomly, running an errand or something? Was he back working there? It was killing her not to know for absolute certain that he wasn't with Bess.

She went back and forth in her mind until she lost patience with herself. Whatever was going on, she had a task, she had something to tell him, and she needed to put on her big girl pants and just do it. She slipped out on her lunch break, walking the few blocks to the clinic in the punishing heat.

The foyer was as chilly as she remembered, the environment as stark. Finn stood at the reception desk in his white coat, deep in conversation with a couple. He didn't notice her at first and she took a long moment to study him, letting her heart flip as she did so. She remembered noticing the thickness of his lashes on that first day, and marvelled at them again. Even more so at the blueness of his eyes. His whole face took her breath away. *He* took her breath away. She tried not to think about how those lips had pressed on hers, about his body sliding against hers, but it was no use.

He looked up and spotted her, surprise and delight flickering across his face. A second later, it was as though he remembered something, and some of the light leached from his gaze. He discreetly held up a finger, asking her to wait, and looked back to the couple he was talking to. They'd both glanced over their shoulders at Marley when Finn had noticed her, displaying identical slightly irritated expressions at finding her standing there.

She wandered slowly towards the sliding entrance doors so that she was out of earshot to give the couple privacy and lingered there for as long as she could stand it. They seemed to be asking an endless stream of questions in low voices, and Finn answered them all with the same smooth, polished professionalism that had put her at ease that very first day she'd met him.

Marley stood for as long as she could bear it. Then, risking everyone's irritation, she strode up to the desk and slid an envelope across it to Finn.

"Excuse me," the man said crossly.

Marley held her hands up, backing off. "I just needed to make that delivery. I beg your pardon."

While they were both turned to her, she saw Finn pull the envelope towards himself and slip it into his coat pocket. He shot her an apologetic glance and then resumed talking to the couple as Marley walked back out through the doors and into the inferno of Sydney heat.

She was trembling as she walked the last block back to work, her thoughts and emotions in turmoil. She felt like running or going to a boxing class—anything to get rid of some energy.

She spotted Mrs Wiśniewska up ahead, walking slowly along with her dog Pavel, his leash tied to her walking frame. Marley jogged lightly to catch them up.

"Hi, Mrs W, lovely to see you out walking Pavel!"

The older woman halted in her walking frame and turned to look at her. "It's not because of what you said." She feigned irritation but her eyes were twinkling.

"I wouldn't have thought any such thing," Marley said, forcing a smile to her face. "Do you need any help with anything? I was just out for a quick walk and I'm heading back to work now."

The older lady shook her head. "No, but that is very nice, thank you." Her eyes trailed down over Marley's body, then came back up to her face. "Ahhh," she said, nodding as though something made sense.

"What is it?"

"I know what's different about you now." She took one hand off her walking frame to waggle a finger at Marley.

"You do?"

The old lady nodded and held Marley's eye, smiling. "You're pregnant."

CHAPTER FORTY-THREE

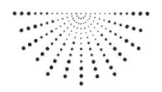

Marley's doorbell rang at 6:30pm that evening. She happened to be walking past the buzzer and unthinkingly pressed the door release without asking who it was.

She barely knew how she'd made it through the day since seeing Finn. Dr Martelle had called her back to earth several times and Marley had even once handed over the wrong file —something that had never happened before. Dr Martelle had been good about it, offering to send her home early. But she hadn't wanted to come home and sit around and wait to see whether Finn would message or call, so she'd forced herself to stay.

Now she was restlessly pacing the apartment. The girls had tried to comfort her, but Lyra had been stuck at the studio and Amy was over at Rick's mother's place so they hadn't had long. Still, they'd done their best.

Marley realised with a jerk that she'd buzzed in a stranger and spent the next minute worrying she'd released a serial killer into the apartment block. Moments later, a gentle tap at her door drew her to the peephole. *Finn.*

Her heart fell several floors and she yanked the door open, surprising him slightly. They stood staring at one another until he stepped tentatively inside.

"Hi," Marley said, breaking their silence.

"Hi," he replied softly. There was so much tenderness in his expression that she had to dig her fingernails into her hand to keep from reaching out to him. "How are you?"

"Good, good," she replied. She would have to tell him right now, and she was not sure at all how he'd react. "Finn—"

He held up the business card she'd placed in the envelope earlier when she'd been to see him. "What's this?"

"Oh." Marley wrung her hands. "Do you want a drink? Shall we sit down? Or is standing fine?"

"Are you okay?" Concern knitted his brows.

"Yes. Uh, that's a business card. For your business. If you still want to open it. I guess you're back working at Repro—"

He quickly shook his head. "Only for a few weeks. Until the new receptionist is fully onboarded."

"Oh. And after that?"

"Bess came to her senses. She's going to help me financially to get started with my own physio practice."

"It's not helping," Marley blurted. "You're owed that at the least."

He nodded. "Yes. You're right. The MacArthur invoices will still be paid."

"I don't—"

"Marley, this card?"

"Dr Martelle is happy to share her office space. It's not huge, but you'd have a room and a kitchenette and a shared storage area. Plus, it's about to be renovated, so you can have a say in that. Nothing big, just new flooring and a fresh lick of paint and stuff like that. The rent is reasonable, and it's a convenient location." She realised she was blabbering and stopped, drawing a deep breath. "But, Finn, there's something I need to tell—"

Finn stared at her. "You organised that? For me?"

Marley looked down at her feet, nodding. "The only thing is, it comes with an office manager. Which is, uh, me. I'm not sure how that would work, since you're back with Bess."

"*What?* No, I'm not."

Relief almost crumpled her legs, and she quickly raised her eyes to him. "You're not?"

"*God* no. Why on earth would you think that?" He shook his head in disbelief, his eyes round with horror.

"Your text message!" She said hotly. "You said 'Bess and I have come to an agreement. Back together it looks like'." She broke off, determined not to cry.

His jaw dropped. "I meant back with Bess *professionally!* Oh my God, Marley, did you really think?" He stepped quickly towards her, putting his arms around her and she melted gratefully into him. "Bess and I are long done," he said firmly. "I'm an idiot for writing the message that way. I didn't even think of how that could have come across. I guess because it wasn't on my radar." A moment later, she felt his body stiffen. He released her and took a step back. "But you were with that guy at the restaurant. The stupidly handsome one who carried you out like a Disney bride."

Marley pulled him to her again, not willing to let him go yet. "That was a big misunderstanding," she said, her voice muffled against his neck. She breathed in the heady scent of him, desire thrilling through her. "We went on one date, a while before our road trip, and I didn't want to see him again. He started dating my boss and thought he had to tell me in person." She tilted her head to gaze at him. "That's all it was."

She didn't know which of them started it, but suddenly their mouths were pressed together and they were kissing hungrily, as though making up for lost time. Marley's mind went blank and all she was aware of was how much like home Finn felt—and how much she wanted him. A moment later, she remembered what she had to tell him, and pulled back from him. They were both breathless.

"Sorry," Finn said, remembering himself. He ran a hand shakily through his hair. "Sorry, I didn't mean ..."

"Finn, I'm pregnant."

He smiled, joy lighting up his face before he closed his eyes, trying to get his breathing under control. He nodded slowly, then opened his eyes to look at her. "Marley, I haven't changed my mind about you. I won't. I know you said you don't want a relationship, but I do. With you. I don't want to push myself on you, but even though you're going to have Tim's baby, I want to be around. I want to be with you. Romantically. If you'll have me, that is. I know I said I wouldn't mention this again, but you did just kiss me and that's given me some hope. I want to be a part of you life. Of ... both your lives."

Marley was momentarily confused, then she pushed out an exhale as she realised what he thought. "No, Finn. No. The baby is *yours*." He froze, his eyes widening. "It's yours," she repeated, taking his hand. "I went to my appointment at MacArthur, but only to tell them I wouldn't go through with it. I wanted to see if I could undo whatever deal they had with Bess. To see if you could walk away with more from her. I didn't have the procedure, Finn. That day in the living room in Darnee ..."

"Oh, I'm *quite* clear on when it would have happened," Finn said, a slow smile spreading across his face and illuminating his features. "Are you *serious*? We're pregnant?"

She nodded and he closed the gap between them, lifting her up and spinning her in a circle.

"Finn, put me down, I'm going to be sick."

"Sorry!" He instantly set her down, still grinning wildly.

"I thought we'd been careful in Darnee," she added.

"We weren't *that* careful if I remember correctly."

"I suppose not." She blushed slightly. "Can we go into the living room? Sit down? This is all a bit much for me right now."

Marley had insisted they sit apart so she could talk without being distracted by his physical proximity. She set her water down on the coffee table and folded her hands in her lap.

"I'm still absolutely terrified," she began, "and I'm not sure what I'm ready for. But … I do know that I won't ever want to get married."

Finn nodded. She could see he was struggling to stay in his seat, the joy on his face refusing to be tamed despite his efforts. "That's okay with me. I've proposed once in my life, that was enough."

"And I think I'll probably freak out. A lot."

"I'm excellent at calming people down when they freak out."

"And there's a slight chance you'll die. Because that appears to be what happens to men in my family's orbit."

"Marley, I hate to break it to you, but there's a one hundred percent chance we'll both die."

She managed a smile at that. "I suppose you're right. I also don't know if I'm any good at relationships. Like, at all."

"Well, my track record is pretty grim, as you know. What else have you got?"

"I don't want to move in together or anything. Not yet. I want to go very, very slowly."

"Finn the Snail, they call me."

She laughed at that, then grew serious again. "Maybe we'll hate each other once the baby comes, and we realise we can't stand the sight of one another."

He nodded thoughtfully. "You're probably right. Pistols at dawn. Or," he held up a finger, "neither of us will like the baby." She lobbed a cushion at him and he ducked, grinning. "I have a question now, if you're done."

"I'm done," she said.

"Why didn't you go through with the plan? At MacArthur? What made you change your mind?"

She gazed down, then lifted her chin resolutely. "I realised my plan has changed a bit."

"How has your plan changed?" His voice was husky, raw with emotion. Slowly, he crossed the room and sat beside her on the sofa. Tentatively, as though she was a deer in the wild he didn't want to startle.

"I met someone I could imagine doing that with. Having a family, I mean." His lips curved and she braved a glance into his eyes. Once she looked at him, she couldn't look away. "Finn, I *should* be scared of losing everyone. Almost everyone I ever loved has died. But I wanted a baby more than I was scared of loss. More than I was scared of losing a child. I want to give that love, even if I break apart if I lose it. And then I realised ..."

"What?" he prompted, his voice barely above a whisper.

"That there was a guy I was willing to brave that for too."

He reached out and smoothed her hair, and she moved ever so slightly towards him. His Adam's apple bobbed as he gulped.

"But, Finn ... I'm *really* scared."

He turned serious. "I know." His voice was husky, and he held her gaze. "We're going to take it one day at a time. That's all we can do. And I promise, on the days you need me to take a step back, I will step back with no hard feelings. And

I'll step forward again when you're ready. On the days you need reassurance or you feel like it's all too hard, I'll carry you a little. On the days when you're freaking out, I will do my best to keep you together. We don't need to rush into anything at all, and we will do everything at your pace. Even after the baby comes. Does that sound okay?"

She swallowed against the lump in her throat and nodded. "Yes," she whispered. "That sounds very okay."

"And on the days you're super horny and—ouch!" He rubbed his shoulder where she swatted him. Then he pulled her close, so tightly that for a second she struggled to breathe.

"Finn, you're going to squash us both!"

"Sorry!" He instantly released her. "I'm just …" He shook his head, tears welling in his eyes. "I've never been so happy in my life."

"Well, don't let go of us all the way." She snuggled closer to him.

He laughed, encircling her with a light pressure. "Is that okay?"

She tilted her head up to his and reached a hand behind his head. "That's perfect," she whispered, grazing her lips over his, her heart skittering at the contact. She felt full. She felt like this was right. Like it was meant to be.

"*You're* perfect," he whispered and they kissed. Slowly at first, and then passionately. A moment later, she pulled back, breathless. "What is it?" he asked, his eyes drunk with desire and his voice gruff.

"You're not scared?" she asked, studying his face. "Not even a little?"

He leaned to plant tiny kisses on her neck, lighting a fire everywhere his lips touched. "Scary is snakes. Scary is Darnee in the dark. Scary is cops busting into a place at midnight. Scary is wondering whether I'll ever get to open my practice. The thought of doing this with you?" He shook his head resolutely, his hair brushing against her cheek and ear. "Not even the tiniest, tiniest little bit."

Satisfied, she pulled his mouth back to hers, to finish what they'd started.

THE END

DON'T MISS BOOK 4: WEDDING BELLS AT LILAC BAY

Happily ever afters rarely come easy...

After trauma and heartache, **Amy and Rick** are finally ready to say I do - but frictions in their families see battle lines drawn. Will the drama jeopardise their big day?

A heavily-pregnant **Marley** faces the reality of her choices and struggles to come to terms with them. Will her principles mean the end for her relationship with **Finn?**

Lyra's on tour, but the distance from **Alex** is a trial. And there's a band member all too willing to take Alex's place... Will it take a tragedy for Lyra to realise where her heart belongs?

When **Silas and Ernie** hit a snag in their relationship, Silas needs to do some soul-searching to set things right. But is it already too late?

As their wedding draws closer, it begins to look like Amy and Rick's "perfect" day will be anything but!

Wedding Bells at Lilac Bay is available now!

THE STRANGER FROM LILAC BAY

YOUR FREE EBOOK!

When a hot paramedic saves Hope's life, she's instantly smitten. Afraid she's just feeling grateful, Connor gives her his number and tells her to make the first move. She meant to hit save, not erase ... for a girl who works in IT, it shouldn't have been that hard.

In a city like Sydney, will she ever be able to find him again?

Get your FREE copy:

https://BookHip.com/TQGLKKT

ACKNOWLEDGMENTS

Once again, I don't even know where to start. A huge thank you first of all to my incredible husband for his constant support and encouragement. And to our baby boy for being my motivation.

To Hannah, Anthea Kirk and Catherine Maloney for being the best betas a girl could ask for.

To N.C., for sharing her donor story with me. Thank you for your trust and your friendship.

To Katharine D'Souza, my brilliant editor—you never fail to make things better!

To the wonderfully talented Ana Grigoriu-Voicu for another stunning cover.

And to all my friends, family and readers who support this dream of mine!

ABOUT THE AUTHOR

Marie Taylor-Ford is a wife, mother, knitter and devoted carboholic—not in that order.

Born in Wales and raised in Australia (Newy forever!), she's currently based in Munich, Germany where she's lived for over a decade.

If she's not writing, she's probably hanging out with her family or friends, traveling, knitting, reading, swearing at her FitOn app or gently coaxing her child into wearing the things she knitted for him.

If you enjoyed this book, please consider leaving a star-rating or a review on Amazon. Reviews are gold-dust for authors and are always greatly appreciated!

You are warmly invited to stop by Marie's website (and subscribe to her newsletter for exclusive content, offers and publication info):

www.marietaylorford.com
or connect via social media:

- facebook.com/marietaylorford
- instagram.com/authormarietaylorford
- tiktok.com/@authormarietaylorford
- bookbub.com/profile/marie-taylor-ford

Printed in Great Britain
by Amazon